SUNLIGHT'S SHADOW

TALES OF THE SHADOW FOLK

Eris Marriott

TYRLADAN PUBLISHING LLC

This book is dedicated to my horse, Andy (Oh Heavenly Moment). Thank you for carrying me in heart, soul, and body. Thank you for teaching me to speak without words.

CONTENTS

GOBLET OF SIN

A LIFE IN THE shadows, as it turns out, is one carved by a thirst that can never be sated without sacrifice. My lips, parched and dry, are cracked from my choice to abstain from sacrificing anyone other than myself. My existence should not burden the true, living souls who do not take from the unwilling, those whose souls have yet to be tainted by darkness.

Mine, now wrapped in the woven webs of Tryta's shadows, is cursed. From the moment I drew breath after Mars changed me, I was a broken thing – something that should be locked away in a cell, left to writhe and starve. Perhaps then, Shadow Folk would learn to subsist on the dust and nothing that occupies empty space rather than sinking their fangs into the unwitting necks of their prey.

Worse yet, my mind still reels with Jupiter's echoing words. *"I have your father's alliance for that."* How could I miss my father's allegiance to a bastard so horrid as Jupiter? Since when would Sunfall ever align itself with the Shadow Folk? The only reservation of hope I have is that Maverick might have slain our father by now. I know for a fact that my brother would never stand for such a thing. Once the foul plot is discovered, I pray to Siralto that my brother is victorious in slaying our father. While I may not trust the man who sired me, I trust my brother implicitly.

Where my father can be bought with ale and coin, my brother will always stand for Sunfall. Always. Even still, my heart feels weak as I consider our sins and the apology I gave to the people of Velyasa. *Did I mean it? Didn't I curse my own kingdom for the shadows they were in league with?*

I swallow, certain my throat is coated in sandpaper rather than flesh. I wonder if it's possible that the two could have been swapped as part of my transformation. Weeks have passed, and I've yet to yield to any of the gilded cups the Shadow King and his servants have brought to me. The frequency of offerings becomes more urgent with each passing day – now, with each passing hour.

I'm getting under Mars's skin, if nothing else, and this alone draws a sick smile of satisfaction from deep within the damned edges of my soul. I can ensure that he suffers alongside me, though I'm not sure why he cares about me or my health at this point. From everything I've read, I can't *die* from not drinking – I cannot cease to breathe by abstaining.

I may go mad, sure, but at least I won't stoop to taking another's life force to fulfill my continued existence. I would rather become a loon they can lock away and show off for sport. They could use me as bait in the arena, knowing I will never die despite all the things they would do to me.

My mind refuses to consider how unfair I'm being. Sherry isn't unkind. Finch wasn't unkind. But I was supposed to be *better* than them, not *one* of them. I also wasn't supposed to yield to that bastard Mars and his power. He promised I would *live* after he punished me. How this can be considered living is beyond me.

The throbbing in my head pulses behind my eyes and all through my neck, the pain growing sharper with each passing refusal. I'm almost unaware of the goblet that's so close to my lips, but my nostrils flare, taking in the scent of something sweet and sinful. My tongue threatens to dart through my sharpened teeth, but I clench them tighter, determined to stave off temptation despite the excruciating pain it causes.

"Adelaide," Mars's deep voice booms, "you cannot continue this nonsense!"

He can hit me with his fists, a weapon, or whatever he chooses, but I will not yield. The thunder in his voice does not frighten me, nor does the brazen fire in his eyes that threatens to consume me if I don't heed his orders, no matter how trivial.

Eating should be an *easy* command. Drinking should be even easier. I can accomplish both at the same time and still won't give in to him. Choosing to deprive myself is hardly a problem for his kingdom, and it can't be declared as a form of treason. Some might consider me ungrateful for the gifts Mars has bestowed on me, but turning me into one of the Shadow Folk was anything but a mercy.

I glare at him, my vision almost incapable of focusing. His pleas will not shake me. Neither will Sherry's. Finch's ghost's pleas won't, though that bastard has yet to visit me. But I suspect if I continue along this path, I'll start to tread along the edge of the mortal and immortal. I don't doubt I'll see him there, a haunting specter, waiting to lecture me about the importance of feeding as a newborn vampire.

But I don't care. I squeeze my eyes shut, tempted to cry if it wasn't for how empty my body feels or how hollow the action would be. Mars will only see it as a call for the mercy of the thick red liquid in the cup he holds beneath my lips. He taunts me like this every day, and every day, I question my sanity and judgment and pray that Siralto will take vengeance on my existence and stamp out the darkness etched into my soul.

My goddess betrays me. Her love, while gone with her to the grave, still burns enough for Tryta to keep me breathing within the tangle of darkness swirling in my veins. In fact, my Siraltona is enhanced by it. She would set me free of this wretched, abominable place if it weren't for the shackles forged to my wrists by a power too heavy for me to counter. It makes me wonder... *Did Mars go easy on me out there on the battlefield? Or am I just weak because I've been born a second time?*

It's a thought I chew on every day, but the ache in my teeth threatens to send me climbing up the walls, shackles and all, into the loving arms of madness itself.

Mars's eyes trace over my thinning body, whose silhouette has become more and more like a corpse. He cannot savor the appearance of a beautiful maiden if there are no curves or soft edges to adore. Instead, the sharp angles of starvation and desperation claw through his gaze and plunge fear into his heart where desire once grew. I know he must despise the look of me now, which is the only satisfaction I can cling to with certain hope – hope that he'll leave me alone and that whatever passion we felt for each other back in Sunfall can die with the mortal Adelaide he incinerated.

A metaphorical fire, of course, as those sharp fangs he now grimaces at me with are the *true* nail in my would-be coffin.

"You said you were putting me to death on the first day of autumn," I hiss, my voice hot like fire. "You call yourself king, even as you ignore the blossoming youth of spring outside my window?"

"*Your* window?" Mars asks, raising an eyebrow. He never lowers the cup from my lips – never easing the temptation gnawing at my throat. "And it is common for elders to flip the seasons. When you've been alive as long as

I have, you'll learn that everything dies. Spring is merely a reminder of the mortality of everything else around you."

The cup rubs against my lips, and I clench them shut. He's tried before to wrench my mouth open, but I've purged the contents every time. I found out quite accidentally from others that it is a great disrespect for a vampire to force another to feed when they choose to abstain. What I am doing is nothing short of a religious fast to them; I've heard whispered rumors from guards stationed outside that there are worries of godly wrath being set upon them if I'm forced to feed. Mars has since ceased any attempts that could be deemed nonconsensual. Instead, he taunts me as I sow the seeds of worry and disrepute into the minds of his people – those same people whose heads I would have stuck on pikes outside my kingdom prior to my capture.

I close my eyes again and see the haunting image of Finch's body scorched there, just out of reach. My lips tremble as I think of where my horse might have gone. I think of the fate of Sira, my phoenix, whose maker now sits in front of me with the watchful gaze of a hunter. I am his prey, but the hunt has gone sour as he realizes his prey has no intent of falling to any arrow. Instead, she has chosen to fall only to herself and the destruction of her own making.

What fun is a hunt when the hunted has claimed Death for herself?

I almost smile. Almost. Instead, I focus on the way his eyes bore into mine as he sits there, holding the cup with unfaltering resolve. It's disgusting the way he matches my stubbornness with a willfulness of his own. He does not sway to my threats.

"When will you accept the reality of your fate?" Mars asks.

We often banter like this over the sinful cup. I've not asked him where the blood was drawn from. I don't want to know the names of the victims who have given so much for me to spurn their sacrifice in the name of some glimmer of glory I've forged in my head. It feels pointless that their sacrifice is in vain.

But then I know it's the hunger talking and I swallow those thoughts, tucking them away in the crevices of my most treacherous thoughts, the cup seeming closer than it ever has.

"You mean the fate where I live forever, regardless of what I eat?" I level his gaze with my own – a stare that used to make nobles wither. Even my father would take a step back when I looked at him like this.

To my disgust and dismay, Mars *chuckles* at the sight of it. He throws his head back. His laughter booms like the thunderous rain rolling in outside my window. *His* window.

This is not your home, I remind myself, regret stinging my eyes like tears that I know won't fall when there's nothing left to give.

Today, Mars surprises me by brushing a soft thumb along my cheek, as though he can sense that tears would've fallen had they been given the energy and spirit to escape their confines. His skin comes up dry of any proof, my suffering still contained to the innermost parts of me.

He fixes me with a knowing gaze. But for the first time in what feels like hours, he sets the cup down. His lips hover over mine. "You are beautiful, even when there is only a ghost of you left, my fire. Even when you are gaunt from your efforts at self-flagellation, I find you to be the most stunning creature I've ever seen. Tell me, when will you finish making me pay a penance for changing you? It hurts me to watch you suffer so."

It's a daring confession to make. He's shuffled our deck of cards that we've spent so long building into something like a house. The walls have been painted with my suffering, and the gaping arches of each delicate card are a cold reminder of how fragile it is. True to its nature, it crumbles the moment Mars takes one of the cards from its place among the structure of what we've built together.

I blink. Words are lost to my tongue, whose dried flesh threatens to reduce to ash in my mouth. I want to yield. I want to drink.

I must stay strong.

"How are you the one suffering?" I finally respond.

"It is not in my nature to treat someone like you in this manner. You are a product of your keeping. You can change. I... long for you as much as I loathe you. It is not fair to watch you writhe against the constraints you have placed on yourself." Mars looks down, considering the shackles on my wrists. "These will not hold your power forever, but they will become far more real the longer you let them shape the way you feel about yourself. Why do you deny the shadows in your soul? They are just as much a part of you as the light burning in your veins."

"Speaking in riddles to get into my pants? I'll pass," I snort. I curse the ache I feel building in my core. I can't swallow that up, no matter how much I hate the bastard looking at me like a feast — a feast fit for a king.

He may not wear a crown, but the regalness of his presence is undeniable. I am in uncharted territory with no compass or astrolabe, let alone a map. I cannot chart the unfamiliar without a drop of hope of discerning direction.

"This is not an effort to bed you." Mars rolls his eyes, but a smirk ghosts the edges of delicate lips I yearn to feel press against mine, despite my loud protests.

The spark we have is undeniable, and with each passing hour, I struggle to stave it off.

"I simply wish you would drink from this cup and embrace who you are. The shadow within means you will live to see empires rise and fall, kings be born and die, and how the world keeps turning despite it. You will be as eternal as the sun, ending only when the gods call you to rest. Does that not excite you?"

As much as Mars is trying to make this sound like a gift, I catch a hint of sorrow in the flames that flicker in his eyes, the roaring heat diminished by some deeper sadness that I'm sure most wouldn't detect.

"But others have to die so I can live!" I sputter. I feel my bottom lip crack and tear, a feeble drop of blood resting on it. I'm numb to the pain; it's only irritating, if anything.

Mars, however, grimaces.

"Please, Adelaide," he begs. His face threatens to contort into something like agony.

I blink, failing to hide my surprise at his sudden change of tone. "What do you gain from me drinking? I'm your enemy, remember?" I ask, my voice soft. I can't believe I'm trying to soothe him when I'm the one torturing myself. And what do *I* gain from it? My thoughts teeter on the verge of betrayal. My stomach coils with rage at the prospect of being filled with death and despair, all so I can traipse about in ballgowns and be the Shadow King's pet.

I've become so much worse, I think to myself, echoing what he told me in the infirmary before he duped me into thinking I would escape his clutches, unscathed by Death itself.

Still, my heart flutters as I reconsider the goblet he holds in front of me. Outside, I'm sure the religious fanatics are plotting against him for trying so hard to sway me. The enemy princess, dead and reborn, is staving off the thing that would return her to her former formidable power. It's ridiculous to pretend I can ever undo the dark magic to which Mars has bound me, whether I drink or not.

The shadows that flit within my veins are as real as the light from Siralto. My throat cries with relief as I seize the goblet from his hands, giving him no warning.

He doesn't even flinch as I toss the goblet back, letting the warmth of some poor creature's blood crash past my lips and slip through to my stomach like a rushing storm of victory.

At once, I feel life flood to my cheeks and resolve forge within my bones, ready to hold me up and keep me going as I face whatever dangers await me in the future.

I look over at Mars and see a thin mist of tears falling from his eyes, but I say nothing. I won't let him celebrate too hard as I polish the last drop of blood and fall backward to the floor, letting the cool stone ground me to the earth.

Things die. Things live. It's all the same, whether I drink or not.

I tell myself this, but my soul isn't convinced that I haven't just damned it to Kohlu. I pray that Tyrladan welcomes me as more than a monster when I'm someday slain or the gods call me back.

But the way the Siraltona surges to the surface of my skin, no longer fettered by the shackles on my wrists, tells me I've made the right choice.

While the shackles don't break, I feel weak spots in the metal. *If I grow strong enough...*

"You can break those." Mars grins, sensing my thoughts.

I shoot him a withering glare, refusing to confirm that he's correct about what I'm thinking. I can't give the bastard that sort of satisfaction. Instead, I push up from the floor as best as I can, given the weight of the metal chains that connect these damned shackles.

To my horror and dismay, Mars reaches out and helps me to my feet. I'm no more coordinated than a newborn lamb, fresh for slaughter. Except the wolf that's taken me from the fold finds me amusing and wants to bed me before he tears into my flesh and ends me for good.

I see the way his eyes flit between murder and lust as he gazes at me, regarding me as though I am a work of art rather than a living, breathing being.

If I can even call myself living, I think.

I don't have much to say to him now. My mind writhes with guilt for taking blood from a poor creature that had no say in their demise or what their blood would be put to use for in the end.

"Sherry will be up shortly," Mars abruptly says. His posture has shifted to the defensive, brooding king I've grown to hate. Without another word, he strides from the room, letting the heavy door to my chambers slam behind him.

If he's any more inconsistent with how he treats me, I might go mad from trying to discern his motives.

I brush thoughts of the brooding king aside and instead focus on trying to use the Siraltona to break the chains that hold me captive. If I can break them, I can set myself free and get out of here.

And go where? I ask myself. Home isn't an option. They would put my head on a spike at the sight of me. My father would overrule Maverick, and I would be used as a beacon of rage to fuel a war they'd be sure to lose.

Velyasa, of course, is the vampire kingdom – not some distant land like my fictional suitor "Idris" promised. How my kingdom never bothered to learn its name is another mystery that will haunt me. And I'm not about to go to Underland, either. My role as a marriage pawn is off the table.

And then there's the fact that Jupiter is still out there, lurking. For once, I'm not as afraid of Mars as I am of that other vampire. Again and again, I see Finch's lifeless body. My stomach churns, threatening to upend the freshly won blood I've managed to keep down.

I wonder if vampires eat anything other than blood. I curse myself for not paying better attention to Finch and asking him more questions when he was still alive.

Why am I so selfish?

I run my hands together as I try again and again to loosen my chains, though I know with each passing moment that the only place I'll ever belong is right here in this damned chamber.

Which, I realize, is *his* chamber. His clothes are lined up in the wardrobe off to the side. Then it dawns on me that he's yet to sleep in here.

Do vampires even sleep?

A whole host of questions about the reality of my changed status begin to crop up faster than I can process them. Why haven't I bothered to ask anything? Here I've been, wasting away for weeks on end based on a foolish attempt at rebellion.

And the only person I managed to hurt was myself.

Before I can make another attempt at loosening my shackles, I hear a soft knock at the door. I recognize Sherry's rhythm at once and move to open the door. When she sees my changed state, she smiles.

"Finally caved, huh? I knew he'd get through to you! Congrats, girl! I was worried there for a minute. Are you ready to start learning how to be one of us?"

I shrug. "Not really, but I can't be anything else, can I?"

Sherry laughs. "I'll take what I can get."

A Mind of Its Own

WHEN SHERRY LEAVES ME alone for a moment to log my vitals, I tilt my head back and try to sort my thoughts back into place. After a month of no feeding, I find it important to reconsider every angle of how I got here.

For one, a mystery is afoot.

Well, several mysteries.

Mars explained to me that, while disguised as Idris, he used thrall to break into the castle and vie for my hand in marriage... but how did *no one* notice him – not even Ivan, a fellow vampire? What is the extent of his power that he can deceive others and hide his appearance? Is that magic easy to attain, or is it something that takes years to develop?

The mystery of thrall and how all of Sunfall was so susceptible to it rests uneasily in the pit of my stomach. I can't imagine a safe way to ask Mars about it. A creeping fear of how I might be able to use thrall gives me pause, then I realize I am no better than any monster living here in Velyasa.

The rain outside still pours, sparing my mind from thinking too loudly above the din of the drops pounding on the tightly-shuttered panes. I'm glad we closed them, though part of me would like to stand outside and let the water coat my throat. It is still parched, despite having finally taken blood.

I wonder how I've managed to stay alive this long. Are there ways to end the life of one of the Shadow Folk, aside from the Siraltona? Surely there must be. But now I question everything I read about them in our history books. I can't count on anything except the power that's shut off to me by these cursed shackles.

I shake them, cursing Mars's name and the way he taunted me, knowing that somewhere within me resides the power to remove them. But I am *weak*. And he knows this. The image of him smirking at me incites a rage down to the very marrow of my bones. I hurl an empty cup across the room. It clangs against the stone wall and falls to the ground, undented and unharmed. Only I am left standing, heaving, having used up energy that was never mine to spend; it was given to me by the life of an unwitting mortal.

Then comes the other mystery to the forefront of my thoughts: How did the Lasira fruit unlock my magic? Why or how did the gods deliver the fruit to me? Was the power always within me, as our kingdom's doctor suggested? Or was something more nefarious at play that led me to this moment?

I hope the gods have not given me this power now as a means of punishment or may even now be watching me for fun and sport. Siralto may be dead, but the thought of her pointing and laughing at me from beyond the grave as some sick form of entertainment makes me nauseous.

Even more sickening, though, is the realization that I may never have answers as to why or how I got these powers. Or why they seem to attract everyone to me.

Jupiter's maniacal smile haunts my mind and makes it nearly impossible to shut my eyes without seeing him standing there, hoisting Finch up and doing the unthinkable. I can't believe how helpless and yet how powerful I was in that moment. I can't believe that monster is somehow in league with my father.

My feet lead me to stand beside the window and watch the rain outside a bit more closely. I imagine once more what life would be like had Finch and I escaped. Where would we have gone? Would Sira truly have led us here? What would have become of Finch once we arrived in Velyasa? Would Mars have given him refuge while leading me away in shackles?

I hope they would have taken care of him. Maybe his sire would have shown up and taken him in. My heart breaks again for my brother-in-law. I miss his smile, his wit, and his humor. It isn't fair that being changed still wasn't enough to save him from Death.

That begs another question: Who was Finch's sire?

My mind tires of all the questions to which I just can't seem to find the answers. I have been a poor scholar in this new kingdom, setting my curiosity aside in favor of self-flagellation for a set of morals I can't begin to define. What does it matter if mortals die so I can live?

I sigh. *It matters a great deal.*

My conscience wins out again, and I am filled with guilt once more. I hope that the death of whatever poor soul I drank from was quick and painless. I hope they were not subjected to the same comedy of torture in which I currently find myself.

Though my hands are sore and my wrists raw from being shackled and fighting against them for a solid month, my hands itch to take notes. I can't afford to lose track of my thoughts, no matter how trivial. Madness will consume me if I don't put pen to paper and record everything I've learned so far. I can't afford to forget the questions I've thought of, either. They're critical if I plan to gain the upper hand against my enemies.

I find sheets of paper laid out on a table and a pen that I don't think Mars will realize is missing. I look about, my eyes darting every which way for a place to hide these papers once I'm done scrawling down my ideas and thoughts.

My eyes settle on the armoire, and I pray to Siralto that Mars won't think to look beneath the rows of long, frilly dresses that are stocked there. I pale when I realize that they've been set there for me – the general shape and measurements are unmistakable.

Unless he's keeping some other woman in his rooms.

This sends shivers and another wave of nausea down through my veins and bones. I almost collapse to the floor, my body still weak from the lingering effects of starvation. For an immortal body, I decide that mine sucks.

I try not to consider too much the reality that I did this to myself.

I frantically scratch things down as fast as I can, desperate to remember it all. I write down how I found the Lasira and my questions about Finch's lineage. Why was he a dragon? Aren't those the most powerful of all? And how did they get their familiars back?

I underline this last question twice, angry with myself for forgetting this little detail. It's hard to remember everything when my mind has been empty of anything but grief and loss for the last few weeks. If Mars were here, I'd slap him and take my punishment with a giddy grin. He's responsible for much of my suffering.

Just as much as I am.

I don't know when I became so self-critical, but it's a truth I force myself to swallow as I continue to jot down everything I can think of.

Satisfied that I've logged it all, I tuck the sheets of paper beneath the long skirts of a wide array of dresses that give me pause the longer I look at them. I didn't write anything about them, but I fear the temptation of asking Mars about who they belong to will become too much to resist.

A small tag on one of the dresses catches my eye, and my curiosity gets the better of me. I pull it out and my eyes land on unfamiliar scrawl, making out a very familiar name: *Adelaide.*

My suspicions confirmed, I pinch myself as the seed of jealousy ebbs away when I realize the dresses are for me. There is no mystery woman. What does it matter who Mars beds?

The flashing images of him writhing between the sheets with an unknown shadow woman make me feel murderous. I grit my teeth, nearly cutting my lip open on the very new, sharp fangs that sit at the front of my mouth. Located where my incisors were, they're much sharper. I wince, realizing that I'll probably make the mistake of biting my lip many more times before I get used to them, despite the pain.

I hope I heal fast from those sorts of injuries, but the aches in my body say otherwise.

I eye the bath and think I might go for a soak, but my plan is interrupted by the sound of someone knocking.

"Adelaide, love, I'm back. I had to log your information for today and make sure we have adequate notes," Sherry says. "Do you want me to come in and help you get into more suitable clothing? I trust you found what Mars left you."

The thought of someone coming near the armoire makes me pause, but I have to trust that the long skirts will do their jobs and that random papers at the bottom won't spark interest. I can't keep them hidden like that forever, but it's the best idea I have.

It's time to put my hiding space to the test.

"Yes, please," I say, feigning a soft femininity that makes me cringe. I've never been one to be soft or gentle. As much as I crave those attributes, they've never been afforded to me by the realities of my life and duties.

When Sherry comes in and rifles through my clothing, I breathe a sigh of relief when she takes a light nightgown and doesn't look down into the bottom of the grand, wooden armoire.

Thank Siralto, I think, praising my dead goddess like she can hear me.

Sherry draws me a bath and promises to answer my questions when I come out. I thank her before going in and peering around at the bathroom. I haven't bathed since coming here – I reek. It's not like me to skip out on cleanliness, but I'd really hoped to die of starvation. Yet here my body stands in defiance of my efforts, and now it's time to give her the care she deserves, whether my soul agrees or not.

I sink beneath the surface and groan as the hot water comes up past my ears. I don't come out for hours.

SHACKLED

S HERRY AND I HAVE spent the last few hours talking. After weeks of keeping my lips wired shut out of pure stubbornness, it's refreshing to hear my voice say anything other than "no." *No* is a wonderful word I've grown to love, but sometimes it's nice to use my voice to ask questions, give compliments, and express my wants and needs.

For instance, I'm able to get Sherry to divulge that there are different *kinds* of blood that I can ask for at any time as a means of refreshing myself. While the goblet Mars gave me was filling, I can already feel the gnawing presence of hunger and thirst snaking their way into my stomach. From Sherry, I learn that vampires *can* eat, but mostly as a vanity thing. The flavors are the real reason a vampire might partake of a meal, since the body absorbs the nutrients too quickly and inefficiently for it to keep them sated and healthy. Blood is the token of our success. Some vampires abstain from mortal foods altogether; others use their heightened senses to master flavor or quest after the best inns and restaurants this side of Velyasa and beyond.

Velyasa, I've learned, is a vast kingdom comprised of several city-states and former countries that have long bowed before Mars's might. The term *emperor* might be better suited to him, but he treats them not as separate countries, but as part of one kingdom. According to Sherry, he has a reputation for kindness and fairness among those he rules. I highly doubt this, but I don't speak my concerns and misgivings aloud. The fact that I am alive, breathing, and full of renewed vigor is enough to keep me cooperative.

For now.

The snaking feelings of rage and betrayal have not left me. If anything, they grow stronger with each passing moment as the fresh blood I've consumed patches over my body, restoring strength to places where I wasn't sure I'd ever feel it again.

The Siraltona is loud, roaring in my ears and demanding the freedom I've yet to secure from the chains still clasped around my wrists. I wonder what sort of dark power has been infused in the metal that I stare at, transfixed, my mind anywhere but the words that Sherry speaks. I think she's talking about politics, but I'm not too sure. Instead, I let the Siraltona hum and sing to the darkness woven in my chains, hoping it might find a way to loosen them.

Still, I know that breaking free will earn me little more than a few feet of physical freedom. My thought process from earlier remains the same. Even if I break free, I don't have anywhere meaningful to go, and my prospects are slim for survival if I try to scale the castle walls and make my way out of Velyasa.

My horse is still missing, perhaps dead, and I'm not in control of my body enough to use vampire speed to my advantage. I wince, wondering if I should have asked Finch about that more before he was brutally murdered by Jupiter.

"Adelaide, are you paying attention?"

My head snaps up. As my eyes meet Sherry's, embarrassment floods my cheeks. I shrug.

Sherry raises an eyebrow. "You're *that* intent on breaking out of here?"

I hate how quickly everyone guesses my intentions, though I suppose that ogling my restraints is probably a good way to let my enemy know exactly what I'm planning. I pinch myself, irritated that I've left so many of my cards on the table and yet gambled so much.

"I'm just... can you blame me?" My voice cracks, my throat still not recovered from depriving myself of blood for almost a month. "Would you want to be captured like this?"

Sherry shakes her head. "I'd rather have my head on a pike and my soul free of the burden of living than be trapped as you are now. But you see, you are being treated far better than any prisoner would be treated in *your* castle."

I recoil from her, daring to sneer. "I disagree. We never took prisoners. Finch was the first, and I fought to give him the best provisions possible."

"But were they the best? Were they consistent?"

I wince, thinking of the ways Finch was tested on and left in the deep caverns of our prison cells while I fought my father to let him have a better set of treatments.

"I'm not sure," I confess. The words sting my lips and the poisonous reality of being helpless in that damned castle becomes more real to me. I was Sunfall's sword and nothing more. Expendable. Someone to be shipped off to produce an heir when my fighting days ended.

But I'm not done fighting, I realize. I just don't know *what* or *who* I'm fighting. *Surely not my own people?*

"Listen, I know eventually you'll break out of those shackles," Sherry says, her voice soft. "I hope you realize, though, this is the safest place for you."

I blink at her, registering her words and mulling them over. "That's the problem," I answer. "I know that. Even if I manage to break free, this is really the only place I can go. The shackles aren't what keep me here. My people and my power are. My head would land on a pike the instant I step outside these walls." I swallow, nausea curling in my stomach and threatening to expel the blood I spent so long putting off. I feel lightheaded. A dull pain begins to throb in my temples.

"Are you falling ill?" Sherry asks, pulling back with surprise. "It's not a common thing for a vampire to do."

"Is it common to reject food for almost a month and have your powers held back by shackles infused with shadow?" I grouse, the pounding growing worse with each spoken word. The sun outside is blisteringly bright, and I want to close my eyes and shield myself in darkness. Ironic, as I feel the divine light of Siralto whisper promises of prosperity in my veins.

"You will break free," it seems to whisper.

Liar, I think to myself, wishing that I believed my retort. Velyasa is becoming more like a beacon of freedom in my mind the more I reminisce on the future I would have if I returned home. A life with my former suitor, Alexander, would see me branded as a witch and kept alive only long enough to produce an heir before I would be put to death. I feel this truth in my bones, which have escaped the grave far longer than any mortal life could promise.

Except Finch died young a second time anyway.

The humility of that truth keeps me from the temptation to imagine how long and amazing my life might be.

Sherry raises an eyebrow. "I think you need more blood and rest. While newborn vampires don't typically *need* that much sleep... I wonder if you've taxed your body too much for it to thrive as it should. Let me place an order for you. Do you know what kind of blood he gave you? He mentioned you took it well. I'd like to stay consistent until your body has more time to recover."

"Moose," Mars answers. His tall frame shadows the doorway, and I freeze, cursing for not sensing his arrival sooner.

His eyes rove over me, concern plastered in the flames that reside in the hollows of his skull. I don't know how they convey so much emotion, but the perception he has of me is unmistakable. Weak. Suffering. Fragile. He walks over to me, approaching as though I am fine porcelain tucked away on the highest shelf in a trove of treasures never meant to be discovered. But here I am, broken and bare and up for the taking.

His hand ghosts over my chin as he lifts my face to look at him. "What ails you?" His voice, though soft, is demanding.

A lump lodges in my throat, robbing me of a response. My tongue dries. I consider how I've spent the past month putting off consuming *anything* he gives me for fear of taking from another living being. More specifically, though, I was concerned about consuming human blood. And now that I know it was a *moose*? I consumed nothing more than an animal I would have otherwise subdued on a regular hunt when my flesh was still mortal.

Now, my soul is in Tryta's shadowy hands, and my future is less certain, save that it will be a long one if I don't meet a brutal end like Finch did. This horrid king, Mars, toyed with me by letting me believe that the only way I could live was to consume an innocent human life.

"Don't you have a court to attend to?" I finally stammer, the vitriol lost in the wake of my growing state of exhaustion and renewed hunger. *Did I not consume enough?*

Sherry's eyebrows knit together with worry, her focus on my sudden illness not swayed by the presence of her king, who stands over me with glowering irritation.

"I do. But I make it a habit of keeping tabs on my enemies, especially after they go on a month-long hunger strike. Besides... the court wishes to see you soon. They want to lay eyes on you. Partaking in such a notable act of defiance intrigues them. They wish to speak with you and understand your perspective," Mars says, his teeth gritted.

Is Mars truly beholden to his courts?

I can hardly fathom the idea of my father giving much care to his nobles for any other reason than pulling at their purse strings. They greatly feared him because of his power. Does Mars have a weakness that would make him a target amongst his own court?

I tuck this idea away to use later, hoping that I've pulled an ace from the midst of so many dud hands. But something tells me I don't have the clearest picture yet.

The thought of standing in front of the nobility again here in Velyasa makes the blood that courses in my veins run cold. I'm not keen on the idea of being a puppet to parade about in front of people who once would have drunk from my veins as one might sip their afternoon tea.

"Well, I'm not in quite the right shape to be seen yet, now am I?" I ask, raising an eyebrow. I hope he doesn't see this challenge as a reason to yank me in front of them as a means of punishment. The flames in his eyes flicker, suggesting that I've landed close to the mark with this guess, though I never speak it aloud and can't confirm if I'm imagining things.

"Perhaps you made yourself sick by violating your vigil?" Sherry asks, breaking the growing fire between us.

No flames sweep our feet, but the temperature steadily rises. I fear we might burn alive here in these chambers he has the audacity to lock me away in.

The power in my veins cries for release, the Siraltona growing weary of her chains. I try to soothe her, but I've got little to barter with. She knows we're trapped, and whatever shadows have held her back have quieted my ability to crack the code.

"I think my power is angry," I answer, and then my stomach makes an awful, loud growling noise to betray my other issue. "And... I'm still hungry." I offer this last confession while facing Sherry, unwilling to look Mars in the eyes and give him the satisfaction of knowing how weak I am.

The sound of his thunderous laughter confirms that he finds my plight entertaining, whereas I am in agony as I realize again that I was standing on the grounds of a principle that was never violated.

That I know of. Maybe he chose moose blood for today, and maybe he's lying. Maybe it did belong to a human and he's saying that just to... what? Make me feel better? Play with me? Give me false hope that I'm not some damned beast that must kill innocents to live?

I suppress a shudder. I refuse to give Mars any more of a show than he's already gotten today.

"Why didn't you just say something?" Sherry asks, her voice incredulous. "Mars says you liked the moose pretty well. Why don't we stick with that? I'll go fetch some more."

As Sherry moves to leave me, I fight every instinct to beg her to stay. I don't want to be left alone in this room with *him,* of all people. I still don't understand why he doesn't return to his throne room to discuss taxation and policy and warfare with his nobles. My father always kept court, leaving prisoners to be dealt with by anyone other than himself. He only ever attended executions and the occasional interrogation.

Truth be told, we didn't keep prisoners, save on rare occasions. I gave more souls than I'd care to admit the mercy of a one-way trip to Tyrladan. Death is far kinder than life, in many cases. A trip to my kingdom's dungeons can be much worse than a visit from Death.

Sherry's earlier inquiry sinks lower in my gut, confirming that she's right about many things I'm not ready to square with, let alone admit out loud. I did my best for Finch and that's all I can claim, though it provides little comfort.

The chill of early spring bites through the open window. I shiver. I slide to the floor, not caring what Mars thinks, tuck my knees beneath my chin, and do my best to keep warm. To my horror, Mars stoops to sit beside me and removes his thick, fur cloak and drapes it over my bare shoulders.

While I'm typically dressed warmly, today I barely had the energy to throw on a nightgown. The fabric covers my body and the sharpened angles of starvation that have begun to peek through my flesh, but it doesn't keep the chilly air from stinging my flesh. I wonder if my gauntness will disappear if I drink more blood. Then I wonder when I began to think of this as a normal act I have to partake in rather than a ritual of the damned I'd once decried so much.

But my body cannot deny how much better it felt after eating. So I hold this treacherous thought of nurturing my body a bit closer to my soul and hope it won't set it alight. I've heard Kohlu is warm, but the chills in my body suggest otherwise.

"Why didn't you tell me it was moose blood? You knew I was abstaining because I thought it was mortal blood... Why not tell me? I would have likely acquiesced sooner," I complain, my voice weary with defeat.

Mars places a firm hand on my shoulder, but he doesn't pull me close as he often does. On days like this, I am certain he hates me more than anything. When his fiery eyes find mine, I know I am correct.

"Why is it so wrong to admit that your morals are founded on a questionable notion of a high ground?" Mars spits, his grip tightening so I can't pull away from the sight of his fangs as they make a more daring appearance.

"How is it wrong of me to refuse to dine on innocents?" I argue.

"The moose wasn't innocent? What quality does a human have that makes them more deserving of life?" Mars asks, daring me to think of a rebuttal.

"Of course it was innocent, but it doesn't have a soul the way a human does," I answer, but the response feels weak.

He hovers close to me. "I think you and I both know that your morals are founded upon mountains of shit lies that you've been fed since you were born. No life is worth any more or less than another, but there are rules... hierarchies. Nature is brutal, and you are a born killer. So, does that change now because your diet is more specific and your life is longer? Tell me, Adelaide, when are you going to accept that life is unfair and you can't play the role of a god and decide what is good or evil?"

"So, anything goes, then?" I hiss.

"You know that's not what I'm saying!" Mars retorts, but I see a flicker of uncertainty in his eyes. His flames tattle on him as a child might, though I suspect I'm one of the first to understand what they're saying.

Before either of us can argue further, Sherry re-enters the room carrying a full flagon. I decide to trust that she's bringing me moose blood and not the blood of a human, though in reality, I gave up on that battle hours ago when I decided to drink what I knew was blood from another living creature.

Mars abruptly stands, leaving his fur swathed around my shoulders. I wait until his back is turned to pull them closer to me, grateful for the way they brace me against the bitter winds of a spring storm traveling this way.

"Close the windows," Mars says. Then he grabs the flagon of blood and returns to where I huddle on the floor, setting it in front of me without another word.

I pick it up, ignoring the way my heart twinges when he turns and stalks from the room, a bitter rage nipping at his heels as he stalks away. Our conversation did more than irritate him; I wonder if I haven't struck a nerve. *Does he really care about the lives he takes?*

I look down, and the smell of blood lures me in and makes my stomach rumble louder. The growing fatigue in my muscles screams to be abated. I pick up the flagon and take a long, deep drink of sweet red liquid.

Only after the flagon is emptied do I look up at Sherry. I can't hide the tears dripping from my eyes that betray my conflicted emotions. "When do you learn to be comfortable being a monster?" I ask, my voice hoarse. The sickness in my stomach settles deeper, still present despite feeling full. My eyelids grow heavy and my arms start to droop.

Her eyes are piercing. "You start feeling comfortable the sooner you realize you're *not* a monster. I put a sleeping draught in the blood. It will help you recover."

Once upon a time, I would've grown angry at medical staff for doing something like this to me. But Sherry calls herself my friend, and I trust her more than most. Besides that, some deep part of me is grateful. I haven't slept since I got here – not truly. The agony of hunger kept my sleep fitful and pained. Now, I feel the true embrace of a deeper dream crawling out from my bones to pull me down into a true slumber.

"Thank you," I mutter.

It's the first step in acquiescence to her. I may hate Mars, but I don't hate her. I can't. She's been honest with me. Kind. She's helped me take feeble steps of hope, even if only in my mind, in a world cast in shadows – shadows I have begun to wonder about.

Were they real? Or are they made up by fearful prey?

My eyes close, leaving that thought to the blank canvas of exhaustion. I wonder if I'll ever return to finish that portrait.

AFTERLIFE

W HEN I WAKE, MY wrists are still shackled and I'm still weak, but the nausea is gone and I feel more alive than ever. This time, Mars is not waiting in my room with another goblet or trying to tempt me to eat. Sherry sits beside me instead, charting notes about my progress on that accursed clipboard of hers. I'm almost certain that the sound of her scribbling roused me from slumber – a dreamless slumber to which I crave to return.

"Time to get up!" Sherry claps. "Too much sleep is never a good thing."

"Says the person who drugged me so I would," I retort.

Unbothered by my jab, Sherry smiles, revealing the petrifyingly sharp white teeth of hers that I'm still not quite used to seeing up close. Finch's never bothered me, but his familiar nature made them seem far less alarming. With Sherry, I'm well aware I am in the room with a predator who takes pride in what she is.

Did Finch have pride in who he was?

It's a morose thought as I look out the window, finding that the sun is high and the spring storm has long since departed.

"How long was I asleep?"

"About a day," Sherry answers. "I wanted to let you rest. It's not common for newborn vampires to abstain from food, let alone for as long as you did. Your mental strength would make most scholars envious, but your body took a significant toll as a result. It will take a while to get you to a point where I'm comfortable. Vampires aren't immune to all illnesses when they're first turned. The body still has to adapt to being changed. While you'll heal, you'll still be... at risk... of feeling subpar and having variable strength."

I blink. "So, my mind and soul have changed, but there's still hope for my body?"

Sherry laughs. "Not hope. It just needs a little... prodding... to realize what it's capable of. Most people think a vampire is most dangerous when they're first turned, and that's partially true. An insatiable appetite with an underdeveloped sense of self is an incredibly lethal combination. I mean, look what happened to Siralto. Poor thing didn't know herself and was eaten alive by her own power."

"Sherry... that's an unproven myth. She was murdered by Tryta, the very god who fills your veins with shadow!" I hiss. I don't take lightly to people poking at my dead goddess. Dead doesn't mean unimportant, and the Siraltona in my veins howls in agreement. I look down at my shackles and grimace. Then her words trickle through my anger. "You're saying you think I can break these?"

"I do. And I'm not worried about when you do. His Highness, on the other hand, should be petrified of you," she chuckles, making another note on her clipboard.

"Why? He could break me like a twig," I complain, my voice full of a dejection I find detestable. Since when did I become a whining whelp?

"Maybe, but you've cracked his resolve, which is even more surprising. Between ogling you and trying to see to the barest bones of your soul, I fear he might go mad. He's already checked in on you five times in the last three hours. He's insistent that we get you fresh air as soon as possible and start training you. You've got to learn to hunt and learn about Velyasa, and we need more information from you about Jupiter."

At the mention of Mars's brother's name, I pale. "What do you want to know about him? I told you everything I know." *I am not a good liar*, I think to myself. Then again, what does it matter to me if they know about his alliance with Sunfall? I am conflicted now, more than ever. I am not keeping the secret for Jupiter's sake, but I fear the punishment that might befall Maverick if Mars storms my kingdom with vengeance on his mind and blood on his flaming fangs. Mars's dragon is unstoppable. I cannot live with the loss of another brother. I resolve myself to silence, if for no other reason than to protect my brother.

Sherry shrugs. "Sometimes we recall things over time. It's worth a second look."

She gives me a knowing glance, and I wonder if she doesn't already know the truth. But I don't prod. Instead, I change the direction of our argument.

"Aren't you worried Sunfall will send an emissary to come get me?" It's something I haven't dared to speak aloud up to this point. I feared saying it for the same reason people don't say their wishes out loud. Now? I fear more than ever that I might become a stuffed mount in my father's grand hall if I'm returned to Sunfall. I am every bit the monster they fear.

"I have a feeling you're more afraid of that than we are. Besides, you didn't tell anyone where you were going, and Mars's thrall duped them.

By the time they guess where you've gone, you'll be a wholly different creature," Sherry muses.

"Are you saying I'd kill them?" I ask, raising an eyebrow.

"When you apologized to the people of Velyasa, did you mean it?" Sherry suddenly asks, her tone sharp.

I look down at my fingers and consider her question, twiddling my thumbs. "I did. I know I was wrong. I know I *must* have been wrong, because my father is every bit the tyrant I delusionally hoped he wasn't. I don't know how I know that, except I saw how he acted during my betrothal ceremony. I caught wind of the politics he kept me out of. But no, I still don't know the extent of what I apologized for. And I'm afraid of what I'll feel when I find out," I admit, my voice a hushed whisper now. "I don't know if I can live with being a killer of innocents when I find out just how bad my father is, or when I learn that the cause of my crusade was little more than the delusions of a tyrannical lunatic."

Sherry looks at me with sympathy, her golden eyes misty with tears I didn't realize were present until now. Without thinking, I get up to put my hands on her shoulders. She doesn't back away from me as I pull her into something like a hug, though my embrace is restrained by the shackles. The Siraltona doesn't hum with a desire to break or bend. Rather, she swoops around us like a gentle wave and tugs Sherry into the warmth of a soft summer's day despite the chill outside. The closed window can't keep it all at bay, after all. Not in this drafty beast of a castle.

"I am sorry for what I've done," I say. "I truly did not know. I killed without knowledge of a true cause. All I knew was that my mother was dead, and a vampire was to blame. And I took my grief out on all of you under my father's banner. But you did not kill my mother... at least I don't think you did." I squint at her, eliciting a bit of humor in this solemn moment.

Sherry smiles. "I don't blame you. You were a victim, too, Adelaide. How would things have ended if you hadn't killed those who attacked you? Your victims were met on the battlefield. The rules of war hardly ever consider the idea of justice."

"So that excuses the thousands I slaughtered?" I ask.

"No, but it gives their death a much more complex meaning. Maybe their deaths served as the changing tide in a war we can finally end. They brought you to us. Maybe you're our salvation," she breathes, her eyes full of awe.

I pull away and look down at my hands. "How can I be your salvation when I don't even know who I am or what I will become? The shadows in me are too strange to understand. All I know is the light, and that light slays you all. Ends your lives."

"And yet you used its warmth to comfort me just now. Maybe the Siraltona can be a balm just as much as it can be a blade," Sherry argues.

"And maybe you're both shirking your duties and need to get down to the garden."

We turn to find Mars staring at us through the entryway of the chambers once again, his hair disheveled and his eyes wide with irritation. I roll my eyes at him. The gesture cracks a smile on those damned lips of his, and I imagine how they would feel on mine. I curse myself for slipping into yet another trap of weakness.

His fiery eyes search me, finding every break in my defenses, and he laughs. "Shall I escort you both downstairs, or do you think you can manage the trip without me?"

Sherry hisses at him, something I've never seen her do. This makes him laugh harder, removing whatever anger he carried with him to the door. A twinge of jealousy snakes into my chest, and I swallow the venom that starts to pool in my mouth. My fangs sharpen, and I resist the urge to bite my captors.

Sherry casts me a glance and notices the change in my demeanor. "He's my uncle," she says.

"What?" I ask.

"He gives me shit because I'm his niece. I'm no threat to whatever is going on between you two," Sherry offers with a knowing glance.

"Sherry, why would I care?" The lie slips from my tongue like honey, though relief bursts free within my chest and sets me at ease.

"For the same reason I would care if someone tried to put their hands on you. You're *my* pet. Well, worse than that," Mars chuckles.

I glare at him. Nobody speaks for an aching length of silence that makes me itch with discomfort. I don't know why I'm so drawn to him or what came over me at the thought of Sherry being Mars's lover. What does it matter to me? Sherry is my friend. If she loved him first, then she could have him first.

But her uncle?

"So, are we heading downstairs or not?" Sherry asks, creating a blissful break in the silence so wonderful that I could kiss her for it.

But I don't voice that aloud. I don't want Mars to get jealous. I can't imagine how violent he might become if his *pet* steps out of line.

Sherry motions for me to follow, and I do. Mars steps aside so we can pass through. As we slip through the doorway, he lands a swift smack on my ass, and I gasp. Before I can turn and say anything, he stalks away from the door, satisfied that he's gotten his point across.

"Doesn't he have a court to attend to? Or is this the life I get to look forward to living here? Does he threaten to kill you like, all the time?"

"Only where you're concerned. And most of the time, it's joking. He's... got a strange sense of humor. I guess he already told you about the swapping seasons?"

"Because spring reminds him of how everything dies?" I ask.

"And because the nights are getting shorter for us. The same way your days get longer for your true spring," Sherry confirms.

We walk together in companionable silence while I consider this and let my eyes rove over the stone walls that travel up to heights I can barely fathom. I wonder if Mars's great dragon familiar ever perches up in the shadows like an oversized bat with anger issues. I almost snort aloud at the thought.

I try to count the stairs, but I'm too distracted to get a solid number. I suspect there are around two hundred, but the reality is that there are likely far more than that.

I note the dark stones and marble columns that litter the hallways and seem to form patterns and tell stories that perhaps only the builders and artists who forged this palace understand. As dark as the stones may be, every hall is fixed with ample windows that let in the light from the outside, bathing the halls in an ethereal glow.

Some of the panes covering those windows are cracked open, allowing me to taste the soft spring in the air and taunting me with the freedom I don't know if I'll ever have again. I can't afford to focus on this. Not here. Not now. I think of something else.

"Why does he want me to stroll outside, anyway?" I ask. "Why not in the castle?"

"Because the weather is nice, and you might be inclined to walk more if you're outside." Sherry shrugs. "We need to get your muscles working and clear your lungs. You've stayed inactive far too long for someone who's been so recently changed."

I don't respond; instead, I digest this information. My legs and arms feel fine, if not a bit fatigued. The heavy cloak of exhaustion still hasn't left me, though, and I know Sherry is right. I'm not worried about bursting into flames upon seeing the sun again; I know better than to believe that outdated folklore. The Siraltona is the only sun a vampire fears. Yet, somehow, I possess both the shadows and light that would ordinarily slay a vampire with little more than a drop of its potency.

Outside, I hear strange birds chirping and spot a flash of vibrant feathers passing by the windows. For a kingdom not far from Sunfall, I wonder how Velyasa is home to such exotic species that I've never seen before. I pause to study a few of them that have perched on the open windowsill. Sherry stops so I can appreciate two magenta birds that stay even as I approach. The song that leaves their throats is haunting, and the way their feathers gleam in the light might tempt one to think they are specters rather than living creatures. But when their feathers brush my skin as they take flight, I know they are just as real as I am.

"Where did the myth about vampires dying in sunlight come from?" The question feels treacherous to speak aloud, but I can't help myself. After years of poring over ancient tomes about my enemies, there's still so much about them that mortals fail to understand. Most of the writers were turned, so the few who live on as undamned have penned their characteristics as a matter of trial and error, not accurate accounts.

"I think it comes from the fact that we prefer to hunt at night. But don't most creatures? We're just... more adept at it than mortals. Night allows you to be concealed from view and operate without as much scrutiny. Vampires delight in the night because it allows them to blend in. As you've noticed, we tend to have incredible power, might, and beauty... many of the traits that make mortals drool and kill for. Not to mention, we are felled by the Siraltona. Is that not a way to die in the sunlight?"

At this last question, her eyes glance longwise at me and I know she's thinking of all the vampires I slayed before being clapped in chains and kept as the vampire king's personal plaything. Her *uncle's* plaything, no less. I wonder why she doesn't hate me. Part of me suspects she might, despite her friendly visage and caring words. I've quickly learned that it's possible to love and hate someone at the same time. The emotions aren't that far from each other in how they feel when they roll past the tongue to coat the throat with passion.

I swallow, aware once again of how thirsty I am. *Is this how life will proceed? Will I always be plagued by this insatiable thirst?*

The pained look in my eyes must be more apparent than I intended. Sherry looks at me and lines of concern paint her beautiful features.

"Are you hungry again?"

I want to lie. I want to tell her that I'm fine and I can carry on with our stroll that's barely just begun. The door to the gardens is wide open. I smell lavender nearby. I wonder how they keep it alive here so early in the season, but the smell is unmistakable. It's a rarity in Sunfall. The vibrant purple hues were always a source of entertainment and a display of wealth to foreign emissaries. Sunfall would be incomplete without its garden of rarities.

The sea of purple beyond the great wooden door where I stand tells me that Velyasa's royal gardens would easily put Sunfall's to shame. I spot marble statues of Tryta and other lesser gods throughout the garden, as well as grand trellises laden with rose bushes that have yet to bloom. It's too early in the spring for many of the species I see, but they were such a rarity in Sunfall that I envy them even without their petals. I yearn for the day when they bloom and coat the air in that gentle sweetness that I craved so often in the gardens of Sunfall. Here, the sensation will be magnified by the sheer volume of varieties. They call to me like sirens in the sea. I am helpless to them, even as my throat constricts with thirst.

"If you need to eat, we'll go back," Sherry presses. Her hand rests on my wrist, prepared to yank me back into the darkness of the castle and the chambers sitting high above us.

"No, I'm okay," I protest, pulling away. Before she can try and hold me back any longer, I'm out the door and plunging into the most magnificent sea of color I've ever seen. All around me, Shadow Folk recognize me at once. The garden is a bustling scene of strange, imp-like vampires, whose colorful skin tones and vibrant hair colors are reminiscent of the tales of fae I'd read about in my studies.

I wonder now if maybe they were fae before being turned. But since fae are already long-lived creatures, why submit to becoming one of the Shadow Folk, of all things?

I'm still puzzling over this quandary when a trio of them approaches. All are about half my height, one red, one green, and one pink, with their eyes full of fear and wonder. They spot the shackles on my wrist and take this opportunity to approach the Shadow Slayer, the name that's being whispered all around me. It occurs to me that I'm *hearing* more than I ever have in my life. I can hear conversations happening several yards away as though they are taking place beside me.

"We thought he'd kill you for your sins," the smallest one says, her ruby red skin and deep amber eyes accosting me with a depth of rage I only felt when I reviewed the sins of my father and thought about being married off as little more than chattel.

This young fae vampire hates me, I realize, and she has every reason to. I consider her small hands and long, black hair, and wonder who I killed that was important to her. Someone drew their last breath thanks to the sharp bite of my sword, while this little girl's soul lives on, long and lonely, because vampires don't die unless they are slain.

And slaying a vampire is hard – something that almost only the gods can accomplish. The gods and their power are the key to ending a vampire's life, and very few can wield them.

I throw diplomacy to the wind.

"I wish he had killed me," I say, not caring what the others think.

The girl blinks at me before nodding, understanding everything I meant, even though I'd never speak my reasoning aloud.

"I'm glad he didn't. You have a pretty shine. The light isn't so scary on you," she says.

The other two vampires nod in agreement, the small green one to my right grabbing hold of my hand with a gentleness that startles me more than a blade would have.

All of them have matching amber eyes. "Are you three sisters?" I ask, deducing that their vibrant skin colors, while different, might also be a shared trait.

They nod. The pink one to my left is the shyest—she won't look me in the eye.

"Do you work here in the garden?" I don't know why I'm asking them a litany of questions like this, other than the fact that my mind is hungry for knowledge and everything I have come to understand about the Shadow Folk is being challenged.

My hands drip with the guilt and blood of the thousands of souls I've slain as these three sweet girls tell me how they spend their days pruning flowers and giving life to Mars's personal garden. Their fangs, though sharp, take pleasure in sweets as any child in Sunfall might, and they delight at the sight of the raw sunshine I pull into my hands.

I can't pull a lot, given the shackles, but I manage to make shapes and creatures dance and flit about the garden.

Rose, Peony, and Violet are all aptly named for the floral magics they draw from, hence their vibrant skin tones. The pink girl, Rose, it seems, is not quite as shy as she is reserved. I realize her silence is her thorns, and I resonate with her deeply. Before long, the girls are tugging me around the garden and showing me their favorite designs and flowers.

I am absolutely smitten with them.

Sherry stands and watches. I catch a hint of something like tears in her eyes as she takes in the sight of the Shadow Slayer playing a hybrid role of parent and sister to three vampire children.

My legs and arms are grateful for the reprieve from sitting still for so long; more importantly, my soul feels refreshed and new. The thirst is gone from my throat, and I have to fight back tears on more than one occasion as the sun's rays hit me and fill me with a warmth I never knew was missing.

There is no threat of betrothal here. Mars himself could enter the garden now, and I would greet him with mirth and joy rather than hate and vitriol. I don't know what's become of me, but as I sit in the soft grass so the girls can braid my hair, I wonder how I ever lived life any differently.

I close my eyes and tilt my neck back, a pledge of trust to the girls as they gather flowers to weave into my hair.

"Getting comfortable?"

Sherry sits down beside me, and Rose takes the liberty of getting flowers to braid her hair alongside mine.

I don't answer right away. Words fail me. Emotion clogs my throat. The blood of ten moose could not clear the feelings that have taken root there, making it impossible to swallow anything other than sadness and betrayal.

I stare at the castle's spires that reach up to the sky, kissing the heavens I yearn to feel on my flesh when I want to flee the most. Today, I don't want to flee. I want to atone. To pray for the souls I've rendered lifeless.

"I really am sorry," I whisper.

"You won't be for long. The stronger you get, the more nobles you'll meet. The Ayesa are always good at setting people at ease."

"Ayesa?"

"Fae who have been turned. These girls are adept at making things bloom and grow. Mars saved them after their parents were killed and gave them a job here. They had to be turned to save them. Fae don't typically consent to being turned."

"And they're called Ayesa?"

Sherry nods.

"How were their parents killed? They were fae... so that wouldn't have been my doing." I don't know why I say this last part aloud. The girls say nothing as they pluck more strands of lavender to weave into my long hair. It feels like we're going to be here a while as I cast a sidelong glance at Sherry's equally long, white mane. It shimmers in the sun, but I know it would put the stars to shame in the moonlight.

"Jupiter," Sherry says, as though that answer is enough. Instead, my stomach curls at his name, and I find that the sense of serenity I was enjoying is tainted with uncertainty and a hint of fear.

Part of me wants to probe for more information – namely, why would Jupiter hunt fae? In Sunfall, the fae are revered as something Other. To kill them and leave their children orphaned is unfathomable. This gives me all the more reason, once again, to flinch at the thought of my father allying with such a dastardly being. I consider whether I should bring this up to Sherry, my loyalty to Sunfall still shaken.

Instead, I stay quiet and let the Ayesa children finish braiding my hair. The instant they secure the end and before I can thank them, they scamper off into the garden, satisfied with their work and unbothered by the importance of goodbyes. I hope that age never teaches them just how precious farewells are.

"Want to head back inside?" Sherry looks at me. I know this is my cue that it's time, whether I'm ready or not, and she's only offering this to sound nicer than the situation warrants.

I nod without a word, but wince as I drop my gaze to the shackles on my wrists. Though the flowers in my hair are beautiful, I am still their captive and a physical representation of everything the Shadow Folk hate.

Truthfully, I hate myself more than they ever could. The fangs in my mouth still don't fit quite right. It's humbling to watch so many stop and stare at me like an animal as we proceed back into the castle.

While I know I didn't kill the girls' parents, I wonder how many other Shadow Folk children now live without parents because of me.

I wonder what my father is thinking back home in Sunfall. Has Jupiter taken up residence there and put my poor brother's head on a stake? Am I little more than a traitorous memory? Without an heir from my brother, our father's line will die with me. The Siraltona will live on only in me, because I will never bear children. I will live the rest of my days here as a prisoner under Mars's keeping.

Maybe someday I will figure out the shadowy puzzle that keeps my wrists locked in the shackles that weigh me down, but today is not that day. With each passing hour, the Siraltona bashes against them, frustrated and angry.

To satisfy her, I create lighted figures that flit all along the pathway that leads back to the castle, just as I did for the girls. I make them take on the shapes of soldiers and wizards and gods, playing out the lore of Siralto and Tryta over and over again for the onlookers who gather to watch.

Though they follow our steps, none of them speak as we reach the door to the castle.

"Go on, everyone. She's going back inside," Sherry says, annoyance ripe in her voice. "She's not a bauble to gawk at!" With a wave of her hand, the crowds move away, and we step back into the depressing shadows of the Velyasan castle. Sherry turns to look at me, her face pinched and obviously annoyed. "Why are you putting on a spectacle?"

I shrug one shoulder. "I'm not. I'm using the little power I have to do something I think is fun. I can't feel my power the way I need to, and it grows more restless with time. So, I grant her the little freedom I can."

Sherry looks at me and blinks. "Does *she* have a voice? Is... is *she* alive? Conscious?"

I think about this for a moment. The Siraltona doesn't speak; I just know what she wants. And she's both within me and separate. Before I can answer Sherry's question, I'm aware of a sharp pain in my stomach. The hunger from before has returned with a vengeance. I double over as pain wracks my body.

"Are you okay?" Sherry swoops over and steadies me before I collapse.

"She's due for another feeding. She'll need a more aggressive schedule until her body adapts to being changed."

Mars stands in the hall, flanked by a few nobles who stare at me like I'm a circus freak.

I lower my eyes, unwilling to look at them as they gawk at me. I am not a piece of art nor a mythological creature. I will not consent to being gaped at.

"Leave us," Mars says, his voice steady. "I need to tend to her."

"But, sire!" one protests. One look from Mars withers any further state-ment from the noble who wisely rushes away from his king. The others follow suit, leaving just Sherry, Mars, and me standing in the hall.

"You can't fend them off forever," Sherry says.

"Yes, but I can give her at least a century before she has to be subjected to such scrutiny," Mars answers.

"Don't try so hard on my account," I argue. "I can take it. I just don't want to today."

His eyes rove over me. "Who did your hair?"

"The Ayesa children in the garden," Sherry answers for me.

I still struggle to find words to answer him. Hate simmers in my soul along with longing, and I hate myself even more for feeling so conflicted over someone who rules the very people who killed my mother. But the blood on my hands still lingers, leaving the wretched questions from earlier fresh in my mind.

Were we really the heroes?

"Would you like to accompany me for dinner?"

This is the last question I expect from Mars, and I force myself to keep from recoiling in open disgust. The rumbling in my stomach makes it impossible to refuse him.

"I think you should join him," Sherry says.

I almost ask her to stay with me and eat dinner with us, but she walks away before I can speak. He stands beside me with his hand outstretched.

The shackles are just long enough for me to take it. I hesitate, a jumble of emotions threatening to swallow me whole as I consider the consequences if I don't.

He waits silently as I render my decision.

I place my hand in his and pray to Siralto that it is the right choice.

Light Show

HE LEADS ME THROUGH weaving hallways before we find our way to a massive dining hall. This early in the afternoon, Sunfall's dining hall would be full of nobles, merchants, and emissaries, all seeking my father's insight and approval when he was most agreeable. Food and ale made him the most likely to accept any odd proposals or lower taxes for those amongst his elite who sought a reprieve.

Jesters and circus performers were hired to come at least once a week. Now, I shudder to think how much such things cost our coffers while so many of our people suffer outside the castle walls.

I didn't consider those things enough when it mattered. Mars's perception of Sunfall is probably closer to the truth than my view of it, which shames me even more, as I am the one who lived there.

Velyasa's dining hall largely sits empty. There will be no distractions of dancing or petitions tonight. It is only the two of us here.

He pulls me along until we reach a large table in the center, its polished veneer bearing the grand, royal appearance I expected.

I wonder if vampires don't use their dining halls because they don't have to eat, or if Mars just doesn't like to be interrupted when he dines.

He pulls a chair out for me and waits until I settle into it before taking the one beside me. His flaming eyes drape over me with a hunger I fear no amount of food or blood can sate.

"Would you like to expand your drinks of choice to things beyond moose? Or do you prefer to stick to the safe option? You'll find that there are plenty of times to feed since you have a longer recovery time ahead of you, but there's no shame in being adventurous."

His eyes flare with challenge, and I consider the reality that I may be trapped in this room with him rather than the other way around. I cannot soothe myself with my usual thoughts that I am the biggest predator in the room.

"What... what are the other options?" Fear creeps into my throat. I wonder how I ever found him attractive.

Then he leans in closer, and that catch in my throat returns when I feel the ghost of his lips on mine, even as he sits too far from me to reach.

But he can clear that distance fast if he wishes. I hold my tongue, willing myself to stay silent.

"I can get you human, turkey, bear... those are readily available at the moment."

I balk at the first option and manage to squeak out *bear* before I lose my resolve entirely and flee the room.

"And what else to eat? I can have bread and ale brought up. I wouldn't recommend the ale, but it might give you some form of familiarity."

I shake my head, nausea threatening to spill my mostly empty stomach onto the table. "Ale does foul things to people. I don't want to start such a nasty vice as a vampire." I don't elaborate. I'm sure he knows why, and I wonder if offering it to me was yet another way to torture me for my past. I'll spend the rest of eternity atoning for my sins and the sins of my bloodline.

Mars snaps his fingers. A young woman enters the room. Her olive skin is smooth, and her dark eyes are full of shadow and mystery. "Kaycee, our guest will have some of the bear that was brought in today, along with some fresh bread. That is all that is required."

Kaycee looks ready to bed Mars here and now, and from the way he looks at her, I have no doubts that she has in the past.

I feel the Siraltona screech to the surface, begging to find the weak points in the shackles and reduce this Kaycee woman to dust, even as she waltzes from the room with a sultry swish to her hips.

He's not mine, I remind myself.

But when my eyes return to his to find the cunning smirk on his stupid face, I know I was too obvious about being jealous.

"We could skip to dessert, if you wish. The food can be brought up to our chambers," Mars purrs.

"Don't be stupid, *pig*!" I answer, although the hiss in my voice is less than convincing.

Mars rolls his eyes and laughs. "Suit yourself. I haven't slept with her in at least a century, though, if that makes you feel better."

White-hot rage threatens to cook my flesh and boil my blood until only flames are left, but I do my best to hide it. Instead, I look away from him, feigning a coolness that neither one of us is buying.

Before I slip any further out of control, Kaycee returns with two flagons of blood and a plate full of fresh, warm bread. My mouth waters as she sets it in front of us, even as I pray for her death. It's wrong of me, I know. I have no claim over Mars and no reason to hate her for a relationship she had with him well before I was born.

Yet, still I sit here, red with rage and full to the brim with sick, green envy.

I grab a piece of bread and tuck it into my mouth, hoping to stuff away the horrible things I would say without it there to plug up those awful words.

"Blood first," Mars chides, his voice suddenly stern.

I look up at him as I swallow a large piece of bread and almost argue with him. But the smell from this flagon is even more enticing than the moose, and I don't have to be told twice that it will suit me better than bread.

I gulp the whole thing down, polishing it off in seconds. Still, the gnawing hunger in my stomach does not find relief.

Kaycee goes back and forth between the kitchens at least four times before my stomach is full enough.

Mars sits back and watches, barely touching his flagon. "You waited far too long to eat. You'll have to stop now to avoid getting sick, because we need to take things easy. No more flower appointments. As pretty as it looks, getting your hair done today took too much of a toll."

I look at him with an incredulity he doesn't expect. He sits back, and his eyes widen. I rarely see him caught off guard, but I know I've done the trick this time.

"You really think I'm that fragile?" I ask. "The Ayesa children were gentle, and I sat the whole time. The real tax was making light figures with the Siraltona."

Mars raises an eyebrow. "Light figures? You're shackled."

He chuckles at me as though I'm foolish, and without thinking, I forge the glowing silhouette of a dagger in my hands and hurl it at him. It flies past his head and shatters into the nothingness it came from so fast, I'm not even sure it happened. But the look of stunned shock on his face tells me I've either gained the upper hand or damned myself to more restrictive shackles.

"How does it get past them?" he asks, gesturing to the very chains that consume my thoughts.

I think for a moment. "That's a secret even I don't know the answer to." I smirk at him before returning to the bread. I reach out to grab a piece when his hand claps over mine.

"Show me more," he whispers.

I look at him and see desperation wavering in his flaming eyes. So I take my hand off the bread and summon flowers shaped by light into my outstretched hands. I let the flower open its petals with slow, deliberate showmanship. Mars assesses the leaves that flutter out past the petals, suggesting that I might start fashioning a stem. Then maybe a whole bush. Hell, I might be tempted to grow a whole garden of flowers right here in the dining hall and call the Ayesa girls back to weave more into my hair.

But the light would fade from between their fingers and even render them ill if it's infused with the right intent. I don't think it is, but I wouldn't risk their sanctity on a guess. I want to test it first... on none other than the Shadow King, who looks at me with the bewitching fascination of which I've grown to have such a mixed opinion.

I extinguish my power. A distinct, awkward pause of silence grows between us. I know he'll break it first. He can't help himself – he always has something to say. Sure enough, he soon proves me right.

"You've gotten past your shackles," he says, raising an eyebrow.

I shake my head, feeling the sudden drain of exhaustion pull on my veins. "It comes at great cost, and that's all I'm limited to... Suddenly, I understand why I was so hungry."

Mars leans back, chuckling. For someone who witnessed his mortal enemy tap into her deadliest power seconds ago, he's at ease, like he's having a nice, hot goblet of blood delivered to him along with some powdered pastries for breakfast.

Does he have a sweet tooth?

I'm not about to ask him. Instead, I reach out with a hunger I fear I'll never conquer and shovel the last of the bread into my mouth just as Kaycee returns with another flagon.

This time, I smell the change in the blood, and I almost choke on the last hunk of bread that's still making its way down my throat.

Kaycee pauses, her dark eyes darting between us, and I notice for the first time the thin sparkle of jealousy held within the shadows that seem to pour from them. I'm almost relieved to know I'm not the only one so deeply affected by Mars.

When I turn back to him, I find his fiery eyes boring holes in me, as though I am the only creature in the room. I shrink away, suddenly shy at the level of scrutiny as Kaycee sets the deep goblet in front of me.

I swallow, already guessing what's in the vessel. I look at Mars. I feel my skin drop a few degrees in temperature and am certain I am as white as the linen sheets that call to me from his bed. I wonder why he has me sleeping in his chambers. Then I wonder if he will take a spot in Kaycee's chambers tonight since his most dangerous enemy is warming his bed.

An enemy in shackles, I grumble, looking down at the restraints.

"You can probably tell that I've had Kaycee bring you the blood of a mortal. He was a criminal guilty of some of the most heinous crimes. His actions were corroborated by many. There was substantial evidence."

"What was his crime?" I ask.

"He killed an Ayesa child. There was a fourth flower girl. Lavender," he explains.

I'm not sure when I stopped listening as I give in to the rage crashing over me. The flowers in my hair feel so much more significant, and I toss back the goblet with an earth-shattering war cry I can't help but release.

Kaycee regards me with open disdain. She hasn't left the room, though her olive skin pales at the sight of my uncouth manners. "Since when do you care for children who aren't human mortals?" she sneers.

Mars cuts her a look that I'm certain could kill her where she stands, but by the look in Kaycee's eyes and the sudden tick in her jaw, it's obvious she's slept with him enough to no longer be afraid of him. This only serves to make me angrier.

I clench my fists, aware that my only weapon right now is myself.

Unluckily for her, that's the only weapon I've ever had. I move toward her before she can react, pinning her to the ground with the chain between my shackles. I press on either side of her neck, ready to choke the life from her horrid windpipe, before massive arms wrench me off her.

"Have you learned *nothing*?" he hisses.

I don't resist when he pulls me off her, and let my body go limp. I have no doubt I can beat Kaycee in a physical fight. The primal rage of jealousy and hatred will fuel my movements. But with Mars? I'm not sure I have the gall to withstand him and his dark shadow magic. The dragon still lurks beneath his flesh, I remind myself. And those fangs he uses to smirk at me are for more than just show. My altered state of life is thanks to those sharp bastards.

"Adelaide, I think it's time we return to our chambers. From now on, I will accompany and oversee your nightly routine to ensure you don't sneak back down here to hunt my favorite waitress."

The word *favorite* makes my blood boil, although I can't figure out why. I hate this man! He's murdered my people and might even be responsible for having my mother killed. I try to remind myself of those things as I feel a twinge of sorrow when he casts another glance at Kaycee. I remind myself of this even more as joy flutters in my heart when he *sneers* at the horrid vampire waitress.

"You should know better than to evoke rage in her. She is *mine*. You do not harass what is mine. Know your place, Kaycee. You are *not* mine. Not anymore. You haven't been for a long time. Let it go and move on." Mars hoists me over his shoulder like a common rag doll.

I squeak a bit at the sudden motion but clamp down on any further protests or insults.

By the sound of the rumbling thunder in Mars's voice, I'd be foolish to test his patience any more than it has been. I *did* just attack one of his royal servants. I'm a prisoner of war, and his pet... and so much worse than that.

More guilt sinks into the pit of my gut, and I fear that I might hurl the gallon or more of blood swirling about in my stomach.

Mars must know I'm on the verge of vomiting because he lets me slide down his shoulder so he can cradle me with both arms, removing the pressure on my stomach.

"Full and satisfied?"

I nod, looking up at him through my eyelids, which have suddenly grown very heavy. "Did she spike my drink? And was it really the blood of the man who killed Lavender?"

"She didn't spike your drink. Not exactly. I had her put a sleeping draught in the blood, my fire. I knew you needed more rest and wouldn't do it willingly. And yes, what I told you about the man is true. A newborn vampire needs mortal blood more frequently than others, and I knew it was a moral dilemma for you. So I thought I would choose someone who would lessen that quandary for you... The fact that you met her sisters today is fortuitous."

"Now I *know* you're related to Sherry," I grumble. "You and your sleeping draughts."

I want to be angry, but sleepiness tugs me beneath the waves, and I know a nap will come crashing over me at any moment.

He steps into the bedchambers, and I don't protest as he slips the clothing from my body and searches the wardrobe for a nightgown. He slides it over my head with ease and tucks me underneath the blankets. He sits back and looks at me, satisfaction wrought in his handsome features, and for a moment, I don't look back at him like a feral, caged animal. Instead, I find myself enamored by the beauty of his face, the sharp angles and roughness.

Before he can get up to leave me, I reach out and grab his hand.

"Let me keep you for a little bit before you go bed someone else," I murmur, my voice slurred by sleep. I'm only half aware of what I'm saying; jealousy still plays a sick song of taunting in my heart, which is torn from watching another woman capture Mars's attention. Even if only for a little bit.

"Do you think I've been bedding others, Adelaide?" he whispers. "Since you've gotten here, I haven't been able to think of anyone else."

His weight settles behind me on the bed. I half expect him to toy with me – to place his hands in forbidden places, and my body lurches, ready to defend my honor to the death despite the drugs coursing through my system.

Instead, one muscular arm finds soft purchase between my neck and the pillow, and the other curls around my body with the defensiveness of a serpent ready to strike.

My stomach curls, and my body relaxes into his embrace. My flesh and spirit are at war with each other as I fight the waves of sleep crashing over me.

As tense as I am, his body sags into the mattress and, judging by the way he breathes, I know he's falling asleep far faster than I, still dressed for court. He only bothered to get me dressed properly to sleep. I wonder if he even planned to sleep or if the stress from today's duties became too much for him to bear.

I also wonder if he's stupid enough to fall asleep with his sworn enemy in his arms when I've already shown him that the Siraltona can worm past the shackles. As homicidal as he makes me feel, my fight against sleep grows weaker with each passing moment. I note the way the world outside grows darker and wonder why vampires aren't nocturnal.

I thought Sherry said they revel in the longer nights because it gives them time to hunt more in the winter. Why isn't he getting ready for the day?

It's the last thing I think of before I finally give in and let the darkness of exhaustion drag me under.

Etched in Scars

When I wake up, Mars is gone. Everything about the day before feels like a fever dream, and I wonder if I am going insane. Why would I ask this bastard to help me? Stay with me? *Sleep* next to me?

As I rub my eyes, the clinking of the shackles still holding me is a constant, itching reminder that this is no dream and I am being held captive by the very monster I swore to slay. The same monster who pretended to be a fine prince from a foreign kingdom, whose name my father never bothered to remember.

Velyasa. The Shadow Kingdom.

With a groan, I roll out from under the covers and curse myself for how refreshed I feel. I don't wait for Sherry before I start sorting through the assortment of fine gowns in the armoire Mars has in his bedchamber. I check to make sure the papers I hid are still there and breathe a sigh of relief when I spot them, untouched. At least, they don't *look* touched. I don't have time to consider the alternative.

His bedchamber is not as pompous as my father's back in Sunfall, but it's undoubtedly royal with its decorated stone walls and the fine furs lining the bed that I've come to cherish so much. Getting cold is still a mortal ailment to which I fall victim. Sherry said that with age, I'll grow stronger and less susceptible to fluctuating temperatures, but the chill passing through the open window tickles the nape of my neck. I shudder.

Clearly, I have a lot of growing up to do.

My eyes land on a smooth, silky gown with silver filigree. It's reminiscent of the dress my father had me wear to the ball on the night I first discovered I could wield the Siraltona. While my brother and his wife wore fine gold and glowing accents, I was tucked away by the less divine color of the moon. The celestial body born to reflect, never to cast her own light.

But here I am, the moon who shines despite the sun and from her own unholy depths. I could shatter the known universe and all the realms that connect it if I could just figure out how to break out of these damned shackles. I curse under my breath as I pluck the gown from the armoire and decide to try it on. I don't care if it's too fancy for daytime; I want to feel every bit the royal I was back in Sunfall, even if it was a dream built on the delusions of a tyrannical madman, even if the madman is my father.

Surely a drop of his strangeness lives in me, whether I like it or not. These are the wild thoughts I process as I tug on the gown and struggle to cinch up the back. It's much harder to do this with shackles than I could have ever imagined. I've never been good at corseting myself, even if this one is less restrictive than the others. I wish corsets could be done away with altogether. If Sherry were here, this would be a much less tedious process. I manage to twist my chained hands in such a way to grab the strings and start trying to tie myself into the blasted gown.

I grumble, pulling at the strings with grasping fingers and praying to Siralto that they're the right ones. I amuse myself sometimes, praying to a dead goddess about corset strings, of all things. What does she care for outfits or catching the attention of a deadly king whose throat I want to rip out most of the time?

When I fumble again, dropping the strings from shaking hands, I swear louder, certain the guards in the hallway can hear me. Vampires have far superior hearing to mortals. I wonder if I'm as loud as I think I am, or if I'm only loud by the standards of Shadow Folk.

Light pools in my hands, startling me from my struggles. In my palm, a small key takes shape. I blink. The key is made of solid light – it does not have a corporeal feeling to it. Yet, when I pick it up in one hand, it carries some heft, despite its odd appearance and physical qualities. It moves about as a real key would, but it glows, but not so bright that you can't see straight through it. It's as if a soft sunbeam has landed in my palm and is waiting for me to do something with it.

I carefully eyeball my shackles, looking for a keyhole that this new instrument of freedom might be useful for. I walk to the window, desperate for the sunlight to highlight any cracks in the shadow metal I can exploit.

There! It's a small opening just large enough for a tiny key of light to slip into it. I almost gasp aloud, but now I'm even more paranoid that the guards might hear me and alert Mars that his terrible pet is about to loosen the bars of her cage and bolt from this place.

I don't know where I'll go if I free myself. I can't go home, and Jupiter is out there somewhere, prowling around. For all I know, he could be lurking within the walls of Sunfall by now, plotting with my father. *I hope to Siralto that Maverick would end him before it came to that.* But maybe, with the powers I possess, it won't matter anyway. Maybe I can let myself be the goddess I know I can be. I only hope Siralto doesn't mind my blasphemies and delusions of grandeur. Just the taste of freedom drives me mad with the promise of power.

I hold my breath, trying not to give myself a false sense of hope as I bring the key closer to the lock on the left shackle. I haven't even thought about looking for the lock on the right one yet. If I have to hurry out of here with one shackle still molded to my right hand, so be it.

Closing my eyes, I push the key into the lock and say more silent prayers. I know the gods must hear me on some level. Why else would they have gifted me the Lasira fruit?

Why did they gift it to me, anyway?

This thought ricochets through my soul and roots me to the spot as I turn the key. When the shackle cracks open and falls from my left wrist, I am left standing, rooted in the realization that I don't even know how I got these powers in the first place.

But the Siraltona does not care for my concerns. She does not care why I was cursed at birth or how the fruit healed me of some unknown ailment that kept her suppressed, unable to roar to the surface as she does now, lighting Mars's bedchambers like a beacon of glowing sin, likely alerting every Shadow Folk that the Shadow Slayer is free.

Where I thought my feet would help me run, I stay planted where I'm at. I eye the right shackle, and the burning, white hot light pouring from my skin illuminates the other lock. I jam the key into it and it, too, cracks open. I stand in silence, key still in hand, as Mars and Sherry barge into my room with wild eyes.

My heart thuds in my ears. Panic dredges through my veins as I consider my options while we all stare at each other in disbelief.

Would my light carry me out of here faster than a dragon? Could this unholy light pierce through Mars's scaly hide if he chased me out of here? Could I live with myself if Sherry were murdered in the fray?

Logic returns to me, drowning out the delirium that freedom deceived me with not moments ago. There is no freedom for a freak like me, I realize, staring down at the burning light shining from my arms and palms.

Mars hesitantly steps towards me, the flames in his eyes wanting and terrified at the same time. Sherry looks faint, her violet skin paling the longer she looks at me.

Monster, her golden eyes seem to say, betraying how she really feels about me. She is terrified of me. I am terrified of myself.

"Put the shackles back on!" Mars hisses.

I look at him, the incredulity of his order dropping my jaw just enough for it to gape. My mother would have made a comment about letting flies in, but I don't care right now. I glare at Mars, rage returning to the surface and giving me second thoughts about leaping from the window and leaving this terrible place behind.

I can find blood on my own, I reason. But then I remind myself what is required when drinking blood from living creatures. Would my fangs puncture through skin the way they should? Will I still be as weak as a newborn?

I catch Mars creeping closer to the broken shackles on the floor, and with little to no thought, I point my hands at the shackles. The Siraltona cracks from my palms and shatters them to dust, narrowly missing his hands.

He cries out and jumps back. Rage contorts his features. He barrels toward me. I don't have time to react, nor is the Siraltona ready to bear the brunt of his shadows as they erupt from his hands like dark flames and consume us in a heated battle of wills.

Where my light stretches out, his shadows meet it to engage in a clash of equals. Mars raises an eyebrow as he watches the stretching tendrils of his shadows get cut down by my rays and blades of light. My heart aches as

I watch my swords of raw, divine light drowned by the shadows of Tryta himself.

Neither of us is winning in the battle of magics, but Mars has the upper hand in brute strength and speed. I curse for being weak and leaving myself open to attack as he tackles me against the wall, pushing my hands above my head and holding me still against the stone wall of his bedchambers.

Both of us are heaving to breathe, the tax of using our magic almost too much to bear. But I'm not one to back down from a challenge.

I push against him, my body thrashing against being held rigid. I hope I don't harm my body too much by bashing up against the wall to try and get leverage against Mars. I'm not sure how strong my body is in its current state. Sherry says I'm susceptible to illness, but what about injury?

Not worried about finding out, I grit my teeth and bear the pain blooming in the back of my head and along my back, arms, and legs. I'm certain I'm bleeding – I feel the familiar wet slick of blood start to stain my dress.

His nostrils flare; his flaming eyes widen. "You're bleeding!" he snaps. "Stop resisting and let me help you!"

"Help me?" I demand. My efforts at holding him off are pointless. The Siraltona has met her match, the shadows she fights going toe-to-toe with her, despite the efforts I make to draw on her.

"Yes, *help* you," Mars grunts. It's the first sign that he's putting forth any strain to keep me trapped here, and I know it's only because of the magic he's using. Siraltona is deadly to them; yet he hasn't broken a sweat, and the single grunt that leaves his lips is the only indication of effort.

Hate pours through my veins, white hot and jealous. Why can he hold himself rigid and strong while I struggle to even think straight enough to keep pulling on my power? Will his shadows consume me if I pull back on the divine light still pouring out on the floor and choking out the few of Mars's shadows that I can best? And what prevents him from shedding his flesh for scales and his fingers for claws? What if he releases his dragon in this bedchamber? He could surely have it rebuilt after squashing me like a bug.

The battle at Sunfall gave me the gift of surprise. There are no surprises here, and I am running out of strength. I curse myself for refusing food for a month and bemoaning morality like it ever mattered to me.

But I know when I am bested.

"I'll stop if you stop," I offer, my teeth still gritted.

He raises an eyebrow. "You can't expect me to go through with that demand when I've clearly won." The smirk plastering his stupid, handsome face makes me want to vomit.

"But I'm not putting the shackles back on," I counter. "They won't work now anyway. I know how to open them."

We stay locked in this feeble dance of resistance while he continues to overpower me. I don't know why I think I have any leverage here at all – he has no reason to honor my wishes. I'm a jailbroken prisoner standing in the middle of his castle, a sea of my enemies all waiting just beyond the walls of the bedchamber.

Was I not just getting ready to try and escape? What stopped me?

The truth of it all is too much to swallow, and I do my best to pull back the tears trying to race down my face. I feel the wounds on my back slowing to a trickle, the blood no longer pouring from my broken flesh.

I heal fast.

But Mars's nostrils continue to flare at the smell of my weakness.

"You are too young to be fighting with, Adelaide. One more step out of line, and I will put far worse than shackles on you. Understood?" He looks at me with a fierceness in those flaming eyes that makes my blood run cold.

I let a moment of silence lapse between us before nodding.

Both of us step back from each other, and I call my light back while his shadows return to his own safekeeping.

Sherry has paled from her usual violet to a light shade of lilac. Terror is still etched on her beautiful features as her eyes flick between her uncle and me, unsure of who she should speak to first. I'm flattered that her loyalty is so clearly split between us when she's only just met me. But it's her uncle that she goes to first.

I feel the sour familiarity of betrayal. I am always picked last, whether it's a battlefield to die on or a group of monsters to slay.

Those same monsters will treat me no differently here. But that's a rebellious thought I tuck away for later. I can't try anything right now or Mars will snuff me out – of that much I'm certain. I'm weak now… but imagine what I can do if I get to be strong like him.

Sherry walks over to me next, ready to give me the once-over, but I pull away.

"I'm fine," I say. I give her a look that tells her I'm unwilling to budge on this. I don't care how hurt I am. I don't want anyone pretending to care about the fact that I'm hurt. I've let myself grow soft, and it's high time I remember where I am. I may wear fangs now, but I did not put them on by choice. These people are still my enemies.

I may share in the magic that makes them what they are, but my soul is wholly unique and different.

"I would like to bathe now," I announce. "I will be in the bath. Do not disturb me."

I don't wait for either of them to protest. Instead, I allow thoughts of how angry I am about my ruined dress, which isn't even mine, to soil my mood as I storm into the bathroom adjacent to the bedchamber. I slam the door behind me, not waiting to see if anyone is looking.

"Adelaide, that's a lot of blood," Mars calls out.

"Yes, and my wounds are not important. *Yours* are. I am your enemy. Don't forget it. I can tend my own wounds. I've been harmed far worse than this and, from what I can tell, it is already healing!" I shout through the door. I keep my voice sharp like a blade. It's the only viable weapon I have left.

Shuddering, I finally look in the mirror. My reflection is visible, despite some of the myths about Shadow Folk having no reflection. My eyes are still the strange, light gold as before, though my hallmark silver is gone. They are a memory of a past that seems so distant, it feels like a century has passed, not a month, since I stole away from Sunfall to meet my doom.

I let my soiled dress slump to the floor and turn to look at my back in the mirror, almost gasping aloud at the sight of the bloody scrapes on my skin. My skin has always been a bit more pliable than most, but this is the first time I've seen it take a beating like it has today. Wounds this bad will live on as scars forever, unless being a vampire can somehow magically etch them from my skin.

Come to think of it, I look down and notice that only a few of my most favored stripes remain. Scars from growth and fights long since won have always littered my body.

Where are they now?

I draw my bathwater and take off the rest of my clothing until I stand completely nude. I begin the arduous process of looking over every scar I've ever earned – at least the ones I remember.

As it turns out, becoming a vampire *has* begun to erase them from my skin. Every line and memory is being eaten alive by immortality. Already, my mortal life has begun to fade in every possible way. Before long, my scars will become a memory not unlike the ones from childhood. I don't remember most of them. I especially don't remember much after my mother died. At the age of ten, it was hard to conceive of that tragedy, so my brain just... shut off. Much of the things that happened before are clouded in a haze of nostalgia I don't dare touch unless I want to become a puddle of tears. *And tears are weakness*, I remind myself, as I find them misting my eyes when I glance back up in the mirror.

Determined to swallow any sobs that might claw their way from my throat, I launch into the bath, not caring about the water that splashes to the floor.

"Please let Sherry tend to your wounds!" Mars calls out.

I jump, startled by the sound of his voice. I didn't realize he was still standing outside my door. Granted, I could have known had I been listening for a heartbeat... or breathing. I can hear both of those things if I listen hard enough. He's not trying to conceal himself, as vampires are apt to do.

I need to be better about using my new skills. If I'm not mortal anymore, then I need to start acting like an immortal.

"No, thank you. I am healing just fine!" I retort.

I grab a cloth and begin to wash off the blood and grime, careful of the scrapes still closing on the backs of my legs. My healing is slower than I remember wounds taking to heal on Finch. Even after that night when I found him in the castle prison... he healed so much faster than I am now.

He was older. And was raised properly. He ate. He drank blood. I...

I shake my head. Finch was a better natural at being a predator than I would ever be. For once, I'm not sure this is a quality I cherish about myself. Groaning, I try to avoid flinching as the cloth reaches the raw skin on my back.

"I'm not leaving until you let someone tend to your wounds!" Mars insists.

I squeal, realizing just how close his voice is. At some point, he let himself into the bathroom, and I completely missed it. I lurch from the water, desperate to grab a towel to cover my nakedness, but he beats me to the chase and tosses it out of reach.

I wrap my arms around my middle and glare daggers at him. I'm almost willing to risk it all and make a break for it, but I don't want to give his nobles that much of an eyeful. Besides that, he's blocking the door.

"Listen, you pig, I know we've had our fun before, but at what point did you get the idea that I would be okay with you ogling me in the bathroom?" I demand. My voice is laced with a fire far hotter than even the flames in his eyes.

"I'm not here to ogle," he huffs. "I... I hurt you. You are still new. You don't heal as fast as I do."

I notice for the first time how he already looks renewed, like he didn't just summon shadows to hold off a magic with the ability to kill him if I were to strike him correctly. *Or can it kill him?*

That's a fear I'm not willing to consider right now. Instead, I focus on trying to cover my naked body.

"If you won't let Sherry check you, then I will. I won't put my niece through the task of trying to tame you and care for you when I am perfectly capable of mending someone. I will do it myself." He plucks a few vials from his pockets and hands them to me.

I look down at them, incredulous. "You want me to trust you to give me something to drink when you've drugged me twice already?"

You expect me to remove my hands from covering my breasts?

"I want you to take these potions because they will speed up the process of mending your skin. They will also serve as an anesthetic and prevent infection. You will feel no pain and you won't risk getting sick again. While you can heal from those things, the longer you remain weakened, the harder it will be to prosper as a proper Shadow Folk. Why make your new life so hard when you've only just gotten started?"

His voice is soft with concern. I can't quite understand why.

"Why do you even care?" I ask. "What do you get out of all this? Are you really that bored for entertainment?"

But my hands fall to my sides. I take the vials from his outstretched hands. I toss the first back and then the second, noting that both are odorless and free of color. It dawns on me that he could still be poisoning me or putting me to sleep again.

But within seconds, I feel more alive.

Mars looks at me like he's seeing me for the first time today and leans down closer to me. He runs a broad hand through my matted, wet hair and chuckles. "You are my fire." He smiles. "Is that not enough? It is my mistake for trying to keep you caged so long. You need to be able to *be*. That is what you need to flourish. Would you like me to take you hunting today? Training? I know your muscles ache for movement. You must promise me that you will let me know when you get tired, but keeping you locked up will not help you grow. We will bring plenty of snacks and blood to keep you thriving while we are out."

His voice holds a hint of excitement. It's tentative, but contagious. For a moment, we are simply two souls who are drawn to each other and nothing else. Neither lust nor hate matters. Only the magic of being with each other is what keeps us rooted here in the reality of existing. I want to get lost in him, and I believe he is so far lost in me that he can never find his way out. The way his eyes rest on mine tells me he is comfortable in their embrace. He does not care that I've tried to kill him, even if it was just moments ago. Once again, we are drowning in the tides of a fate far bigger than either of us could ever hope to resist.

I breathe in, letting the scent of him tickle my nose. He's been close to me many times now, but never for any reason other than letting our tongues dance or in fits of rage and battle.

As his hand snakes down my back to feel the depth of my wounds, I note the scent of cinnamon and earth and fire. I would never have pinned him for having a sweet spice in the fabric of his essence, but there it rests, pulling me in. He is as deadly to me as any poison. But the vials he gave me, true to his word, start to ease the pain of my wounds, and I feel my skin start to renew at a much faster pace.

"I will miss my scars," I blurt, wondering why I would ever bother to tell him something so sensitive.

"Your scars?"

No longer caring about my nakedness, I begin to point out to him the few that remain.

"I got these when I grew. My body was not ready to grow tall, and it happened so fast. I ached all the time," I explain. "They are sort of like my tree rings. I've always looked at them as a sign of how I managed to grow despite everything life threw at me. Despite losing my mother. Despite my father hating me and using me as a sword, then leaving me in the shadows." I pointed to my arms. "These are from when I first learned to train with my father. Once upon a time, he cared that I knew how to fight and was not powerless, even without magic. I don't know when the rage from my mother's loss found him at the bottom of his flagons of ale, but they did. After that, we did not train anymore. I trained alone."

I don't wait for him to ask questions. I move on to the next scar, displaying the few I got in battle maneuvers. I show him the ones I got saving Ronald's life in battle so he could return home to his wife and children.

As I'm showing each battle scar to him, I notice how many of them are being drawn out of my skin, replaced with new, more supple flesh that does not bend and scar as easily as mine did.

Finally, I show him the one right above my heart at the rise of my breast. It's the one I talk about the least – the one where my father nearly split me open the first time I asked him why my mother's power couldn't stop the Shadow Folk from taking her head. It was the first and only time I opened up to him, tears spilling from my eyes, wanting to tell him how badly watching her die had affected me.

"Alaric blames me," I say. "I know it is my fault."

Mars places his thumb over the scar, and the two of us watch as it begins to fade. He bends over it, speechless, and places his lips to it. "A last farewell to it," he whispers. "May a blade never touch you like that again. May even my hands never harm your flesh like that again."

Finally, it fades, the last scar and testament to the life I had as a mortal.

I don't remember when I started crying. I don't remember when he plucked me out of the tub or when he started to help dry me off.

But after a few moments, I've collected myself, and he's helping me find something to wear after ruining the pretty silver dress that still sits in a bloodied mess on the bathroom floor. While it lies forgotten and permanently stained, my skin has overcome and moved on.

Mars helps me find riding pants and a more suitable top. It's one of his, I realize, but it must have shrunken in a wash done too hot, so it fits me more appropriately than it would his hulking, muscular frame.

I hope he will train me, I think, but the thought is treacherous to even admit to myself, so I tuck it away where I can't see it again.

For now, I have to trust him enough to go hunting with him.

I can only hope that I won't become the hunted once again.

FLEDGLING

O F ALL THE PLACES I expected to have a meltdown beyond the castle walls, the stables weren't first on my list. But the grief of finding my beloved Challenger missing hit me like a brick wall, and I've yet to stop crying.

Mars, at first concerned, now regards me as someone might look at a petulant child. "Adelaide, crying is not going to bring him back," he scoffs.

Gone is the tenderness he displayed while bathing me and inspecting the scars that once littered my body and are now *gone* thanks to his treacherous shadow magic. I am cursed with smooth skin, though it feels softer to the touch than it should. But I don't dwell on that. I'm sure that will disappear, too, in time.

"Adelaide, perhaps we should hunt later," Mars growls. "You're making a fool of yourself in front of the entire kingdom."

I consider him through a sheen of tears and blink. "Why do you care? I'm not a royal. I'm your stupid pet! Let them think I'm pathetic. I miss my horse. I miss my scars. I miss my life as a mortal! Besides, isn't this supposed to be my punishment? Isn't this what you wanted?"

Mars knits his eyebrows; I see him process several retorts, but no words leave his lips. Instead, another sigh of frustration passes through his gritted teeth and he runs a hand through his copper locks, tousling them to a degree of attractiveness I find disturbing.

I can't bed him here. *I can't bed him, ever.* I curse myself for letting him do as much as he has up to this point. *Thrall must be a hell of a drug,* I think to myself, ignoring the possibility that much more sinister magic might be at play. Thoughts of enchantment and curses come to mind, but I can't trust any of the literature I've studied up to this point. Everything I learned about Shadow Folk so far has proven to be mostly lies with skinny truths peppered in between. If I could throttle the past scholars of Sunfall and the kingdoms before for their ineptitude, I would.

I think back to the notes I have hidden in the bed chamber and wince, scolding myself for being such a hypocrite.

"While a punishment, the choice for whether that stays a punishment is up to you. You are one of us now. Do you really want to spend the rest of your life running from what you are? From the powers you now possess? You spent almost a month starving yourself to the point that you inspired religious fanatics – and yet you do not serve our god. Is this the legacy you want for yourself? And your horse is gone – that was not my choice. Are you really going to blame me for that, too?"

The tears slow and I glare at Mars, finally deciding what I want. "No, I want you to teach me. I want to know my powers. I don't want a legacy of moping or never coming to grips with what I am, but this has been such a big change for me. And is it so horrible for me to grieve my companion? I loved that horse. He was among the few friends I had back in Sunfall. For all I know, he became your brother's lunch!"

I shudder at my statement. His flaming eyes soften a bit, but the rigid stance of annoyance and urgency remains in his taut shoulders.

"Shouldn't we be hunting at night? I thought that was the whole point of you older vampires calling spring, autumn, and autumn, spring," I grouse, not caring how brash I sound. Mars doesn't seem offended, but when I see the odd stares from people passing by, I decide I should probably think twice before acting this way with their king in public.

He is their king. Should I care about his reputation? Why should I cushion him from the blows of judgment?

"That is from an era long past, hence why we *aged* vampires reference it more than the modern generations. The freedom that we enjoy now came at great expense, Adelaide. A great expense that you and your mortal friends were more than happy to impose on us."

Mars glares at me now with a putrid disgust that almost makes me shrink away from him. *Almost.* Instead, I let the rage at being sneered at like a common rat push me forward, stopping any errant tears still streaming down my face.

"Fine. Let's get on with it, then. Why do we need to ride horses to hunt? I thought our kind were fast."

To test this, I take a shot at running from my current spot to the stable doors. I'm faster than I've ever been, but Mars still beats me to the entrance. Any sign of his earlier vitriol is gone, replaced now with simmering amusement.

"We are, but you are still young and tire quickly. You're regaining your strength, which is fantastic, but I don't want to place too much trust in your growth just yet. You *did* just take a healing potion," he reminds me, the barb sticking right in the softest part of my soul.

Whether he meant to jab me is a question I don't care to ponder. Instead, I stick my nose up in the air and push past him. When the pungent smell of manure slams into my nose, it takes everything in me not to double over and puke all over the barn's floors.

"You'll also find that your senses will sharpen. Of course, this means smells will be stronger." Mars chuckles, passing by me without so much as a sniff to betray whether the smell affects him the same as it does me.

I cringe when I realize that during my stubborn fast after first being turned, I didn't bathe for a month. He could *smell* all of that on me. Then again, he's probably used to it. I take a moment to steady my roiling stomach to avoid retching. By the time I'm standing again, through a sheen of tears, I see that Mars has begun to saddle two fine steeds.

One is a small bay mare, and the other is a large gray destrier. I don't have to guess whose horse belongs to whom. My fingers itch for Challenger's reins, and it feels like treason to even touch the saddle that sits on my new mount's back.

I don't ask her name. It's a sin to skip over this detail, but my heart can't stand to be broken again. To acknowledge what I'm about to do is to admit defeat and confess that my horse is never coming back. Somewhere deep in my chest sits the small girl who still believes in fairytales and miracles. There, in the delusion, Finch always walks up holding Challenger's reins. Together, we ride back to Sunfall, where my mother still lives, and vampires live only in fantasy books.

But the harsh reality hits me when Mars hands me the bridle after tacking up for me. Turning, he gets his own horse ready for the hunt. I note how careful Mars is with his selections and how cautiously he approaches his horse. If I were anyone else, I'd assume this is how horses are often handled. But I know better. A person's treatment of their horse reveals a great deal about them. What they tolerate, how they communicate, and what tack they prefer... It's all a way to map them down to the finest grain of their soul.

I wonder what Mars sees in me as I take the bridle and slide it onto my horse's head, careful to place a thumb in the crook of her mouth so she'll accept the bit. It's not a harsh one, for which I'm grateful. While it's not one I'm familiar with, I note how easily it moves and how the bar is linked to relieve pressure on the tongue.

I check the cheek pieces and cavesson, making sure that everything is cinched properly, and take one last look at the girth to make sure it's not loosened now that we've been standing here for a bit. To my surprise, the mare doesn't seem to have puffed herself out at all to avoid tightened straps. She's a horse with little stress.

They must take good care of them here.

It's not uncommon for horses in the royal guard to exhibit signs of stress over time. It comes with the territory of what we do. With the exception of horses like Challenger and Shadow, the horses in Sunfall were prone to all sorts of issues caused by being overworked.

I note the way not even Mars's horse flinches and, once again, am confronted with the reality that Sunfall might be the kingdom of real villains and monsters.

"What–what is her name?" I ask quietly. This girl deserves to have her name called, even if I'm unwilling to admit the reality of Challenger's demise.

"Dya," Mars grunts, swinging up into the saddle. "The gods' word for *dream.*"

I nod. I look into Dya's eyes more closely this time and find kindness there – a warmth that is not unlike the one I found in Challenger's. I'm still wary of her, but I am firm and kind with my hands. My discomfort should never be her lived reality.

I flinch as I see how close Mars's head is to the rafters above once he's mounted. I don't think being beheaded is a feasible way to kill him – at least not like *this* – but years of having it drilled into me *not* to do things like that keep me honest enough to walk Dya to the doors of the barn.

A horse named *Dream* feels fitting for the view I bear witness to when I step out into the light. The cerulean sky and lush forest ahead are breathtaking; behind us the spires of the castle look almost crystalline in the light from the sun. I stand there, letting the world wash over me, rather than mounting up. "It's a beautiful day," I whisper, half to myself. But it's enough for him to hear. The Shadow King turns to say something to me; instead, Mars's eyes widen when he realizes I'm still not on my horse.

"Hold on. Let me help you – I was foolish. That was very ungentlemanly of me," he starts.

But I don't wait for him to dismount. My foot finds the grip it needs in the stirrup and I pull myself up. I make it quick so I don't pull too much on her back and settle lightly into the seat, my rear held firmly up against the cantle. I'm disgusted by how well-suited I am to a saddle I've never ridden in. We never had such fine tack in Sunfall.

"Next time, wait for me," Mars grunts, riding up alongside to assess me more closely. His eyes rove over my legs and stirrup leathers.

But I'm already adjusting them before he can say anything or make even the slightest movement to help me. I'm still angry with him for being so impatient with my grief. I almost laugh aloud when Dya pins her ears at him when he tries to come closer.

He reels back, feigning shock. "I had a feeling she would pick your side. Come on, then. I see you've got things handled," Mars sighs.

I almost detect disappointment in his voice, but it's gone as soon as I sense it and neither of us is eager to wait around for more of it to return.

We pick an easy pace. Without the urgency of battle, riding is a relaxing thing. I know that some creature during this hunt will come to take its last breath, but the knowledge doesn't bother me right now. Instead, I allow the steady motion of Dya's smooth trot to sway me into a false sense of comfort.

"How far out do we ride?" I ask. "I've never been hunting before."

Mars looks at me, shock now prominent on his handsome features. "Never? Not even as a mortal?"

"Don't get me wrong, I've hunted out of necessity when we were out on patrols. But not... not for sport. I only hunted out of necessity," I admit. "My father often went on royal hunts. I presume that's what this is?"

Mars shakes his head. "This is also done for necessity. You must drink blood, Adelaide. This is not some pompous royal hunt, and it is no different from when you hunted for your men when you were out on patrol." He gazed into the forest. "Regarding how far out we'll go, I try to go a good ways from the castle." He glances at me and narrows his shrewd eyes. "Why? Planning to slay me out here in the woods?"

I blink. For once, I am not thinking of homicide. Despite our earlier bickering, no animosity hides in my bones... at least not right now.

"No. I was merely curious as to your customs."

I wish I had a notebook to write in when I am not in the castle with my precious papers. I've learned and written a lot about Velyasa and its customs, but hunting is an entry I haven't catalogued yet. I hope I will remember everything by the time we return.

I wonder if this is why scholars have struggled so much to keep accurate accounts. Though I have a sneaking suspicion that prejudice and fear have played a larger part in the fanciful lies and tales I've read about the Shadow Folk.

He is unconvinced. "Why do you suddenly care for our customs? Planning a cultural revolution to spite me?"

Normally, I'd find this sort of question as an opportunity for verbal sparring, but I detect the humor in his tone and decide to play along.

"Yes. I plan to instill the will of my people and have you all worshipping Siralto by next week," I say, barely stifling a chuckle. I've always done a poor job of conveying sarcasm unless I'm angry. For the first time in a long time, I'm not angry.

I am at peace as the feeling of Dya's body swaying beneath mine rocks me into a sense of calm. My eyes grow heavy, but I am not willing to put my life completely in Dya's capable hooves. It's not fair to make her pilot this trip alone. I keep my body in an appropriate position and ensure I am aware of her every move.

"What is your horse's name?" I ask.

"Tye," he grunts.

"Like... the Mansalo word for *paper*?" I snort.

Mars shoots me a grin. "He's the right color for it. I wasn't very inspired when naming him, but he seemed the sort of blank canvas just worthy of the name. He'll grow lighter with age, as many grays do, so he will naturally age into his name."

I'm laughing even harder now. I'm not sure if it's the humor of a horse named Paper or the fact that I have finally dropped all pretenses and thrown caution to the wind, but it is a deep belly laugh that leaves my body aching once I manage to stopper it back up.

Even Mars's shoulders shake a bit as we enter a tall copse of trees. But then my humor is swallowed by a tenseness that arrives and seizes me by the throat. All at once, the memory of losing Finch in the woods washes over me until I fear drowning in it. Dya stops and refuses to move forward, and I'm grateful she's not a flightier steed. I know she senses my fear; if she were younger, she might take this as a prime opportunity to flee. And who could blame her in a vampire-ridden forest?

"Why don't you all feed from your horses?" I curse the way my voice chokes on my question, further betraying just how terrified I am.

Mars whips around to look at me. "What's got you startled?"

I shake my head. "Answer my question. It helps keep my mind off things. Do you?"

"Not typically," he cautiously answers. His flaming eyes narrow, and he urges his horse closer to me. "What are you frightened by?"

My neck cranes up to the trees whose tops I can't see, and I'm convinced the sun will leave us behind. Siraltona starts to pool in my hands. I'm careful not to explode here like I did the last time I was in the woods.

"Finch died out here," I finally mutter.

At this point, I know it's time to slide from the saddle. My legs have turned to jelly, and I'm not going to push my luck with Dya's steadfast resolve. She and I don't have the rapport that Challenger and I did. At least... not yet. I can't hold back from her on account of a horse I can't have.

Mars follows suit and rushes over to me, placing his firm hands on my shoulders. "Do we need to go back?"

I shake my head in protest a bit too violently, but it gets the point across. I am unashamed as I crash into him and let him put his arm around my shoulder. His warmth is a hedge of protection, and in this moment, we are nothing more than a young couple on a romantic outing in the wilderness. He is not the Shadow King, nor I the Shadow Slayer. Together, we are searching for the perfect place for our picnic.

But when I look up at his flaming eyes and the sharp teeth in his wicked smile, I am reminded again why I must work hard not to let my guard down around him. I am safe in his arms from all but himself.

"He cannot find you here, my fire. He found you when you were still young... weak... mortal. You are none of those things now. And *I* am here," Mars growls, the flames in his eyes growing dark with flickering shadow at the thought of his brother trying to come back for a second round.

I am overwhelmed by the urge to kiss him and let him do vile things to me here in the woods, but I will never speak these desires aloud. I'm sure he knows of my arousal anyway. It's probably some sick vampire trick I've yet to learn. I'm still angry he never mentioned to me that I *stank* for a month. I could have bathed in between fighting him about drinking blood.

"So... what do we hunt for?" I ask, trying my best to change the subject and ignore the trepidation growing in my legs, which shake so badly, Mars must steady me. I am almost incapable of controlling my body now.

"Whatever attracts your taste buds most, my fire. You will easily smell prey here in these woods. That's half the battle. Then, you will learn how to subdue prey and consume their life force. It's important to note that you do not have to *kill* them. There are plenty of trophies to be had here in the woods, but letting a few go so they can regenerate their lost blood supply and have young is critical."

My skin pales. "You... don't have to kill them?"

"Adelaide, surely you know that we do not need a lot of blood to keep going and that you..." He trails off and gives me a quizzical look. "Have you never done bloodletting on account of a doctor's orders? It astounds me how readily you'll believe anything about us except the truth," Mars complains.

Before I can retort, I note a shift in the air and a drop in the temperature. I smell it before I see it–another spring storm has come to join us on our outing. I cringe at the thought of our tack being sullied by the rain.

"Maybe we should head back," I say. "I don't want our stuff to get ruined."

Mars shakes his head. "Not until you answer me. Do you really think we are all monsters?" His gaze intensifies.

Suddenly, his fangs seem sharper and the fires in his eyes burn hotter... brighter. Fear seizes my throat and I search for an answer. "No," I finally manage to choke out.

I know he doesn't believe me, but I also believe what I said. Anyone can be a monster. I hope he sees the truth in my eyes, as my throat is too dry to plead with him.

"We will finish the hunt before we return. Our tack is imbued with magical properties... it will not be soiled," Mars says.

There's a harshness to his words that tells me I won't be able to argue with him. For once, I'm not in the mood.

I'm disgusted with the effect he has on me. To avoid having to further confront these conflicting feelings, I return my focus to the hunt. "How do I know what I'm smelling? Do... do I just know?"

When the vampire king chuckles, I'm relieved the tension between us has faded. For now, I don't have to fear breaking into a fight or trying to jump his bones here beneath the trees and risk being caught in the act by the very citizens who wanted me dead. Despite my very real punishment, I'm sure many would rather have seen my head on a spike. Finding me pleasuring their king in the woods is certainly not the way I want to be remembered.

First impressions, even among enemies, are everything.

"A lot of it is instinct, but I would encourage you to breathe deeply. You'll find that your sense of smell is much sharper than before. Let your senses be the guide that leads you to your first caught meal."

I can think of several things I'd rather do than breathe deeply, but I follow his lead and wisely keep my mouth shut. Instead, I focus on my hearing and smell, praying to Siralto that I can quickly get it over with and figure out how to do this. Hunting for myself is a skill I can take with me if I ever find the courage to escape or hatch something of a real plan to be out on my own.

Several minutes pass. Mars darts off and disappears several times before returning to my side, blood and satisfaction smeared on his lips. While he is a natural-born vampire, I struggle to drown out the cacophony of voices and ideas scrambled in my brain.

Mars chuckles. "You're trying too hard."

He looms over me, eyeing me like someone might look at the last piece of a delicious cake. But I can't afford to be distracted right now, as much as I would love to let him pin me to a tree and have me in every diabolical way I can imagine.

His nostrils flare and I wonder if he can *smell* what I'm thinking. Just in case, I dust away my lustful thoughts and refocus my efforts. As his arms snake around my shoulders from behind, I sense a different scent in the air. I freeze; Mars loosens his grip and lets out a low, rumbling laugh.

"You've got something in your sights," he whispers. "Go now. You can do it. When you get back, we can celebrate."

I don't dare ask him what it would mean to celebrate. I can't be shaken from my focus now. I take another deep breath and note the fresh scent of something *warm...* savory....

At once, I'm taken by a deeper instinct I can hardly control. One moment, I am fighting against Mars's sinful game of touch and taunt; the next, I am an apex predator in a game of chase with a creature I've yet to see up close. But as soon as I'm locked onto its scent, I'm aware of its heartbeat and the thudding of its feet... *hooves.* But these hooves are cloven, unlike those on Dya and Tye.

I hook a corner past a tree, my feet lighter than air and swift as the wind before I descend upon my poor, hapless victim. A doe. My teeth cleave through her fur and flesh and find purchase in the sweet nectar hidden in her veins. She is far more savory than a moose, and the warmth of blood straight from the source is a new sensation for which I am insatiably hungry.

I don't know how long I drink. It is only when I feel her heart start to slow that panic overtakes my selfishness. I realize too late what I have done as the heart stops beating, and she falls limp in my grasp. My arms drop. She slumps to the ground. Tears fill my eyes, and I stumble back and away from her. *I killed her.*

It's not the first deer I've killed, and I doubt it will be the last. But to have been so intimately involved with her end... This was a much more brutal death than an arrow.

Yet, she didn't thrash. She didn't even seem frightened when I took her down and made her my next meal. I hear Mars before I see him. Already, the effects of being changed have overtaken my mortal senses. I wonder how long it will be before every inch of the mortality I once clung to is scrubbed away by the monster who now wears my face and parades about in my flesh.

Am I even still myself?

"Well done, Adelaide," Mars praises me.

But the words feel hollow and ricochet through my chest like a stray bullet. Guns are rare in our northern provinces; considered pointless because they do little to harm vampires. But the harsh steel of reality cannot be denied.

"I could have let her live," I say, my lip trembling. I hate how emotional I've become since moving here.

Mars crouches beside me. I don't remember when I got this close to the ground, but I am determined not to cry in front of him again. One meltdown is enough for today. I take a shuddering breath and steady my nerves.

"Adelaide, it is okay to be overwhelmed. You have been through a lot of... change."

I know his words are sincere, but I shoot him a withering glare just the same. We both know who is responsible for the *change* he mentions. But I don't say it aloud. I let him slide his arms around me and hoist me up, ever the damsel in distress, and he walks me back to my horse.

"Let's get you back to the castle," Mars says, his voice hushed.

I'm quiet the whole ride home, but I give Dya special attention when we return as a thanks for tolerating my shaken nature. I promise her that, if I'm ever given the chance to ride her again, I will be much more alert.

I swear I hear Mars say something about being careful of promises I can't keep, but when he catches me glaring at him, he stops whatever hateful thing he was saying before it finishes passing his lips.

"Not so fun when I start to 'embrace my senses,' as you say." I offer a saucy wink, unsure where I keep finding the bravery to taunt him as I do.

He holds out his hand and I note the way the guards look at us with suspicion when I take it. If I try anything, they'll end me without a moment's notice. The reverence these people have for their king is astounding. In stark contrast, my father was always greeted with wary glances and fear shining in the eyes of his people.

Where my father's people had fear in their eyes, Mars's people have admiration. Some bow. Some kneel as he passes by. He greets each one with a grateful nod and a smile as he sweeps me back into the castle.

I almost have the courage to ask him about familiars and magic and all the things that have haunted my people, as well as the people who lived centuries before and logged all those strange and erroneous facts about them. But the desire to ask those things dies when I remember the stacks of paper I'm still hiding from him in the armoire. If I don't trust him not to search for those written accounts, what makes me think it would be wise to ask him those questions aloud?

I decide I'm better suited to figuring those things out in passing. I will collect facts like trinkets and tuck them away for safekeeping. Only after I've finished the puzzle will I reveal my cards, if at all. I have always been a brilliant strategist; it was my father's fatal flaw to exclude me from politicking. I would have known Mars's face despite the thrall.

My heart is not so sure of this when we reach the bedchambers, where our lips find their way into a passionate game of tug of war. Where sadness has ached in my chest since we left the hunt, desire now snakes through my core.

"You were brilliant today," Mars whispers, his tone sultry. The flames in his eyes darken as he lets his hands wander down my frame. "Seeing you hunt while wearing *my* clothes..."

He doesn't finish whatever statement he's about to make. Instead, he tugs his tunic from my body, leaving my bare flesh exposed to him. I feel no shame as his eyes rove over me, drinking in my half-naked frame.

"I wish to celebrate your accomplishments today, Adelaide, though I will not bed you in the traditional sense. As I said before, I will not do that until I take you as mine. But do you trust me to treat you fairly and leave you satisfied?"

My cheeks flush. I remember him saying something about mating rites when I was first in the infirmary with him, but I don't have time to properly recall them before I'm nodding and letting him unfasten my trousers.

"Lie down on the bed," Mars hisses.

I stumble forward to the bed, awkward with my gait, as nerves start to take over my senses.

"Trust me, Adelaide. I won't hurt you," Mars says. This is a time when I believe him, despite all the times he has hurt me.

My body shakes, the tremors of nerves overtaking me more than I realized. I've never been naked like this in front of a man. I had my fun as a young royal without a husband, but I've never taken things *this* far. I never had the time to think about such things, nor has anyone like Mars ever taken an interest in me.

"Let's get you a bit more relaxed," he says.

When he removes his shirt, I am transfixed by the way his muscles ripple like those of a sleek panther as he moves to hold himself over me. Our lips crash together again, and we spend what feels like hours letting our tongues and lips explore each other until they are numb. He stops to slide the trousers from my legs, exposing the rest of me to him, and seeing I am ripe for his taking.

There isn't an inch of me that he doesn't explore with his hands. I try several times to spread my legs for him. I beg him to take me, but he still resists.

"Not until the proper Rites," Mars huffs. But his resolve is diminishing. *What happens if he violates the Rites?*

But then his lips pepper down my frame. "You are still too thin," Mars murmurs against my left breast before taking my nipple into his mouth and suckling with gentle persistence.

The yearning in my core is unbearable. I slip a trembling hand down my body, ready to do what I must to relieve the pressure if he won't ease my suffering. But he smacks my hand away.

"Sweet fire, you mustn't spoil the fun just yet. I will get there... have patience."

He has the audacity to *nip* the lower flesh of my breast, and I yelp. Before my irritation gets the better of me, he takes his other hand and snakes it right where I need it.

He has no trouble finding just the spot. I cry out, pleasure wracking my body. The relief at finally feeling his touch is so overwhelming, I am almost in tears.

This must be a sickness. This cannot be a normal case of infatuation!

"You make the loveliest noises," Mars croons.

In response, I let out another squealing moan that I'm certain can be heard all the way home in Sunfall. But I don't care. My body arches when he suddenly brings his head between my legs and plunges his tongue between my folds. Gone is the patience he demonstrated moments ago.

He is ravenous, but gentle. I hardly remember my name as he performs ministrations down there that have me questioning why I ever hated him. Between his fingers and tongue, I am certain I will die like this. They will find my naked body, and I will not be ashamed.

When an orgasm tears through my body, I don't have time to warn him before my body convulses around him. Never has my body rocked and shaken such as this, but the look of sated satisfaction in his flaming eyes tells me he doesn't mind.

I slump against the bed, my body sore and spent, but I have a duty to repay him. I start to sit up, but he stops me.

"You don't owe me any return favors," he says, guessing my thoughts. "I suspect you and I will both be pleased and angry with ourselves for this in the morning. Let's not add to the guilt where it is not necessary. Should you choose to repay the favor at some other point, let it be a time when you feel less hatred for me than you do now. Or... perhaps when you feel more. Surprise me."

Anger flashes in my soul, but I stamp it out. If he doesn't want me to take him in my mouth tonight, so be it.

Why am I so determined to repay his service anyhow? He did me a favor... nothing more.

Still, my heart sours when he puts on his clothes and exits the room without another word. Rather than finding solace in the sheets while basking in the afterglow, I cry myself to sleep.

What have I done?

COURT

I 'VE SPENT THE BETTER part of a week holed up in this blasted bed-chamber since we returned from the hunt. Neither of us has spoken of the steamy encounter we had after, and Mars has rarely come to see me. I'm certain now that he must have a second bedchamber somewhere in the castle... or else he is spending his time with other women.

I can't stomach the second option, so I choose to believe that a king can have more than one bedchamber. A part of me remains self-conscious, wondering if there was something I said or did that night that would push him away or make him seek refuge in the arms of another.

Sherry and I have taken to visiting the Ayesa girls on a regular basis. They have redone my hair at least four times, and each time is more intricate than the last. One of the girls brought a replica of the Narlasha last time — a famed instrument of the gods — and actually wove strings from blades of grass on which to play it. While not woven of stars as the mighty Siralto once played upon, it is still a magic I am blessed to behold.

The Shadow Folk are not bashful in their use of magic, nor is it used in a way that is always destructive, as the Siraltona often is. I envy them and how free they all seem as they snap their fingers or speak aloud incantations that give life to color, freedom, and happiness.

Magic, as I've always understood it, comes at some cost. Siraltona is rare in that it draws from the energy of what it strikes. Lesser magics always come at the eventual cost of someone's life, if not worse, depending on how they use it and if they anger Fate too much. However, it seems these laws only apply to mortals.

The Shadow Folk use magic for everything from baking bread to mending clothes. No one is burned at the stake for practicing illicit witchcraft, a law I always found hypocritical in Sunfall, and no one is treated as an outcast or breeding stock for future lines of magic. At least, those things don't happen to my knowledge.

My stacks of paper grow higher as I write down all the things I learn about the Shadow Folk. I know I can't keep them hidden in the armoire forever, but I am proud of the knowledge I've amassed in the month and a half since I was turned into something... *other*.

As much as my comfort grows with handling the Siraltona, I am still wary of the shadows that flit around it and caress my divine light with promise of immortality that I can't shake. The worst part is that the Siraltona doesn't rise to fight off Mars's shadows every time. Sometimes, it extinguishes these vile thoughts as soon as they're conceived by whatever dark magic keeps me alive. Other times, she is no better than I am in avoiding the temptation of stealing moments of lustful exchanges, the few times Mars and I aren't trying to kill each other.

Those peaceful times have been few and far between lately, and I fear how I've begun to feel during his absence. I should not crave a man I hate with the same fervor with which I hate him.

"Is something wrong with me?" I ask aloud, sitting next to Sherry while she and I both read. Mars is not opposed to me reading from their library. I have voraciously consumed hundreds of pages of literature about Shadow Folk. Some of the accounts still seem dubious, and I don't understand the context of everything, nor what I'm even looking for, but what I've learned is fascinating. Today, I am enjoying a small volume about familiars. While it doesn't reveal why that magic disappeared, it gives me a great idea about what different familiars mean.

True to his seismic power, Mars has a dragon, which represents that he is at the top of the proverbial food chain. Challenges to his power are rare since he possesses magic almost certainly granted by Tryta himself.

I wonder about the power Finch might have possessed if he'd lived long enough to see his magic flourish. Would the small red dragon I saw have become a great, fire-breathing monster?

"What do you mean, is something wrong with you?" Sherry's question drags me back to the present, and I look at her, pretending I wasn't lost in deep, spiraling thoughts about my brother-in-law's death.

"I... I know it's probably gross because he's your uncle... but why can't I stop thinking about him when most of the time, I want to kill him? Why is it hard to breathe when he's not near me?" I ask. "Is it because he's the one who turned me? Is it natural to feel this much of a... *draw* to him?"

Sherry looks at me for a long moment before chuckling. "I have my theories about what's happening, but it's not my place to speak on them. And I don't know that he's ready to acknowledge the situation, either. He's been in a state of ruin since you both went hunting last week. Spare me the details, though, please. You're right. He is my uncle; that's gross."

Though my cheeks flood with embarrassment, I'm not deterred from pushing for more information. "You mean you have an idea of what's wrong with me? Meaning there *is* something..." I let the sentence trail off, hoping Sherry will finish it. Instead, she shakes her head, the knowing smile on her face filling me with irritation. "Sherry, please, this isn't funny. I am being eaten alive by a desire that is not mine! I love him as much as I hate him, and I'm not sure if the love part is even real!"

I am terrified of how weak and needy I've become. Over and over, I've played the reality of being replaced by another woman in my head. Rage coats my bones. I am rigid with fury and cannot find my way out of the chasm of fire and jealousy.

"He won't talk to me, which means I must have done something wrong. Either he found someone else, or he found me to be unlikable. How do I fix that?" I look at her and find a sick sense of satisfaction when the smirk is wiped from her face and replaced by concern.

Instead of waiting for her to put me out of my misery, I put my book down.

"I'm going to walk in the gardens. If you're not going to tell me, then I need to clear my head and free myself of this madness. There are other things I must consider – chief among them is why the gods gave me fruit to heal me and then left me with my magic in this hellhole!"

Sherry winces like I've slapped her, but I don't care. My body is a bundle of bouncing nerves. I can't keep them trapped in my body like a jar of bones anymore.

My feet do the work for me; my mind is miles away as I race to find the door to the garden and step out into the green, fresh growth of spring. The smell of fresh flowers and the cool waters of the kingdom's countless fountains and streams will surely refresh my soul. Perhaps those very same waters can douse the fire that burns in my heart and soul for a king whose life is an insult to my very lineage.

Except now, my body also courses with shadow. I am even more perplexed at how I have managed to carry the Siraltona with me.

The instant my feet touch the grass, I breathe a sigh of relief. At once, pressure and fire are released from my lungs. I feel like a whole person again. No longer am I trapped by the lonely voices of my anger. The sun's rays cast their warmth on my shoulders, and I shrug off the light fur wrap I wore inside the castle's drafty halls. Not even closing the windows in my bedchamber has stamped out the cold that seems buried in my marrow.

I try not to obsess about where Mars is or what I could have done to send him away this long. I try not to think of how I cried myself to sleep the night before and feel starved of him like one might be starved of oxygen.

The longer I stand in the warmth and glow of the sun, the louder my power thrums in my ears. No longer am I a slave to my feelings for Mars; instead, I am caught up in the realization of just how much energy is concentrated in my veins.

I pay the shadows that flit there no heed. They are a power in which I have no interest. Instead, I grab hold of the hilt of the Siraltona and wield it in my hands like unforged blades, ready to be brought to cruel life with only a snap of my fingers.

My feet don't know where they're heading now, but my eyes recognize the familiar path to the stables. It stands to reason that I would seek a ride into the forest on a day like today.

Maybe I can hunt down a meal and sate the endless, ravenous hunger of the gnawing fury that grows with each day I remain Velyasa's prisoner. Maybe I can douse the fire that eats me alive.

This time, when I pass through the doors to the stable, I don't bend over when the odor hits me. It is more bearable this time. I know now that Mars is a master of experience and nothing more — he is not more powerful than I. He has simply been here longer, hence how he can stand, unfazed, by the things that bring me to my knees.

To be a fledgling vampire is to be a student relearning the art of living. I wish more than ever that I had pen and paper to scratch these things down like the desperate thoughts of a madwoman.

Instead, I look through the rows of stalls in the hopes of finding Dya. I won't take Tye, and my heart can't bear the thought of befriending any other horses. One betrayal against Challenger is enough.

I notice that most of the stalls are empty. In Sunfall, this usually meant scouts were out on patrol and something sinister was afoot. I want to ask someone about this, but I doubt anyone would readily share that level of intelligence with me.

That, at least, is not that different from home.

I swallow the bitter memories of being a princess in a castle made of glass. While everyone else could see through the fragility of its walls, I was blind to the truths I now witness every day.

We were doomed. We never stood a chance against the Shadow Folk. My father and brother were brief spots of respite granted to mortals by the gods. That time of benevolence is coming to an end.

I believe the Lasira was given to me by the gods to mock me. It was given so that I might serve as a reminder to others how I am still not a god. Wasting their gifts to become tyrants is folly. It still astounds me how the Siraltona does not eat us alive when we use it to slay perceived threats to our kingdom.

But watching my father crumble and my brother lose his health tells me it might be eating at us more than we think.

Still, I remain unscathed. So far, anyway. As one of the Shadow Folk, I have a lot of life left to burn.

I've been up and down the rows of stalls twice and don't see any sign of the bay mare I bonded with. She must be out on a hunt or otherwise engaged in battle. I pray to Siralto for her safety and decide to set off towards the woods on foot. A mount would be helpful, but not necessary.

While I know I could get there in no time with my newfound speed, I decide to take an easy pace. All along the road, I explore the softer side of the Siraltona I first used to entertain the Ayesa children. I make little figurines of lovers dancing, butterflies, birds, and even tiny dragons that play chase along the worn path that stretches to the woods.

It occurs to me that my Siraltona is really only useful for slaughtering and destruction or feeble feats such as this. How I'm supposed to wield it for anything like mending, creating, or anything else escapes me. It's ironic, considering the Siraltona was born of a Creator.

I resolve to try and learn those things, if I am able.

"I am more than murder and destruction," I whisper aloud as a challenge and a promise.

When I reach the edge of the woods, I stop and take a deep breath. At once, I catch it: the faint scent of cinnamon and smoke.

Mars.

The vampire king is out here hunting. Part of me yearns to turn back, but the other is renewed in her quest to kill him. *After* he tells me why he's been avoiding me.

I press on, letting the twigs and roots of the tall, slender trees caress me in the shadows that slink beneath the sun and give us night in the day.

I listen, though I don't need to strain to hear his heartbeat. I soon catch it, along with the others who are with him. This must be where all the horses went.

Before I can turn and run, I hear a shout.

"Your Majesty, your prisoner has escaped!" a deep, booming voice calls out.

My eyes widen. "I've done no such thing!" I hiss back, certain they can hear me. "I'm out hunting, not escaping, you senseless dolt. If that proves too difficult a concept for you to grasp, I'll go hunt in other woods."

In the distance, I hear laughter. It's genuine, pealing laughter that tells me I've somehow managed to get them to lower their guard and relax.

"Hunting without me?"

His voice makes my breath still. I almost swear aloud for losing my resolve so quickly.

"You've been otherwise occupied this week, so I took it upon myself to clear my head. Sherry did not let me go willingly, but she refuses to give me the information I need, so I don't need her company today." There is a sharp edge to my words that leaves dull wounds in my flesh. It hurts to speak of her this way, but I am irritated that she won't set aside tradition to help me understand the inexplicable draw I have to Mars.

Then again, I used to be their greatest fear. Which begs the question: Why aren't the folks in these woods all afraid of me? Why don't they hate me even more now that I am in their midst?

But since Mars is also in these woods, they have no reason to be afraid. I held him off for a small while in that room and back in Sunfall, but he recovers quickly and can hold me spellbound if he wishes. Truthfully, they could easily use the same tactic now to slay me. My magic is still new and unruly, and even a fool would realize that I have nowhere to go. All of Sunfall's alliances are in my father's hands, including the one with Jupiter. I was only ever a pawn in his game. As such, I would be surrendered immediately. My fate would be just like Finch's.

Swallowing, I try not to pay too much attention to the conversation they're all having. It's a mix of male and female voices. Jealousy churns in my stomach. I cannot control the reaction. I want to disappear into the trees forever rather than acknowledge the growing fear that something is wrong.

Why else wouldn't Sherry tell me the truth?

But then I hear the thundering of hooves—Tye's—and goosebumps ride up my flesh as Mars rounds a corner and I catch his gaze for the first time since our last night together. My throat, now dry, constricts, and I struggle to find air.

"You shouldn't be out alone, Adelaide," Mars chides. "My niece is merely protecting her kingdom. Is that not an asset to be valued?"

"Yes. Which is why friendship is out of the question for me here," I sneer. "Now let me get on with hunting. I'm hungry and over with entertaining people who only pretend to care so the show can continue. I am *not* a performer, *King Mars*!"

I turn my back on him and start to stomp away, doing my best to catch the scent of something to otherwise occupy my attention. But then all the king's soldiers arrive, and I realize they are not soldiers, after all. They are nobles. This is their first opportunity to behold me as Adelaide the vampire and not Adelaide the Shadow Slayer.

Whatever hopes I had of hunting are dashed. Now I must put on a mask of poised nobility and grace. In the sea of faces, I recognize none but Mars, but everyone here is astonishingly beautiful. Lithe. Strong. Men are chiseled by the fires of Tryta himself, and women possess the grace and light of Siralto. At once, I realize I was never in Mars's league in the first place. Our passionate night a week ago was an accident.

The Siraltona roars in my ears, shooting warmth and strength through my veins. I stand up straighter, ignoring the way my skin glows.

A few nobles pull their horses back. One of those nobles is riding Dya. She's a princess, I think, and a far more accomplished one than I ever was. Long golden tresses adorn her precious head, and her bright blue eyes are deep like the oceans I've read about in so many stories. She fixes me with a wary glare before Mars rides up beside her.

"Charlotte, this is Adelaide. Adelaide, this is my daughter, Charlotte."

My eyes stretch wide. It's not a ladylike response, but I'm so startled by this revelation that I stumble back a bit. "I didn't know you had children," I stammer. "It's... It's a pleasure to meet you." Despite the sincerity of my words, they fall flat. Charlotte's glare doesn't lessen. If anything, the oceans in her eyes grow more tempestuous.

But I still can't get past it. *A daughter?* Of all the things I expected to learn about Mars... this hadn't even crossed my mind.

"I have many children, several of whom are here today," Mars explains. "My sons Adalius and Ewing, and my other daughter, Grace, are also here. Much of the nobility are heirs to the throne."

As each of his children nods and bows in my direction, the wind leaves my lungs. I'm certain it will be a miracle if I breathe again. *Are they all from the same woman?* But by scanning their faces, I note the marked differences between all of them and realize that Mars has been busy creating heirs throughout his existence. I wonder how old they all are and how their ranking system works. Does their birth order dictate who inherits the throne? The rank of their mother? Their power?

"That's lovely that they go with you," I stammer. "Now, I am off to hunt. It is apparent that you seem to have suddenly developed a worry over me being alone, but I thought we both understood that I am not in the business of running."

Overhead, a crow calls out, mocking me at the insincerity of my words. If I were a crueler sort, I might try to shoot it. Of course, that would also make me a foolish sort. Crows have gods of their own keeping; I'd rather not invoke their wrath, even if I am blessed by Siralto's light.

"Why don't you ride back with us, and I'll take you back out later?" Mars suggests. "My children and friends have been *dying* to make your acquaintance." He grins, flashing his fangs at me in warning.

It's obvious he is threatening me, but sometimes the urge to be head-strong is greater than I can deny.

I plant my feet deeper into the soil and give him a startling, wild grin in return. Beside him, Charlotte pales.

"I think I'll sate my hunger first and *then* meet you. I shouldn't want to meet your family in my current state. Sherry already bore the brunt of my rage, poor thing. I was horribly rude and snapped at her. That's not very fetching or becoming of the king's *pet*," I snarl.

I don't even realize I've done it until it's too late, nor was I aware I was even capable of such a noise. But just like when the Siraltona erupted from me that night when I fought off his dragon form, a growl leaves my throat.

I expect fireworks. Instead, Mars tips his head back and laughs. And everyone else *joins in*.

"My goodness, it is good to see someone give my father a run for his money!" laughs Adalius. "Tell us, how did it feel to give up on your moral tirade? Did hunger finally get the better of you?" His rich brown hair and eyes look like amber in the light that peeks through the trees, and I see the resemblance between him and his father. The same sharp, chiseled jaw and swagger are unmistakable. I would wager Mars is not only a father, but a grandfather as well.

I clasp my hands together, unimpressed by their response to my anger. His jab at my hunger strike rankles. It seems not everyone was as worried about divine consequences as Mars pretended. If this were a different time and place, I might have cut them down where they stand, which frightens me most of all. These are the thoughts of an insecure madwoman. These are the thoughts of my father's daughter. I pray penance upon myself through Siralto, but the way Mars has turned from me is punishment in itself. Once again, I am a flower starved of the sun, even when that sun is woven by darkness incarnate.

But those bright flames in his eyes, when they return to me, are all the light in the world I need. Jealousy brims within the Siraltona. I steady her, recognizing and fearing how intimately aware of me my power has become. Is she a reflection of me, or is she truly sentient?

My fingers twitch, desperate for the relief of a writing instrument and notebook that I still can't seem to remember to carry with me. Documenting my experiences and theories out in the open would gather too much attention, but moments like these create quite a spark of rebellion.

Mars lifts one brow. "Adelaide, you will accompany us as we return to the palace. That is nonnegotiable, or else I shall return those wretched shackles to your wrists."

"Will you?" I ask, raising an eyebrow. "Then I will shatter them again. And again. And again."

With a snap of my fingers, light cascades into my palms and takes the shape of a long, sharp blade. She is far more lethal than any sword I have carried before.

Now, the air of carefree fun is gone; in its stead is tension. I am a destroyer of peace, and I take comfort in knowing they will not seek me out as an easy target.

"You will let me carry on and get something to eat. I have been locked up in that room for a week with little to do but wonder why you *left* after my last hunt, and I won't wait around for you to figure out why you don't like me!" I snap.

"You're making a fool out of yourself," Mars sneers. "Put the blade down and accompany us. You will be punished for this."

At his threat, I throw my head back and laugh. The sound is sharp, piercing, and unconvincing, but I do it anyway. "I'm not scared of you, Mars. You've already taken everything I once thought I cared for; what do I have to fear now? Death? It would be a respite from the hell you've left me in."

I turn on my heel, ignoring the low hisses from his gathered court, and hurry through the trees, abandoning any hope of decorum. The hunger thrashing in my veins is unbearable. If I don't consume something soon, I will start to deteriorate as I did the first time. I am blinded by the anger that pounds in my temples while I try, to no avail, to sense any scent of prey on the wind. But I am wild, free, and willing to keep going until I find something.

It occurs to me that a trip to the kitchens might have been less disruptive, but I am not here to make Mars's life easier. I will make it as difficult as I can for as long as I can to pay him back for changing me against my will. This, I vow.

Suddenly, I sense something else erupting alongside the Siraltona. My skin, while cast in burning white light, is caressed in the arms of a shadow I've never seen before. I realize, too late, that the shadow is not mine. Not in its entirety.

Mars.

I don't turn around and give him the satisfaction of seeing terror contort my face as I thrash against it, but some of the shadow *does,* in fact, belong to me. It grabs hold of his shadow magic and clings to it, desperate to be united with him with the same fierceness as I felt about him all this past week, against my better judgment and hatred.

Before I reach the crest of a steep hill, I am overrun by a fight against myself and Mars's snaking shadows, which seem to creep and reach for me from every corner of the woods. But I will not go down without a fight.

I call to the Siraltona, but she is deaf to my cries. My power's attention is fully engaged with the shadows that flit along my body and curl over me like a cage.

Caged. Like a beast or a monster.

I don't stop thrashing until the world goes black.

Heavy is the Crown

When I wake, there are new shackles on my wrists, just as he promised. Except these are not as forgiving as the ones I had the first time. These bind me to a bed that is *not* in my bedchambers.

His bedchambers, I remind myself.

Through blurred vision, I spot Sherry standing and staring at me from a corner in the infirmary room where I met her the first time. I wonder if everything I've experienced up to this point has been a dream. Maybe I'm waking up before my execution again. Maybe everything I dreamed is a sick premonition to tell me just how terrible life will be when I wake up, changed and monstrous.

Then I look down at my hands and spot scars – new ones – etched into my flesh by none other than Mars's shadows. The memory of the woods and his court comes surging back to me. My throat dries up.

"Need this?" Sherry asks.

There is a glass of blood ready for me at my bedside. I lick my lips, but determined to punish myself for failing again, I shake my head, refusing to take a drink.

"He's not going to like that," Sherry cautions. "You just finished healing."

"And he hurt me again, so who cares?" I spit. "None of you do. I am here for entertainment purposes and for him to fuck on the occasions that he likes. Shall I carry any other heirs for him? That's all that seems to be my purpose, anyway!"

"Enough!" Mars roars as he bursts into the room.

He rushes over beside my bed and grabs the glass of blood with fury contorting his handsome features. Even though his fangs are sharper than I have ever seen them, I couldn't be any less afraid of them than I am now.

"You will drink this and stop this nonsense! I was not aiming to hurt you. You were acting like a fool in front of my entire court over a foolish desire to go hunting *alone* in a wood you don't *know,* and because you're bothered that I ignored you for a week. That's childish, Adelaide!" he hisses. "Now drink this and shut the fuck up."

My eyes widen, and for a moment, I swear I feel the raw power of the sun explode from within my soul. The shackles on my wrists shatter. The room is bathed in a light so terrible, I fear I may have blinded everyone in the room.

But to my surprise, only Sherry falls to the ground and covers her eyes. Mars, whose eyes are made of flames, stiffens. He holds his stance, still clenching the glass. He is poised to strike if I try to move against him. Instead, we stare at each other, breathing hard and heavy like we've just run the entire length between Velyasa and Sunfall.

I don't know how to catch my breath. "I don't want to like you," I say. "What have you done to me to make me want to be with you every waking moment? What do I need to give you to make it stop?"

Silence ensues. I wait for him to offer an explanation. An offer. A deal. *Anything.*

"I would ask the same of you," he spits.

"You're doing a fine job without me!" I roar. "*You've* been out cavorting with all the lovely women and breeding mares you seem to have around here while *I've* been rotting alone and cursing your name while imagining all the terrible ways I wish you'd have me to yourself, you filthy *pig*! I am not a common courtesan, and I have never acted as such. *What have you done to me?*"

I fling a stray, lit dagger at him; he catches it barehanded. His skin does not curl up in smoke as I've seen happen to every Shadow Folk I've struck before. I realize I am *not* sure he is killable. Heirs are a joke. He doesn't need them. Mars must be eternal.

I swallow, refusing to betray how terrified I am with this knowledge, but shrink back when he looms closer, prowling like a panther. I am a sheep in a cage, waiting to be fed to the beast before he goes on to perform before a circus. In this case, the circus is his court.

"Leave me alone," I demand. "I will not drink blood any longer. I will wither away to nothing. Put me on display. Tell your religious scholars that I am back to abstaining in the name of the morals that mean nothing to me anymore. But I will *not* be your pet any longer."

He cages me between his broad arms and shoulders and arches over me. The light from my flesh grows brighter, blinding him from my vision. I can't bear to look at him. I can't bear to watch as his arms snake around me and crush me into his chest.

But at the feeling of his touch, my resolve breaks. The light dims, and I am left weeping in his arms. My strength evaporates, and my knees buckle. I sag against him, nothing but dead weight, and depend on him to steady me and keep me from crumpling to the ground.

"Please," I sob, "I beg of you. Heal me of this. Break me if you have to!"

"I have not cursed you, Adelaide," Mars says, his voice hushed.

But his arms grow tighter around me. All I crave is to stay right where I am. And I *hate* myself for it. "Why did my shadows rise to meet yours, then? Is that not evidence of a hex?" I force myself to pull away, wincing at the sudden loss of contact.

"Adelaide, I have *not* cursed you," Mars repeats. "Are you going to listen to me? Will you let me explain what's happening?"

My eyes crawl along the soft colors of the infirmary, and how barren it seems; devoid of true light and vibrancy and all the things a patient needs to cling to hope. But perhaps there is no hope here.

"What, you'll tell me?" I ask. "Sherry won't. What makes me believe that you'll tell me?"

"It isn't her place to tell someone when they've met their mate, Adelaide. I mean it when I say the mating Rites must be observed. I meant it when I said you thralled me just as much as I did you when we first met. It is called *mutual-thrall*. You are in my thrall, but I am just as much in yours. We are what are known as Lafura by the gods. Soulmates. You are bound to me just as tightly as I am to you," Mars says.

I note the way his features become wan with stress and grief, like he has been fighting these truths harder than he has ever fought anything in his existence. *And that's a long time.* Disbelief crowds my judgment, and I stare at him as though he's just admitted he doesn't believe in the gods and magic isn't real.

"That's not possible!" I hiss.

"Then explain how you are beginning to wield my power," Mars answers.

When he reaches out and grabs my hands, the shadows in my veins rush to the surface as soon as our flesh brushes together. More importantly, I catch a much more damning sight.

A small pinprick of light pools in his hands.

"Why do you think your power does not obliterate me, Adelaide? It has blinded me before, yes, but your little stunt at Sunfall that first time *should* have been the end of me. I couldn't figure out why it didn't. I figured I'd been blessed by the gods to live another day and slaughter you for that hateful attempt on my life. Instead, I find that the gods have damned me to do nothing but love you, even through the eons of hatred I have for you in my soul."

He shakes his head, his frustration palpable. "I have not been cavorting with other women since I met you. I cannot take pleasure in it, knowing you live and breathe and sleep in my chambers every night. I want to put your head on a spike. I want to fill your womb with my children and parade you around the kingdom in my lap for all to see. I am just as conflicted as you. I thought staying away from you would alleviate this feeling, but now I realize I was wrong."

My chest heaves. I don't know whether to slap him or repay him the favor I owe from last week. I am too conflicted to know what I want or why.

But the sun in his hands is all the truth I need to know – I am not being deceived. I now know that the truth is the most damning weapon you can use against someone.

"I wish you'd just kill me," I blurt.

"I wish you'd stop saying that when you know it's not an option. I would mourn you forever until my soul shattered to dust like Tryta's did when

Siralto ceased to live," Mars says miserably. "Don't you realize that our powers are theirs? It is where we got them. Of course mine is drawn to yours. It is the nature of how life itself was created."

I am his captive audience. I can tell he has pondered these heavy thoughts alone for quite some time.

"Do you think I'll really be your wife and queen here?" I ask. "Your people–your children, most of all–will not accept a woman who once tried to slaughter their father. More than once, not to mention. I defied you in front of them all."

"And I bested you!" he laughs. "They know I am unstoppable, and they know what you are to me. I have already briefed them on the realities of the fate we cannot escape. The more we fight it, the worse this will get."

I narrow my eyes at him. "Is this your way of getting into my pants?" I demand. "If so, this is a ridiculously elaborate plan, especially when I have already given you plenty of opportunities to do just that."

"Please stop. *Both* of you," Sherry pipes up, finally finding her voice in the midst of our twisted lovers' spat. "I don't want to listen to my uncle confess to wanting to bed my best friend or vice-versa. Besides that, you two are stupid!" Sherry snarls. "You're upending the natural order, all because you're both too cowardly to admit you love each other. Love is unavoidable. You choose to stay in love, but you do not choose to fall into it. And you can never deny it when it is as sacred as the bond you two share."

She turns her ire to Mars. "Uncle, vampires greater than you have thrown away their entire legacies when they found their mates, and here you are, shackling her like a common dog!" Not finished, she whirls on me. "And *you*, Adelaide. If you don't stop talking about us and our kind like we are some kind of vermin, I will personally gut you like a fish! You like me, right? Are we not friends? Don't you love the Ayesa children? Over and over, we have shown you that we are not the villains your kingdom painted us as. So why hold onto these salacious ideas of us that you know aren't true?" She fixes me with a pointed glare. "I've read what you write about us."

I blanch and flinch like I've been slapped.

"I know about the notes, Adelaide," Sherry continues. "You should read them, Uncle. They're much better than any I've seen to date. It's clear she knows we are more than what the fables say. So, give it up. Stop fighting what you cannot possibly win against. Try *courting* each other and maybe plan a wedding. We all know it's coming. The people are not opposed to it. Have you seen the way they look at her out there, Mars? They love her and the way she makes the children light up. I've been bringing her out as much as possible so they can see she's not a monster." Sherry pauses. "Now, I wonder at what point she will accept that *we* aren't monsters, either."

Sherry cuts me a look that makes me wither like a common weed being tossed from her garden. I want to apologize, but I'm having trouble finding the words. She is right. Guilt and shame bleed through my cheeks, and an uncomfortable warmth makes it markedly hard to breathe.

Mars looks at me like he's never seen me before. "You've... you've been documenting our habits? Our rituals and customs?"

I shrug, frightened of the consequences of admission.

"Where are these notes, Sherry?"

"Up in your armoire. Now, I'm leaving you both alone. Go read them together. Ask Mars your questions – many of them are good. She'd be a brilliant strategist if she weren't so busy feeling sorry for herself and bemoaning the fact that you aren't buried to the hilt inside her at all times. Gods, I hate newly mated vampires most," Sherry grumbles.

"We aren't mated!" Mars protests. "I haven't even–"

"Get on with it then, fool!" Sherry says. "Maybe once you've had each other enough, I can have my friend back and she can stop acting like a hateful moron. I had her convinced there for a while that we aren't half bad until you started trying to deny your feelings for her."

Before Mars can argue, Sherry storms out of the room, abandoning us to a stunned silence neither of us ever saw coming.

It feels like hours before I can bother to look in his direction. "I'm sorry!" I blurt. "I'm sorry for everything. I'm sorry for killing your people. I'm sorry for treating them like they're an inferior species. I'm just... I don't know how to feel. I don't know anything about the Shadow Folk. Everything I've been taught is false and stupid. I'm trying hard to learn, but you make me so *angry*. All I want is to learn from you and be with you, and you hate me so much, but then tug me along on a string..." I growl in frustration. "I don't know how to please you."

Mars sighs. "I'm sorry I forced you to navigate a mating bond alone and left you in the dark about who and what you are, Adelaide. And I'm sorry I ever made you feel like you're not enough, because you're all that and so much more."

The sincerity in his words freezes me. I see raw emotion in his eyes and know I would be foolish not to tap into it.

"Will you let me show you my notes?" I ask. "I'd like to learn from you, if I can. I know it's probably foolish to let your enemy know your plans, but I'd like to help you, Mars. I don't want Sunfall to be the future for your people. My father is a tyrannical fool. Maverick and I were planning to overthrow him, even if we only hinted at it. I would put Alaric's head on a spike long before yours."

It's odd confessing these things aloud. "I am only the Shadow Slayer because I was forced to be. It was slay or die. But I never should have chosen my life over the lives of your people."

"*Our* people," Mars corrects, his voice soft. "And I would have you make that choice in every lifetime if it meant that you could make it back to me safely."

He closes the distance between us and presses his forehead to mine. We stay like this for quite some time. My soul sings a song I've never heard, and yet I feel that I've known him my entire existence. I suddenly know Mars is the answer to every problem I've ever had... while also being the cause of those problems in the first place. My treacherous heart betrays my mind every time I am in his presence. Now is no different.

"I will read them, but only if you let me help you heal the cuts my shadows left on your skin."

I look at him, breathless. "Okay."

He takes my hand and together, we leave the infirmary.

SCRIBE

I STAND AND WAIT for Mars to say something. While the tension between us has eased, I know it can return with a snap of our fingers. Conflict awaits us, lurking just beyond the corner of our odd stalemate. I think of all the ways I can apologize to Sherry for being so hateful and holding Shadow Folk in such poor regard because of Mars's actions and the way he and I become so enraged with each other.

Sherry and the Ayesa children, along with so many others, have proven to me that this kingdom is full of *good* people. What's worse, if I am his mate, it means at some point... *I might be their queen.*

The thought sends shivers down my spine. I can't picture Mars as my husband, even if he was my suitor not too long ago. That charade was nothing more than deceit and trickery at play, not true love.

Or was it?

I feel as though the gods have suspended us like puppets on strings. I want to hate the man who stands before me, holding several pieces of paper in his hands as he reviews my notations with a laser focus that makes me jealous. But watching his eyes sweep over the paper with so much attentiveness and care makes my heart flutter.

Another part of me feels like I've been caught committing treason. Will being his mate be enough to convince him not to have my head cut off for writing down what might be sacred knowledge of his kind?

When his eyes finally reach mine, full to the brim of all the things I've documented in the past week, I let out a huff of breath, my lungs still full of trepidation.

"Why do you act like you've committed a crime, Adelaide? I've found no evidence of treason in these notes you've taken. Knowledge is not forbidden in Velyasa. I'm not sure what Sunfall was about, but even if you had plotted to take my head, it's not like your hatred for me is a secret. Besides, I'll always be able to match you in battle." Mars winks.

Whether it's his attempt to calm me down or a real statement, my cheeks flush with relief and embarrassment. It's strange to hold both things in my heart so closely, but I cradle them just the same.

"I've never been permitted to have thoughts about policy and history and law," I stammer. I inwardly cringe at how weak my voice sounds. I sound like I've been without a drink in weeks. Then I realize I *haven't* had blood in a week. My hunt was unsuccessful, and I refused the drink I was offered in the infirmary earlier. I've been so busy learning this past week that I haven't been taking care of my basic needs. But I don't complain.

"In Velyasa, you would be encouraged to do so. Your notes are critical pieces of information. Much of our history has been written by others. As you well know, most of what's out there is counterfactual or contains wild exaggerations that paint us as something else entirely. There are a few questions in here that I can probably help you answer... but Adelaide, I believe you've proven that you'd be incredibly useful to the kingdom as more than just my bride. How would you feel about being our official record keeper?"

My eyes widen. I stare at Mars as though he's asked me to dance for him naked, rather than take notes.

"Have I asked something inappropriate? Your cheeks are scarlet." Mars chuckles, though his gaze roves over me with concern.

I clear my throat, struggling to find the right words to say. "How could I possibly be qualified? I'm sure there are plenty of errors in my accounts. Not to mention, don't you already have scribes?"

Mars shakes his head. "We have a few young scribes, but none as thorough as you. Much of our records have been lost over the years. I am the first king to secure this kingdom's safety. It came at great cost to me – the story of which I cannot reveal to you just yet – but rest assured. Now that our power and might are solid, it would be good to have official documents to record who and what we are. You're new to being a Shadow Folk, so your perspective is fresh and less likely to miss details we take for granted – like autumn and spring being swapped out, or the fact that our familiar power was missing for so long. You even catch how some of us aren't as susceptible to Siraltona as others and ask important questions about the Ayesa and why they submit to being turned when they are already long-lived and, in some cases, immortal."

I swear I see a glimmer of pride in his eyes. I don't know whether to run or laugh as he fixes a predatory gaze on me and licks his lips. "I must admit that your records about our sexual appetites are biased. That might be best reserved as a discussion between the two of us, not for the history books."

Now I know my face is on fire. I tug at the collar of my dress and wonder why I ever set out to hunt in it in the first place. I miss the looseness of his tunic that I wore the first time. If I wore something looser, I might not feel like I'm about to drown in this oppressive heat, even if I know it originates from within.

"We will remove that from the record, then," I concede. "What... what should I write about Lafuras? I don't fully understand the concept of a soulmate. Can... can you explain? Why am I carrying some of your power, and how can you wield mine? I should have killed you, as you yourself admitted... How do I rectify that in our records? Or is that something I should exclude?"

Mars raises an eyebrow. "You want to ask if you should write about how I evaded death? Of course you should. This provides further evidence that our union is the result of divine intervention. My scouts broke through your barriers and magic to poison your kingdom's ale, and yet, you still stand. Why didn't you take a drink that night before your powers were discovered?"

I shrug. "I don't like to be out of control. Being drunk..." I grimaced. "I'd be no better than my father."

"Still, I'd call it a divine intervention of sorts. You outwitted me; I outwitted you. I did what had to be done to find the power I needed. The cost, it seems, was being bound to the very thing I wanted to understand and destroy. The only way to destroy my enemy was to love it... *her*. But now it makes sense," Mars adds with a growl.

I barely register as he closes the gap between us and cups my face in his hands. "Had I known Alaric would beget such a beautiful daughter, I might not have tried to kill him so frequently all those years ago."

My senses become blurred again and I am putty in his hands as he presses his lips to mine. We finally pull away, my thoughts still yearning for answers about how I am filled to the brim with shadow as much as I am light. How can I stand, a newly changed Shadow Folk when my magic is antithetical to it?

"Were you supposed to kill me instead of changing me?"

"Had you not been my Lafura? Yes. But by then I knew... I knew you were bound to me and would come back," Mars says, his voice cracking. "It was the only way to appease my people *and* keep you to myself. I fretted until you drew breath, and I would never take such a risk again. But no, Adelaide, the shadow in you should have wiped you out as your light should have cleaved me in two that night on the battlefield."

"I thought you were as surprised as I was by what Sherry told us. You mean you've known the whole time?"

"I had my suspicions, but no. It was news of what I... couldn't seem to register. No, Adelaide, I risked your life on the simple knowledge that you were etched into my soul regardless of whether the gods ordained it or not. *Lafura* implies the gods chose you for me. I knew I would choose you anyway, even as much as I hated you."

Hated. Not hate. *Hated.*

Heaviness constricts my throat. Tears threaten to burst from my eyes. I swallow, but the effect is not what I want as a few of those damned tears slip free. He wipes them away with gentle thumbs, the roughness of his hands soothing against my heated skin.

"Why is this so difficult?" I ask, my breath short and my chest heaving.

"You have been taught your entire life to hate me, and I have spent millennia slaughtering mortals who would otherwise stuff me like taxidermy and use my body as an example to scare their children. Yet the gods decided that our souls belong together. That is what makes it so that we can exist together, Adelaide. Your soul is mine. Mine is yours. The longer we fight this, the worse things will get. The sooner we embrace it, the more powerful we stand to become together."

"What do you even have to fear?" I ask. "Jupiter? Sunfall is yours for the taking now." I choke on those last words, my tongue still unwilling to repeat the truth of the alliance my father supposedly forged with Jupiter. A sob sputters past my lips. I imagine the way he might slay my brother and decorate the walls of the castle with Beatrice's innards, her womb still barren of children. I know the cost of Siraltona for Maverick was his ability to provide an heir more than any wound from war. The more I have contemplated the costs of magic on mortals over the last month in Velyasa, I know it to be the truth. Part of me wonders if it's why my mother was so weak when the Shadow Folk overtook her. Otherwise, she would have snapped her fingers and slaughtered them.

"How is my father not dead or absent of power by now?" I ask, not waiting for him to reply to my first question. "So much doesn't add up, Mars. Why do you care what they're up to?"

Mars shrugs. "*They* do not concern me. But my brother... my brother does. He has meddled with *dark* magic, Adelaide. Corrupt magic, wherein he uses his immortality to evade the consequences of manipulating others. That is magic that the gods have not ordained to use, save in extreme circumstances. He kidnaps my people and robs them of their will to build an army of fledglings to overtake every neighboring village he can. He is thirsty for power and every bit the vampire you and your people fear. My people have been on edge because of him. It's why they don't seem to mind you as much as I worried they would. Once I proved to them that I had your power under control, they knew you were nothing to fear. I had to parade you on a leash for them to accept you. Jupiter... Well, Jupiter represents the death of their very soul."

I feel faint, the color draining from my face. "How... how did I not..."

"The Siraltona makes you immune, Adelaide. He works in shadow. You... you present a very ripe opportunity for saving our people if you would let us ally with you. Our marriage could be more than just pleasure in the sheets. It could be an opportunity to right the wrongs of murdering innocents on *both* sides and addressing the real problems in this world," Mars says, his voice grave.

I know there will be steep costs. He needn't say them aloud. I don't know how my power could be used to shield everyone... except... *I do.*

"You want to protect your people?"

"Yes!" Mars laughs aloud. "I thought that much was obvious."

I wave him off. "No, stupid. I mean... I have an idea. Do you have a necklace that isn't particularly loved or valued? I want to demonstrate my idea."

Mars frowns. "I do. But... I'd like to try something, too. You see... I want to marry you. And in order to let the nobles know you've been persuaded to cooperate, I'd like to have them see your proposal in person. Would you be willing to present your idea to them? It would serve both as a help to my kingdom and a way to legitimize our marriage so we can publicly perform the mating Rite. I can do so regardless, but their approval would help keep things... peaceful."

I stammer. "M-marry me?"

"Was I not clear? I thought the Lafura revelation was enough to convince you, but..."

Before I can say anything, Mars is on one knee, taking my hands in his.

"Adelaide, I love you far more than I hate you. I can't promise there won't be many more fights ahead, but I would be honored if you would fight by my side as much as you choose to fight me over personal grievances," Mars says.

The humor in his voice is refreshing. I feel like I've been doused in ice water, but I nod yes before I process that he's back on his feet and kissing me again, his mouth greedier than ever.

"You vex me so, you little witch," he breathes.

"Like *you're* innocent!" I hiss back, nipping his bottom lip.

He moans, and my knees buckle as he moves me back toward the mattress. "I can't go as far as we want," he breathes, reminding himself of his earlier promise.

"Your precious honor didn't stop you from railing every maid you could find in your kingdom before me!" I whine. "Why am I different?"

"Because you're my wife-to-be. You will be the last I ever bed," Mars swears. "The others were nothing more than a distraction. You deserve to be treated with the honor and purity you deserve. Mating rituals are sacred."

Irritated, I huff. "I don't consider myself pure, Mars."

He freezes. "Have... have there been others?"

I shake my head, and his shoulders slump with relief as he pushes me onto my back. "So it's a big deal for *you*, yet *I* have to put up with the fact that you've had others?" I pull away before he can continue to pepper me with kisses.

"I would take you either way, Adelaide. I just... You're younger, and I've been alive far longer. Loneliness is a vile curse."

His answer, while satisfactory, still leaves me frustrated that he won't just have me the way I want him. I add it to the list of reasons that I *should* behead him, even though I know I won't. I don't think I even could, at this point. His magic knows mine, and my magic knows his. I swear I hear my magic purr as he begins to lap at my throat and suck. A sick part of me hopes he leaves a mark so everyone knows that I am the object of their king's affections.

"I believe I owe you a favor," I whisper.

Mars pulls back, laughing. "Not tonight, my fire. If you do that, I can promise you I will violate the sanctity of the mating Rites. Hold off on that favor until later. Truthfully, we should stop now while we are ahead."

My heart, thrumming in my ears, screams. Valiantly, I manage to wire my lips shut to prevent that scream from echoing across Velyasa. "You're insufferable!" I spit.

"Yes, but I promise to make it up to you tenfold once we are wed." Tossing me a wink, Mars stands and helps me to my feet.

Every part of me throbs with aching want. My legs wobble when I walk to him. He catches me in his arms, helping me stand up straight while I collect my nerves.

Neither of us speaks as we bask in the silent tension that curls between us, though this time the tension is sensual rather than murderous.

"So, will you come see my court later? So we can... show them your idea?" Mars's voice sounds strained, and judging by the hardness pressed against me, I know he is struggling just as much as I am to abstain from further action between the sheets.

"Yes," I breathe. "Mars?"

"What is it, my love?" he asks. Not his *fire*. His *love*.

"When can I eat?"

Before he can answer, my stomach lets out a rumbling growl that makes my cheeks flush. I don't know why it's more embarrassing than the idea of being laid out naked for him on his bed, but I shun myself for the bodily mishap. I think it's detestable that an immortal should be capable of such a thing.

But when Mars laughs again, I am grateful to see the mirth return to his face. It's odd how fast my emotions shift, when a handful of hours ago we were at each other's throats in the infirmary. My soul is at rest, though, and I know the truth of our bond to be indisputable.

He smirks. "I will take you to the kitchens. Would you like bread like last time as well?"

My mouth waters, and I nod. "No Kaycee, though. I don't share."

Mars regards me with pride and chuckles. "I don't either, love, so that is fine with me. However, I haven't had anyone since meeting you. That, I can promise."

My heart soars.

"So, tell me of your plan while we walk, and I can tell you more about what to expect of becoming the kingdom's scribe. We can discuss discrepancies in the notes and decide how we want to categorize some of the entries you've put together."

It's an entirely domestic conversation between a king and his future queen. Even so, I doubt the Shadow Folk will take well to the idea of the former Shadow Slayer becoming their queen.

But Jupiter... Jupiter is the real threat. I was never the monster they feared. Maybe I was for a short while, but I do not rob my victims of their free will. If the stories Mars told me are true... Jupiter is far worse than anything I ever was.

I curse Mars's brother beneath my breath as the king and I reach the dining hall.

A Presentation

W E EAT IN SILENCE. I don't know what to say to Mars. All I want
to do is bask in the fact that our bond is beyond our control. Still,
I have so many nagging questions. Worse still, the burden to tell him the
truth about Jupiter and Sunfall lingers. But true to my nature, it is my
jealousy that spurs my first question to leap from my tongue.

"How many children do you have? And how many different mothers are
there?" I blurt before stuffing another piece of bread into my mouth.

Mars gives me a wolfish grin. "I have hundreds of children, Adelaide.
Not all of them are noble in the way you've met so far, but all of them
are well-cared for. I have never shied from my appetites before, especially
in my youth. I was a hell of a fledgling." Mars laughs until he catches me
scowling at him, at which point he shrugs. "Immortality is a lonely way to
live, Adelaide, and to be able to provide heirs is a blessing. Prior to securing
immunity to the Siraltona, the pressure to secure my line was just as important as it was to your father in finding you a suitor. Maverick's barrenness

was enough to push him to put you up on the chopping block, and that's with few active threats at your door – at least by Alaric's perception. I had pressures from Sunfall *and* my brother to consider."

His answers may be satisfactory, but I still can't fathom how he has *hundreds* of children.

"How... how old... how old are you?" I finally ask.

"You act as though you are trying to murder me again. And this time... I dare say you aren't fond of the idea," Mars teases.

"No, I'm not... I just don't know what's appropriate to ask and what's not. I don't want to offend you," I stammer. It's hard to look him in the eyes when he stares at me like I'm the last piece of bread on the dinner plate. Especially when I know he will continue to deny me my carnal desires until we are officially "mated," by whatever standards are expected within his culture.

Speaking of, I don't really understand his culture, other than what I learned about customs and such while watching the Shadow Folk in Sunfall. They are more active at night, despite being able to move about during the day. Their nocturnal habits are the lasting effect of being forced to operate in the shadows for centuries to avoid being slain.

Their different familiars, while unequal in power, hold no bearing on the friendships they seem to forge. Where mortals might be expected to mingle by type or power, Shadow Folk appear to thrive in mismatched groups.

Ayesa are few and far between, as is to be expected since they are already immortal, but they seem to be revered by other Shadow Folk for the mystical lore that comes with them from before they were changed. The flower girls always seem to have onlookers and almost worshipful admirers who ask them questions about how to make their gardens flourish and their crops yield more.

But I still don't understand what drives them. How can they worship a god who slew his wife in a fit of rage? Or are those texts wrong, too?

"I am at least a millennium old," Mars says. "I have watched empires rise and fall. I brought my people to this place to protect them and give them life in a world that would stamp them out. I'm not sure of my exact age, Adelaide, but you truly are a gift. I have never experienced companionship like this in my life. Loves, yes. I cannot pretend I have not loved before. But I have not met any whose soul cries to mine as mine does to hers."

He reaches his hand out to me, stretched wide so I can clasp my fingers with his. My heart thudding, I look at him and try to understand what he's just said. I slap his hand away, instead rushing to him and jumping into his lap. This time, the tone isn't sensual; it is a desire to be close. One I have spent too long suppressing and can fight no longer.

I curl up against his chest, my belly full and my heart content, and we sit in silence. He begins to rock me back and forth in his chair, humming unfamiliar tunes that seem nostalgic all the same. His voice is tender and beautiful, something I hope I never forget.

"Did you get your fill?" he asks, his voice rumbling against my ear and sending a pleasant shiver down my spine.

"Yes," I answer. "I believe I owe your court an explanation of my idea on how to protect your people. Other than killing Jupiter, of course…"

I grit my teeth at the last statement, unable to quell the rage that pools in my veins as I remember how Finch was disemboweled before my eyes and my firebird slaughtered in the name of some foul feud between family.

How old is Jupiter? Do they share the same father? Does Mars know that my father might be allied with his brother?

These are questions I don't dare ask just yet. I tuck them away, determined to ask Mars for a notebook so I can keep track of them all, save the last one. That one nags at me because it is the one truth I can't afford to tell myself. But it still lurks there, waiting for me to let the truth bleed from between my teeth, staining the floor with my deceitfulness. Mars's next question breaks my train of thought, releasing me from the spiraling, agonizing thoughts that haunt me. His voice is a sweet caress that pulls me from the depths of despair.

"Are you sure you want to summon them just now? Learning we are Lafura is... overwhelming."

"Do you need a break?" I ask. Pulling my head back from where it was tucked beneath his chin, I raise an eyebrow.

He offers me a knowing smile. "No, but I defer to your wants and needs first."

"You have a kingdom that might take issue with this. You've spent over a thousand years carving out the world for their success – to make it fit for them even if it wouldn't let them. Why risk it all for me?" I ask, my voice quavering.

"The gods would not have gifted you to me if your love was not equally valuable to my people's success. Adelaide, you are woven within the fabric of my soul just as I am in yours. We have spent so long fighting it, but it is the truth we can no longer deny. If my kingdom cannot accept that their king has found his other half from the land of sunlight, then that is an issue they can take up in their prayers to Tryta. As far as I am concerned, to deny you is akin to treason. You are a gift sent by Tryta's mate. You must be here to bolster our success, not our failure," Mars whispers. "Besides, even if you were here to level us to the ground... if that's what the gods decided, who are we to question it?"

It's a startling thing for him to say. He's so... willing... to rest the fate of his life in hands that belong to gods who may or may not know his name.

I frown. "What if the gods were to tear us apart someday?"

"Then I will defy the gods." Gone is the rapt adoration of Tryta's strongest warrior. In his stead sits my future husband, his devotion unwavering.

I don't know how he can freely offer me such a thing when I nearly killed him. Were it not for those gods, I would have succeeded and mounted his great dragon head on a spike.

And then I would have been sent off to marry Alexander from Underland. I would be a mother to a bevy of nameless heirs, and the Siraltona would have eaten our lineage alive, leaving our bodies unfit to rule under the oppression of magic that was never ours. How did we get it in the first place?

"What troubles you?" Mars asks.

"I only wonder how I have become so lucky," I say, not fully lying. I *am* lucky. Lucky to have him. Lucky that the one person in this world who can kill me is driven by a desire to love and mate with me rather than putting me in the ground or having me for dinner. "I appreciate you putting me first, but I'm perfectly happy to meet with your advisors and give them my plan. Though I have to ask... What are your plans for Sunfall?"

Mars shrugs. "I haven't really thought about it. My focus has been on Jupiter and his forces."

I squirm. It dawns on me that Mars may not yet know what Jupiter told me in the woods. In my selfishness, I've been concealing something that might now be putting my Lafura's life at risk. As I consider him, I wonder how angry he will be if I tell the truth. I hope I can find a way to let this truth slip free. It ails me – pains me – to carry this secret now, where I once gave little care or thought to it. Betrayal is a currency I'm familiar with. Love and loyalty that transcends a kingdom is not.

I nod. "I should like to deal with Sunfall. My brother would make a great king. Once we are done with Jupiter, would you help me slaughter my father?"

His eyes widen; he chokes on a laugh. "You want my aid in committing patricide?"

"Yes," I admit. "I want that kingdom's future secured in hands more worthy than my father's. Even if my brother dies young as a consequence of using the Siraltona... I want him to have the choice to rule it as he sees fit. Not Alaric. And I... I need to tell you something. Jupiter has an alliance with my father."

Mars blinks, his eyes growing wide. "Who... who told you about this?"

It's my turn to be shocked, my mind going blank. It takes me a moment to gather my thoughts. It is already hard for me to so readily give him intel that would undo my former kingdom. But to register that he's known about my father's sins the whole time?

"From Jupiter himself in the woods that day. I wasn't sure if I should tell you... Until now, I didn't even want to accept it, let alone give you something that would undo my former kingdom. But now that I know the truth.... I was scared you would punish Sunfall, and I would lose my other brother. Losing Finch was bad enough. To lose Maverick, too... I don't think I could survive that." My throat clogs with grief. It's the first time I've fully considered my father's ultimate betrayal.

To align with a despicable Shadow Folk specimen like Jupiter, all in the name of seeking vengeance against Sunfall?

My eyes sting with tears as that reality shatters the last sliver of love that might have been left for my former kingdom. Knowing the truth I do now, I could never let my mate's kingdom fall to ruin on behalf of some awful secret.

Mars stares at me with sympathy in his eyes, which is hardly what I should expect, given the circumstances. I've confessed to *lying*. To concealing the enemy.

"We knew about this ages ago. Or at least the potential of it. The good news is that my spies are constantly collecting information, and their alliance never came to fruition. Jupiter was bluffing when he told you that in the woods. Do you really think I would stand idly by and never consider such a possibility? Your father's drunken stupors ended it long before it could begin. Your father has never been the agreeable type. Fear not, my fire, you have not concealed something too deadly from us. I have eyes and ears everywhere. The shadows are my witnesses, as Tryta would have it."

"I'm glad, then." A weak sense of relief settles in my shoulders, though a part of me still doubts he is telling the truth. The idea that Mars already knew and this awful secret I've been carrying was for nothing is almost too much to fathom. How can it be that simple? How do we know that Jupiter hasn't tricked us into believing he's not working with Sunfall as we speak? But I can't afford to consider this idea. I tuck away this possibility to consider later and instead return my focus on the fullness of my belly and resting in this new, quiet normal with Mars.

Mars reaches over and grabs a goblet of blood, taking a long sip before fixing me with a bold grin. He tilts the cup to my mouth, and I accept, taking a long drink. He makes me finish it.

"What was that for?" I ask, licking my lips.

"To celebrate your first good decision for Sunfall. Choosing Velyasa's interests over your own is a big first step. Well... It's your *second* good decision. Your first was leaving it behind to come find me, whether you meant to or not," Mars chuckles. "But then again, I may be biased."

I roll my eyes, but I find myself laughing anyway. The lingering edge of discomfort still rests in my chest, but the more I look at Mars and the way he smiles without a care in the world, the more I am put at ease.

"I will help you in that effort to punish and slay your father. But first, we need to handle Jupiter or all will be lost," Mars says, seriousness returning to his tone.

I nod. The thought of someone like Jupiter taking over Sunfall fills me with unease.

We return to our silent meal – what is left of it – and I appreciate how secure I feel. I have no desire to even move out of his lap.

Only when I hear approaching footsteps and conversation nearing the dining hall do I return to my seat, ready for the potential confrontation with nobility. I know how Mars and a few of his children feel about me, but I didn't get much of a read from the nobles I ran into in the forest. I curse myself for wasting that chance to assess my potential opponents in favor of throwing a tantrum over my unrequited feelings for Mars.

Well, not unrequited…

I suddenly realize my dress is still in tatters. My eyes widen in terror. I look at Mars, who seems unbothered by my sudden distress until his gaze lands on me. He raises an eyebrow. "Have you seen a ghost?"

"This is hardly a dress to address the court!" I hiss. "Why did we not think to let me change?"

Mars chuckles. "You have not been the fancy dress sort since the day I met you. You've always been a woman of more practical means."

I glare at him, but I know he's right. Still, sometimes I wish I could wear fine silks and satins and feel like a princess rather than a warrior. But I keep that thought to myself. I sense a shift in the way Mars looks at me, but he doesn't get a chance to speak further before a swarm of nobles breaches the doorway to the dining hall. I sit up straight, temporarily casting off my embarrassment at my meager clothing.

I instantly recognize Mars's children, who lead the pack. Charlotte is at the front, her sharp blue gaze slicing through me like a hot blade. I meet her gaze with equal ferocity. I refuse to wilt, even for his daughter. The truth of it still doesn't sit well with me. I don't understand how *I* ended up as his mate, rather than whatever beautiful woman gave him his current heir. I assume Charlotte is the first in line to the throne by the way she carries herself and how her siblings defer to her as the unspoken leader.

"Charlotte, Adalius, Ewing, Grace..." I say, remembering each of their names. "I'm afraid I didn't get to meet the rest of you earlier. I apologize for the slip in formalities."

A few of them bow and curtsy. Charlotte merely nods.

"What do you need?" Mars asks, interrupting the tense staring contest between me and the nobles.

"We came to ask about what to do about Jupiter. There's been another attack, Your Highness," Charlotte crisply announces.

I do my best to school my response, wondering why she doesn't address him as *Father* or something similar. Perhaps I was more impertinent with my own father than I thought.

"Daughter dearest, you've come at just the right time. Adelaide has an idea about how we might better protect our people until we can hunt my brother down and extinguish him."

I resist the urge to whip around and glare at him for putting me on the spot when several eyes land on me, all different in color and very much full of confusion and caution. I can't escape them now. Charlotte squints at me with open disbelief, which I scoff at aloud.

"You all act like I haven't driven hordes of Shadow Folk away before! I even managed to hold Jupiter off in the woods – let's not forget how I became a captive held behind your walls. None of the Shadow Folk had managed to accost me until Jupiter, but my mind and my will remain my own. Your father's power is in my veins, and he knows it to be true."

A few of them gasp, confirming that Mars had *not* let the mate conversation slip to them quite yet, or at least not in full, but I don't stop to consider whether it was the right decision to admit that our powers were binding. A few whispers of "Lafura" make a ripple through them before Adalius interrupts.

"How did you fend him off? And why do you think your guidance now is enough to place our trust in you to save our kingdom? Not even a month ago, you were plotting to have my father's head cut off and leave my people without a leader!" Adalius sneers.

I smile at him. "While I have no doubt that Charlotte would lead you well in his absence, I have no desire to destroy my mate. Besides, I believe my power would go with him. His kingdom is his pride, and to cut it down would be to harm the other half of my soul."

Adalius blanches, but wisely says nothing.

"As for how to fend him off," I continue, "I have a theory. Does anyone have a piece of jewelry that they don't mind sparing?"

A few of the nobles squabble before a small necklace is tossed at me. I take a deep breath and channel the energy stored in my veins, reaching for it the same way my father and brother used to when they infused my blades.

I touch the metal and Siraltona bursts forth, surging through the chain and pendant, filling the light silver with a faint, pulsing glow. I smile, satisfied that I've done what my father and brother did and that this light will last. I look up and see that everyone has taken a wide step back from me. The only person still in the same place is Mars.

"You expect us to use that demon goddess's light to protect our people?" Charlotte spits. Her blue eyes are wide with rage. "That stuff will *kill* us!"

I shake my head and roll my eyes at her. A snaking, shadowy tendril races up my arm and coats the metal one last time, concealing the glow beneath the metal and making it appear normal again.

"Who wants to try putting this on so I can demonstrate my point? Your father and king won't be a good candidate, as he is immune to the Siraltona," I say, grinning. "So, anyone hoping to use me as a weapon against him will find themselves sorely disappointed."

Ewing steps forward, his dusty blond hair disheveled and his olive-green eyes wary. "I will risk being struck down."

"You are a *royal*, Ewing!" Charlotte argues. "You cannot afford to lose your head because of her stupid quest to trick us by offering help when she's *never* done anything of the sort. Just because you've earned my father's affections by gobbling his cock doesn't mean you've tricked the rest of us."

Mars's flaming eyes burn brighter. He slams his fist on the table hard enough to send vibrations ricocheting across the table and rattle the plates and silverware. "You will *not* speak of her that way, Charlotte! We are waiting to observe the mating Rites, which is really none of your business! Suffice it to say she is as under my control as I am hers. Do you think I would let her undo all I have done to secure this kingdom?"

I bite my tongue, remembering how minutes ago, he was promising to defy the gods in my name and honor. But his children needn't know that detail. Charlotte dips her head in shame and steps back, motioning for Ewing to continue.

Ewing walks to me, kneeling so I can place the necklace over his head, as there is no clasp. It slides down his neck and leaves no marks or burns. I breathe a sigh of relief, glad that his skin is unmarred by the Siraltona. Part of me wonders if it would have hurt him at all, given the intentions woven into it. Intentions mean everything in spellcraft of any kind. It can't guarantee results, though, and I refuse to be reckless with my mate's child.

When Ewing stands back up, he brushes his fingers along the necklace, admiring it with wonder as light winks up at him but remains dormant.

"How do we know this will work against Jupiter's will-theft magic? The Falahle is what we are up against, not his shadows, or else there is no point to this," he says.

I ponder this, wondering how we might test such an idea when Mars stands. "I think it is time I confess to you all that Jupiter is not the only one with this power."

Ewing looks up in time to see a slithering serpent of shadow strike at him, its red eyes glowing and its fangs dripping with venom. Venom that *glows* from within the purest shadows I've ever seen.

But before the fangs can cleave through Ewing's flesh, the light from the necklace bursts forth, shooting angry blades of divine rage through the serpent's neck. The shadow bursts into smithereens, leaving nothing but memory in its wake.

No one speaks for a while. Charlotte's gaze falls on me again, but the rage there softens. Her brother, Ewing, remains standing despite the outburst of light that would have once cleaved him in two. As it turns out, the intention *did* matter. The light touches his skin as it drips from the necklace. The shadows carved into the metal snake down his arms to meet it, luring it back into the pendant for safekeeping. It pulses once, and the light goes dim.

And just like that, I have gifted the Shadow Folk the one thing they feared before Jupiter. I have given them the Siraltona.

I only pray they will not use it against Sunfall.

A Plot Hatches

Several minutes pass. Still, no one speaks. Ewing's face is ripe with relief that he hasn't been turned to ash and dust, and his head remains firmly attached to his neck.

From the way the light shifts in the hallway, I can tell dusk is fast approaching. I'm grateful that my belly is full and resentful that I cannot go to bed with my future husband and enjoy him as I truly wish. Instead, I remain a spectacle for him and his children.

"You didn't kill him," Charlotte finally says. "Why?"

"What good would that do me?" I shrug, meeting her eyes with honesty. I do my best to let no rage slip through and give her the idea that I am trying to undermine her. I don't know why I have given up the mantle of moral superiority to which I held so steadfastly when I first arrived here. Unease curls in my stomach. I want to retch, but I know my body cannot afford this. Healing potions can't be that easy to come by, even if this kingdom is forged in magic, unlimited by mortality. Mars can't keep buying me out of the damage I've done to myself out of pure stupidity.

Shame threatens to coat my veins, and I shiver. At once, Mars stands beside me and places a hand on my shoulder. My thoughts begin to spiral on me, and I fear I'll collapse as they cave in. I am often a victim of my own terrors while rarely a victim of anything else. Perhaps that is why losing to Jupiter stings as intensely as it does.

"So, do you mean to outfit the entire country with these baubles?" Adalius asks, his eyes sparkling with amusement. "You do know that, even as an immortal, magic taxes the body. You'd be spent within a week trying to charge your weapons."

I shake my head. "Not so. Do you know how many weapons my father and brother can infuse light into at a given time? You may not be familiar with the Siraltona, but she is alive. While your darkness relies on structure and planning, the Siraltona can do many things at once."

I reach out my right hand to one of the plates on the table and focus my left on forging the small figures of light I once had dance for Mars here in this dining hall. As recently as that was, it feels like an eternity ago as the Siraltona soars from my veins and infuses the dinner plate with light, being careful to coat it in the afterglow of the shadows that follow suit. They are the Siraltona's most persistent lover; I'm not sure I can stop them from following her anyway, and I am proven correct when the shadows flit about with her and the creatures I made with my left hand. Now, rather than just figures of light, figures of shadow have joined in the dance while I let the last of my power charge the plate with its finishing touches of divine inspiration.

When the plate stops glowing and the figurines fade, I remain standing. A bit of hunger gnaws at my stomach, but I'm careful not to allow them to detect weakness. It is concerning that Adalius may be correct, but I can't let my weaknesses cause us to fail in a war waged against Jupiter. I don't know if it's because my soul is tied to his or not, but I sense just how desperate Mars is for a solution.

Even more than that, I have a renewed appreciation for the surly king standing next to me, a hard focus glinting in his flaming eyes. Then I remember...

He can rob people of their will.

"When were you going to tell us you possessed such a power, *Father*?" Charlotte snarls.

That's how I would expect her to address him... I wonder why she called him 'Your Highness' earlier?

His daughter continues, "Are we at risk of wielding such powers ourselves? Should we be more considerate in our practices?" A few of the nobles shift uncomfortably, confirming that only four of Mars's children are present. The nobles step away from them, fear plainly stamped on their beautiful features. "Should we check Sherry to ensure she isn't at risk of manipulating you or Adelaide?"

At the mention of her name, I find myself wondering about my friend.

"I escaped Jupiter, did I not? And I detect none of Jupiter's magic coming from your father. He is immune to him as much as I am. He has my light," I say. "Siralto was the goddess of free will. It was why the world was a disaster until Tryta created consequences. Because of her, we could choose. Because of her, we could kill, steal, and do so much worse. Do you not remember this to be her truth? Tryta destroyed her when she gave the people free will and ensured that people could die as a result of their folly. Your immortality is yours only because he granted it to you. It is because of him that it was taken in the first place."

None of them says anything in response, but I detect I've struck a nerve by the way they avert their eyes and refuse to speak to me.

"Rest assured, I will help defend this kingdom. I will work to craft you the weapons you need. It is in my best interest to do so. Free will is a gift from the goddess who gave me my power in the first place. I cannot spurn what she blessed me with by ignoring such an outright threat. Sherry has no influence on my decisions there, I promise. And your father and king has not been swayed in such a manner, either. He is decidedly the biggest pain in my ass I've ever encountered!" I blurt.

Behind me, Mars chuckles. A few of the nobles seem aghast at my words, but I don't care enough about their feelings and traditions to spare them from my fierceness. I am not made of glass, and I do not belong on a shelf. I belong on the center stage.

"What will you do if you fail? You'll fail not just the nobility, but the people of Velyasa. You'll fail your kingdom, too, undoubtedly," Adalius challenges, his fierceness returning despite my surge of strength.

Intimidation isn't a currency I can rely on among the Shadow Folk. I respect them for their temerity, but I won't be shaken.

"You think the failure alone won't be penance enough? Is not the change of my soul and magic sufficient to say that my tides and allegiances have changed? I drink blood as you do. I am bound to the very king who forged the realm you cherish. What more do you want as a pledge? Whether I wish to give my loyalty or not, it has already been purchased by the gods themselves. Siralto is not alive to barter with Tryta on my behalf, yet her power flows in my veins and cries for the shadows I was never meant to wield. What more do you want from me?" My voice, now hoarse, cuts off. I stand, breathing heavily as I consider my own words.

Was being changed all it took to change? Yet... Finch stayed loyal to the cause of Sunfall. Or... did he?

I shake this last question off before I can ponder it further; I refuse to judge the dead. At least, I'm not ready to. Finch's motives hardly matter now. He's gone, and the earth feasts on his bones as they give new life to worms, ants, and flowers.

I make a note to consider the flowers in the gardens a bit more carefully the next time I stroll through them. When I feel Mars's strong hands clamp down on my shoulders, I know he means to whisk me away.

I miss the part of me that would fight him for this, but my ankles are weak with fatigue. I fear I might collapse to the floor, further bolstering Adalius's hesitations as to whether I'm capable of saving Velyasa. Incentives aside, the limits to my power have yet to be explored. I know they exist, yet I can't feel the end to the eternal, yawning stretch of the Siraltona as it roars in my ears, demanding to be loosed.

"Adelaide and I will work together to devise a plan on how to best implement her proposed plan. You all know I detest the very idea of robbing anyone of free will; the fact that I possess the power does not mean I would use it. I only revealed it because I believe in Adelaide's power as much as I do my own. I will return to discuss the matter of mating Rites before long. Right now, I need to consult with my medic about whether Adelaide can carry out her plan without risking her neck."

Mars doesn't wait for answers from the gathered nobles. Instead, he places a steady hand in mine and almost drags me out of the dining hall, people cowering in his path and staring at him, awestruck, once his back is turned to them.

Even after they have witnessed the lengths of the evil of which he is capable, they trust him not to fall victim to the siren call of power. It warped my father and turned him into something incomprehensibly evil. My father consorted with the worst sin of all: complacency. He gave up. He gave up when it was never his place to do so. Tens of thousands of lives rest on his shoulders, and he chooses to spend their loyalty in the tap room on cheap ale.

All the coins in Sunfall couldn't buy my loyalty or respect back for my father. As I watch the way Mars sets his jaw as we pass through the shadowy hallways of the castle, I know now what it means to be royal. Or, at least, this is how I'd like to imagine it's supposed to look. I refuse to accept deviations from this. I only hope Maverick will follow in this vein should he depose Alaric as we subtly planned to for so long.

I realize my empty hand is clenched in an angry fist and do my best to calm my rage as it snakes to the surface. I don't know why my mind is preoccupied with a kingdom that planned to sell me as a breeding mare. I don't know why I care to think about people whose souls I no longer mirror – whose aspirations are limited to decades and not centuries.

And yet, my soul weeps for them all the same.

~*~

The door to our room barely clicks shut before Mars has me in his arms. His embrace is restrictive, but not full of the lustful desire to which I've avidly become accustomed. If he holds me any tighter, I fear I may shatter under the weight of his broad arms that crush my arms against my sides like the coils of a python.

"Mars," I choke, "are you okay?"

"You were outstanding out there. But Adelaide... I cannot allow you to risk your life this way. You want to arm the *entire* kingdom with your magic? Do you know the toll that will take on your body?" Mars pulls back to look at me, the hungry fire in his eyes brighter than usual, lines of concern painted between the spot where his eyebrows knit together.

I swallow. "Mars... I have slaughtered so many of your people. They will never accept me if I do not offer something equally as grand."

Deep down, I have no idea why I've brought it upon myself to prove my loyalty to them, but the flutter across our divine tether tells me the mating bond is, yet again, to blame. I curse the gods for daring to conceive of something as stupid as love.

"So your change of heart comes at the potential destruction of yourself?" Mars crosses his arms.

"It doesn't have to be at the destruction of myself — I just have to learn to be efficient in how I use my power. Besides, the biggest cost of the Siraltona is death when you're *mortal*, which doesn't even apply to me anymore," I scoff.

"You are fallible, though," Mars warns. His face is grave as he moves to sit on the edge of the bed. "You can still be killed. Don't you worry that the very power that gives you your strength might be your downfall?"

I shrug. The thought doesn't often cross my mind; I simply know it is one of the risks you accept when you use magic. I sit beside him and try to ignore the way my skin glows brighter when I'm closer to him. It's disgusting how even my power yields to his presence — how it calls to him without my permission.

"I know that the Siraltona comes at a cost, just as your shadows do. Don't you worry that the power you possess to rob others of their will might swallow you whole? Don't you worry that you might become a puppet to the very magic you use to rule your kingdom?" My words roll from my tongue with careful sharpness. I hope they won't cut too deep, but the way Mars pulls away tells me he's perturbed.

"Keen observation," is all he says, his mouth tugging into a grimace.

Before he can continue, a soft knock sounds at the door. Sherry.

I get up to open the door, but he grabs my hand, making me fall back onto the bed to sit and wait while he opens the door to our chambers.

When Sherry enters, her eyes are wide. "Adalius said I should come up and examine Adelaide for signs of magical wear. What did you do to her today, Mars? I thought the goal was to keep her alive! She's *your* mate," Sherry complains, her voice cross. She clucks her tongue before approaching me, her wide, pale eyes full of concern.

Mars ticks his angled jaw, and I note the way his veins protrude. He's irritated by her. But the softness of the flames in his eyes betrays him. I know he would never hurt his niece.

"They also mentioned that we should be examining *you* for perverted incentives. Should I be worried that you'll harm me or Mars?" I ask, not caring when Mars turns to look at me like I've thrown a dagger at Sherry rather than asking a question. His nostrils flare. I know he's conflicted, his eyes darting between the two of us.

Sherry levels me with a glare, but I serve it right back. I don't care if I've offended her — I can't let these questions linger in my mind. If Sherry is a threat to me or Mars, it's my business to know it.

"What makes you think I would betray my kingdom — my uncle?" Sherry's voice is an angry shockwave, the silver glint to her hair set aglow with rage. Her hand reaches out like she might try to grab me, but I smack it away.

"Sherry," Mars warns. He shifts his stance and his muscles twitch, eager to be loosed into a fray that's not yet broken out.

"She doesn't know." Sherry's voice rises another octave. "She doesn't know what I've been through to get here. The things I've seen."

"Sherry, I'm not trying to hurt your feelings, I'm just trying to understand why Adalius would say that. I'm not worried if you *do* try to harm me, to be clear," I sneer. Light crackles in my palms as an affirmation of my confidence.

"You're such an egotistical prick!" Sherry shouts.

Before she can lay her hands on me, Mars springs. He grabs both of her wrists and yanks her back, forcing her to stand still as her golden eyes burn with white-hot rage and shadows creep like tendrils down her arms. I know they'd like to sear through me, ripping the flesh from my bones and leaving ashes in their wake.

But I don't rise to the occasion to confirm her desires or fears. Instead, I tilt my chin up and smile at her. "I don't know your past, Sherry, but I've not done anything to conceal mine from you. Shall I recount everyone I've slain in the last year alone? I've never shied from my past. What makes you think that I won't ask you to reveal yours if there's a hint of a threat? Am I wrong to ask about the things that might harm this kingdom?"

Tears spring from Sherry's eyes and I take a wide step back, my heart panging for her. Regret forges a new seat in the depths of my heart, and I take a breath. I've never felt such a thing before – regret – for a Shadow Folk.

Except for Finch.

My mind has never counted Finch among them, though. I wonder what my father and brother might say if they saw me now, my hands outstretched and my eyes wide with concern for Sherry as she falls apart, thick sobs ripping through her chest as she slumps into her uncle's arms.

He doesn't react, save to hold her closer and pat her head reassuringly. He looks at me, his eyes almost pleading – begging – for me to say something as recompense for upsetting her.

"I'm sorry to upset you, Sherry. I know you mean well. You've been kind to me since I got here. I only meant to try and understand what Adalius was saying. Am I wrong for trying to keep track of the threats to this kingdom, real or not?"

"No," Sherry stammers. She takes a few shuddering breaths as an attempt to stop crying.

I procure a handkerchief from the small end table by the door and give it to her. With a mumbled thanks, she wipes and dabs at her eyes. Mars steadies her arm; I motion for her to sit in one of our armchairs. The soft, aged fabric is something I can't stand – the texture is far too soft and slick for my taste – but it doesn't seem to bother Sherry when she sits down.

"You're right to ask. It just infuriates me that they still question my loyalty." Sherry's eyes land on Mars, and she scowls at him. "Your children are insufferable."

"Your cousins haven't gotten to know you as I have." Mars sighs. He walks over to stand beside me.

My feet stay planted a firm distance apart. I refuse to sit in the chair next to Sherry's. As much as I want to let my guard down and trust her as much as I can, I can't just yet.

"I suppose I need to tell you why I'm always suspected. It is because I am Jupiter's daughter," Sherry confesses.

I shrug. "I suspected as much. I never saw Mars as being someone with several siblings…"

Sherry's eyes widen. "You mean to tell me you've suspected this the whole time and never said a word of it?"

I roll my eyes. "I haven't really been asking questions until recently. I was busy chasing a moral pinnacle that doesn't exist. But seriously, Sherry, is that what Adalius is worried about? Does he know of some betrayal by you?"

Sherry shakes her head. "No. Mars rescued me when my father first started to go mad. I alerted Velyasa that he had… changed. He'd always spoken of wanting a throne of his own, but he couldn't rally people as Mars did. I never thought my uncle would prove to be the deciding factor for my father to begin pursuing such dark deals with the gods, but that is how he acquired that awful power of his." Sherry lowers her eyes. "I'm lucky I was spared. I barely escaped with my life and will intact."

"And you are welcome here, still," Mars says. The resolution in his voice is unmistakable, but the look Sherry and I share betrays our doubt.

I shake my head. "Clearly, your people still aren't on board with her being here. What prevents them from trusting you?"

Mars chuckles. "Rich, coming from the woman who slaughtered thousands of them on behalf of her mother..."

His comment lands heavy in my soul. I step back from him, falling into the chair beside Sherry.

"That was low, uncle," Sherry scolds.

I grip the slick, silken fabric and steady my breathing. As much as I carried my mother's death as a beacon of strength and motivation, I don't like to think of her much. Just as I can still see Finch being ripped open by Jupiter's dark, horrid magic, I can still hear the thud of my mother's head hitting the castle floor. I can still hear the earth-shattering scream that left my lungs that day when she drew her last breath.

My eyes land on Sherry, and I blink. "I understand your plight more than you know. The people here will never trust me, either. We're more alike than you would hope, and this fool here wants to make me his queen."

I glare at Mars, my heart still stinging from his lancing words. I can't believe he would say something so brash, but not an ounce of regret can be found in his handsome, chiseled features. Instead, he nods at me.

If his goal was to get me to commiserate with Sherry, he accomplished it. But once again, I'm not so sure of my allegiance to him. I lower my eyes, refusing to look at him. I take a deep breath and consider all that I've learned.

"So, if she's not a threat, how do we convince the people that our efforts to arm them are genuine?" I ask. "And how do we make it so that I can do this without expending myself too much?"

Sherry turns to me, a grateful smile plastered on her features. I won't keep this page of our conversation closed forever; deep down, I know I'll still struggle to trust her. As much as I want to put my faith in her, the knowledge that she is descended from that creature, Jupiter, is earth-shattering.

Then again, look who I'm related to, I remind myself. I'm not a fan of this sort of introspection, but it finds me more often than not lately.

"We need to assess your body now that you've been turned. Your body is still more fragile than most, but it gets stronger with age," Sherry comments. She stands from her chair and motions for me to give her my hand. She presses her thumb to my left pulse point and hums, her eyes grazing over my veins with thoughtful detail.

"Your heart is racing," she says. "Is it normally elevated like this?"

I nod. "I... tend to stay on edge."

But that's not the whole truth. This bout of fatigue and a runaway heartbeat is worse than usual. Only now that my focus has been lifted from Sherry and the revelation of who her father is do I realize that I feel like my heart is about to crack through a rib and run away into the woods on a hunt of its own. A hunt for sanity. For provisions that will keep her sated on anything but the horrible Shadow King and his wicked fangs and tongue.

He growls at me, knowing that I am yet again affected by his presence. Sherry rolls her eyes. "You two are impossible." But there is a glimmer in her eyes and a smirk that tells me she's having fun mocking us just as much as Mars and I are struggling to navigate our feelings for each other.

"You both still owe me for that horrible outburst of power earlier, by the way." Sherry's tone changes so fast that I barely have time to register that she's scolding us again. "Letting you both use your powers to such extremes like this has gotten out of hand. Uncle, I know you're powerful, but the Falaleh is still dangerous. Why would you even *bother* with a demonstration of that today?"

For the first time, I notice a thin sheen of sweat has broken out on my mate's forehead. My heart lurches, its speed becoming even faster – something I didn't think possible. I struggle to take in air, but mask this as valiantly as I can as Sherry turns her attention to the king, leaving me to writhe in anxious agony.

But his eyes never leave mine. Mars calls my bluff without speaking a word. I know by the way he fixes his jaw that I'm in for a *long* argument about whether my plan to save the kingdom will work.

It's my call. Not his.

It occurs to me that my defiance may be my downfall someday, but today is not that day. I intend to take full advantage of Mars's weakness for my advantage... and that weakness is *me*.

Sherry has her fancy pen and notes out again, scribbling things I'm sure would make my head spin as she looks Mars up and down. Neither of them speaks, but a heated exchange of wills passes between them. His face very much says, *I'm fine, leave me be.* Sherry's face says, *Shut up and let me make sure you're okay.*

Mars doesn't strike me as the type to continue cooperating for much longer. I'm hopeful we can return to the conversation regarding how I can arm the Velyasan soldiers against Jupiter. The power in my veins pleads for answers on how she might be set free once more. She cries for the battlefield; my Siraltona is ever the warrior.

"What can we do to speed up the maturation process?" I ask.

Sherry, who is dabbing the sweat from Mars's forehead and taking his pulse, doesn't respond. Her focus is entirely on caring for her uncle.

"That's a conversation we can have later. Right now, I need to examine both of you and make sure you haven't drained yourselves too much and ensure you get the right amount of blood to recover."

"Sherry, your father could arrive at any moment. Velyasa needs protection!" I argue, my voice sputtering. I flex my fingers, doing my best to contain the electric jolts traveling down to the tips of my fingers. My skin twitches against the angry brush of lightning, trying to burst free of its bottle.

"Our defenses remain solid," Sherry mutters.

Mars looks at his niece and raises an eyebrow. "You've never been one to be so calm about your father's potential arrival."

Sherry shrugs. "Now we have you two. He knows that even if he takes down the whole kingdom, you two would still be standing... and he has to conquer everything before he can be satisfied. He won't arrive until he deludes himself into thinking he can win."

I throw my hands into the air. "Forget I asked. That kind of attitude is what got us in trouble at Sunfall," I grumble. I bolt from the chair and sweep from the chambers, ignoring their pleas for me to come back. For far too long, I sat idly by while Sunfall fell to ruin and became barren for the Shadow Folk to prey upon. By the time we realized our folly, it was too late.

I need to think, and the bedchamber where Sherry and Mars are still arguing is hardly the place for it. Velyasa cannot afford to fall to that bastard Jupiter, and I can't afford to let my magic consume my life.

"Let her go, Mars," Sherry says. It's the last thing I hear as I step into the hall and take purposeful strides to still my mind and sift through my thoughts. I don't know how long Sherry will hold him at bay from following me. I suspect my freedom will be short-lived, so I need to think hard and fast before I'm swept away into the burning desires for Mars and his embrace once more. I yearn for the blasted mating Rites to be over more than I think even he does.

Groaning, I scold myself for being so fickle as I consider my options for protecting Velyasa. I refuse to let it become another Sunfall. I refuse to be like my father and ignore the harsh reality that safety is never guaranteed. It must be earned. And it is never equally shared by all.

But I am powerful enough to take on danger. The innocents of Velyasa might not be, especially since their free will and power are at stake. I still wonder how they managed to regain the power they have. How did they lose it? What dark bargain did Mars make to get their familiars back?

I yearn for the tomes in the vast library back in Sunfall, even knowing how erroneous the records on Shadow Folk are. What wasn't erroneous were the records on the Siraltona.

Then again, none of the wielders were ever... vampires.

I swallow, my tongue glancing over the sharp fangs on either side of my mouth that I try with desperate delusion to ignore. What business do I have with such things, anyway?

But the sweet caress of blood across the tongue and teeth can't be stressed enough – it is an offer of peace and hope from the gods themselves. At once, I find myself ravenous as I scour the hallways of the castle, intent upon finding my way to a hunt or the dining hall once more. I know my stomach cries as it does because of the power I've expended in the last few hours. I wonder how many thousands of gallons of blood would be necessary to keep me standing, as I hope to infuse everything I can with Siraltona to protect the very people I once swore to destroy.

How many must die to keep me living? Will the lives saved outweigh those deaths? Surely many must die to give me that much blood. Surely donations alone would not be enough.

Still, I consider the prospect of finding the right token with which to arm the soldiers. Should only their weapons be infused?

But their souls must be protected. The trinket must be just as the necklace was on Ewing... How can I fashion that many necklaces? How many soldiers are there? How long would it take a smith to make things of that nature?

I look around and realize I don't know where I am. The long stretches of dark hallway never seem to end; they are a maze I've yet to learn. I wonder if Mars and Sherry are keeping up at all. I glance over my shoulder and find that only my shadow has accompanied me this far. It's odd that they are letting me have space such as this. How can either of them trust that I won't betray the kingdom in a moment of rage? All I have to do is slip once, and it could cost everyone in this kingdom their lives.

But I think of Rose, Peony, and Violet and how they lost their sister Lavender. I think of Sherry, who narrowly escaped losing her soul to the clutches of a madman who chose to defy the gods.

A bleak part of me wonders if I should have continued to abstain from blood. Maybe it was a sign from the gods to resist the very thing that would strengthen me. The stronger I get, the bigger a threat I become. It suddenly occurs to me that I might not wish to walk alone in the castle. The Shadow Folk I pass stare at me for what I am: *a monster*. How long before one of them becomes emboldened enough to strike me down, especially since I am only a fledgling vampire?

Creeping, anxious thoughts snake through my mind. I jump at the barest hint of whispers. *Should I run back and hope to find my way to my bed chambers?*

I look up to try and steady my nerves, hoping to count ceiling patterns as a means of refocusing, but find that the ceiling remains shrouded in shadow. It is high up there and, once again, I imagine how Mars might perch up there as his mighty dragon familiar and gaze upon the subjects below, his eyes unburdened by shadow.

Mine, on the other hand, remains weak.

I can't go back there. I won't find my way. I can't listen to him. He'll talk me out of this. I need someone who can tell me what sorts of pendants make sense. How strong must the chains be? How many can I infuse at once?

Up until now, I've only infused a few things at a time, today being the most ambitious example of my power that I've ever pursued. It is strange to come into power as late as I have. This new body has no memory to guide it. I only have an inkling of what I might be capable of, and most of my grand demonstrations only came out of dire necessity or pressure to perform.

Now, in these quiet corridors, I pass countless faces of people I know nothing about, while they all stare at me as though I am a god. And this god has no idea if she even understands her divine power, let alone how to use it. I am a failure to them just as much as I am a nightmare.

My shallow breath quickens. The ceiling feels like it is caving in on me, and I stop to lean a hand against the wall. My heart, while slower than earlier, still races. My body begs to be rested after using so much power today, but greed and ego threaten to befall my success. I wonder now if the Siraltona can be used to create *solid* things. Perhaps *I* could be the smith who weaves the very protection amulets this kingdom needs. Perhaps I could equip *everyone* and not just the soldiers.

Just as I am about to pull on the raw power singing in my veins, I feel strong hands on my shoulders. My freedom is gone once more as Mars turns me around to face him.

I greet him with a sinister smile.

BARGAIN

"**D**ON'T EVEN THINK ABOUT it," he hisses.

I look down and see light dripping from my hands, drops of raw power spattering on the floor before dissipating into nothing. "I can do it!" I argue. "I can save this kingdom. I can't save my own, but I can save this one."

Mars shakes his head. "Perhaps you can, but not like this. Not at the expense of your sanity and health. I did not just find my Lafura to have her wink out like some common star in the sky! You should burn longer than that before going home to Tyrladan. Please, let me keep you – at least for a while."

His voice is unsteady. Fear writhes in his tone, and I'm alarmed by how fiercely he clings to me. His hands clamp onto my shoulders. His eyes sweep over my face as shame floods my cheeks.

I have no idea what it means to live *thousands* of years without someone you love. He says he has loved before, but to know that he has existed without *this* depth of yearning in his heart – without *this* knowledge of someone being made for them by the gods themselves... I can't imagine it. It's a hard thought to wrestle with. As much confidence as I have in my power, I lack any sort of love for myself. It's a truth I've left to rot within the deepest parts of my mind and heart since my mother died.

Yet here Mars stands before me, staring at me as though I am the answer to every prayer he's ever dared to think or whisper.

"Fine. I will rest... for now. But I have questions, and you owe me answers." I tilt my head and stare directly up at him. I'm not one for trying to push a man to the edge, but if it gets me more information and helps me figure out how to save his kingdom without dying, I'll do what I must.

His lips crash onto mine, and he nudges me up against a wall. Our tongues dance, and we rob each other of breath as our bodies writhe against each other. Neither of us cares that other Shadow Folk pass by. I don't care whether they are disgusted or happy that their king is clearly enamored with his former enemy. Finding solace in his lips and ecstasy at his touch, I'm unwilling to surrender either of those things.

We finally pull apart, panting. Had things continued, I would have been stark naked in this hall and working on another heir for him. It's a startling feeling – the idea of having his offspring someday. I've never considered becoming a mother or one capable of mothering.

Will he expect them of me? Or will the children he has now suffice?

I know I am not ready for them now, and make a mental note to ask Sherry what their methods for abstaining from childbearing are here. Is it different for vampires than for mortals? In Sunfall, there were teas and herbs to ensure one did not become pregnant.

His copper hair is disheveled from our passionate encounter, and I reach my hand up to help set it to rights, returning it to its graceful, wavy nature. He smiles down at me as I stretch up on my tiptoes to finish styling it and runs his fingers through my auburn locks as thanks, the smile never leaving his face.

"I wish you would trust that I seek ways to save my kingdom just as much as you are. You've only known the dangers for a month. I have known them since I founded it over a millennia ago," Mars whispers.

His sudden return to our earlier argument jerks me from the remaining high of our kisses with aggravating force. I was not ready to return to talks of politics and defending the kingdom. I was content to bask in the joy of being with him, but he is right to reel me back in.

I fix him with a grimace. "I know you care for them. I do, too. But you must remember that I am a warrior first, not a princess. My thoughts always stray to the battlefield. I was never taught to rule – only to secure my kingdom's safety."

It's the deepest truth I've ever shared with anyone. I have always known I was a pawn on the chessboard – perhaps a knight, at most. But a queen? Never a queen. The thought of something as heavy as a crown on my head, as metaphorical as it might be, makes my neck twinge with the pain of so much responsibility.

"Come," Mars says. When he sticks his hand out for me to take, I oblige him, settling in the rough comfort of his worn hands.

I can tell from his calluses that he is no stranger to labor. He has toiled, though I have no idea where. The hunts are not scarce of prey, and his crops yield bountiful production based on what I've seen of the royal gardens. I've not seen reports or complaints from the peasantry as we had in Sunfall, though I suppose he could be hiding them.

We walk together in silence through the halls. I count my steps and track the different chips in the brick for a clue about where we are headed, but I cannot decipher where we are, relative to our bedchambers. I curse my mind for not being more quick-witted in moments like these. At times, my mind misses nothing; it is what empowers the scribe that Mars would have me be. Other times, I am as useless as a newborn – a child who's broken into their parents' inkwells without a clue how to form words on a page, let alone within their mind.

"What are you troubling over in those thoughts of yours?" His voice caresses my mind with the same gentleness as his shadows.

"I'm just... my mind isn't what it should be," I sheepishly admit. "I feel lost and don't know where I am in this blasted castle. I was just a prisoner, and in many ways, I still am. I can't commit the bricks and steps to memory, so I count things. I note the differences. It's how I find my way. But now I must confess, I am lost," I murmur.

I expect him to chuckle or toss some joke at me, which is our way. Our banter always seems to land a barb in the other's heart, whether we speak those truths aloud. But this one brings the greatest shame. I am supposed to be Sunfall's greatest warrior, but here, I am lost, alone, and without any sort of bearing to guide me. I don't even have the privilege of calling somewhere home.

"My fire, has anyone ever taught you to use your magic to do anything more than cleave through things? Those spells take the greatest toll, but they lack the finesse and spark that more creative magics possess. Have you ever considered a tracking or mapping spell?" His voice is kind, curious.

I look over at him and laugh. "May I remind you, Mars, that I only got my powers right before you arrived to court me? The arrival of my powers marked the reason you even visited Sunfall in the first place. It is the reason I survived meeting you for the first time, but that was the first time I've ever wielded. My father taught me grounding. The general *way* of magic is not new to me, but how to shape it and use it as my own *is* new. I have only ever borrowed."

I anxiously chew my bottom lip, careful not to cut through it with my sharp incisors. I wonder how long it will be before I forget to be careful. I wonder how long it will be before I stop caring to be careful in the first place.

Then again, Mars possesses a gentleness that defies those ever-present expectations of Shadow Folk that I can't seem to shake. I can't overcome the way I've come to view them in my head as easily as I'd hoped. I remind myself to write down some of these thoughts later.

"We need to teach you how to use yours for all that it is, then," Mars says. "Come. There are some scholars in the library who might be able to help. They are followers of Tryta who have dedicated themselves for ages to the study of magic and how we can best utilize it. I want you to learn from them and write down the things you learn. We are haphazard in how we document our magical practices, and I need you to change that when you begin to scribe for us."

His tone is unapologetically pleading. He is resting something sacred in my hands regarding his kingdom; the simple act of *writing* things down is something he needs. If it's all I can do, it is what he will get. I only wish I could do more. It kills me the more I think of how far I've fallen.

Even worse, my mind can't escape a scarier reality than I've allowed myself to ponder until now, as we stroll between the flittering shadows of the halls whose curves I still don't know or understand. Mars is more powerful than I gave him credit for, but the ultimate power he has is the one he strays from. In a moment of dire recklessness–perhaps bravery–I do the unthinkable and pluck up the courage to ask him.

"I'll work with them, but first... I don't mean to patronize you, but how did you acquire the Falaleh? Like... how did you and Jupiter acquire such power when it is the antithesis of what both Tryta and Siralto stood for?"

The question sinks into the ground between us. I feel the yawning gap between king and prisoner open. I await the descent to some dungeon or pit where the shadows might swallow me up and never let me see the light of day again, save from the stuff that lives in my veins. Even then, I worry she may not be enough. Resistant or not, I am not capable of holding him off on my own. In the end, he is still far older and sharper than I am. It is uncomfortable to have met someone who can truly best me as he has.

I almost resent him for it. Almost.

But when his eyes meet mine, I catch a note of delight and surprise there. Once again, I am reminded he is not my father. Where my father detested questions, Mars seems to rejoice in them. I can't tell if this is a strength or weakness of the Shadow King. Would he be so willing to confess these things to others?

He wouldn't tell his own children earlier. What makes you think he's comfortable telling you?

His lips part, and I am proven wrong, yet again, about where I think the limits of the mating bond lie.

"I bartered with Tryta," he answers. "And that, my love, is a secret you are stuck keeping. It is a condition of the deal, you see, that only my Lafura and I might have knowledge of the Falahle."

"So, let me get this straight," I push back. "Tryta gave you a power that he is opposed to and granted all your familiars back in the same breath? Who took them in the first place? How did you lose them?"

Mars laughs. "That, my love, is a secret I must keep a bit longer. I hope you'll forgive me. But as for why Tryta granted me such power? Jupiter acquired it through ill means – by bartering with the darker gods of Kohlu who robbed it from the clutches of the Neylka itself."

At the mention of the Neylka, the hairs on the back of my neck stand on end. The thought of being erased from existence doesn't settle well in my stomach. I never stopped to ponder that goddess – that *thing* – for very long. It's largely regarded as where Siralto went. I shudder to think that my goddess died in the clutches of that wretched entity. Why would I ever want to ponder it as anything more than a wretched godslayer and destroyer of dreams and light?

Still, the power hums in my veins, alive despite the death of her creator.

"So, you'll tell me that Tryta armed you in an effort to stop Jupiter... you'll tell me that your bargain with him is the reason you found me – you admitted as much before – but you won't tell me how you got your familiars back? Or how you lost them?"

Mars grimaces. "There are stakes involved in that discussion that would put you at risk, as well as the fate of this kingdom. I won't risk either without having extinguished certain threats who would use that knowledge to destroy this kingdom."

I stare at him, dumbfounded by his answer. I don't know why his reticence shocks me as it does, but I suppose I have grown used to how candid he's been with me. I frown.

"I promise you, the reason is... far more complex than you think. Just trust that we lost them for reasons beyond my control that were, at the same time, directly my fault. And I had to work hard to make amends for sins that I couldn't atone for in blood alone."

The heaviness in his voice stops any follow-up questions I might have asked. I reach out and place a hand on his arm. "I trust your judgment," I lie.

Mars grins at me. "No, you don't, but I appreciate your pretty words, anyway."

"So, you need me to learn my powers, then? Rather... the extent of what they're actually capable of?" I ask.

"As a future queen, your goal should be to assume all of your power, not just the part that's the most familiar or convenient. You will have duties. As a scribe, your understanding of our magic will be far richer if you explore your own with the diligence of a scholar." His explanations, unfortunately, make sense. "Tell me, do you want to be able to do more than make figurines of light? To be capable of more than murder? You've already demonstrated that there is nuance to your abilities... Why not explore that?"

I blink. "I mean... I haven't really had much of an opportunity, but of course I do." My tone reveals my defensiveness at being scolded, and I'm not a fan of what that says about me. I hate that I am so readily thrown off course by a simple question. A humble offer shouldn't be the basis for how disgruntled I've become.

Still, I anxiously wring my wrists and consider all the ways I am failing, both as a princess of Sunfall and a future queen of Velyasa.

"I don't believe that your people will accept me as queen," I mutter. Then I wonder why I let something so personal slip through my teeth. Why I would speak such a thing aloud is more beyond my understanding than anything I've uttered thus far.

But my cheeks flush with rage and embarrassment as I struggle to meet Mars's outraged gaze. He puts a hand beneath my chin and forces me to look up at him. I place my hands around his arm, but find I am too weak to wrench him away.

"They will accept you, as there is no other option. They may hold misgivings for centuries, for all I care, but they will bow to you and call you their queen just as they call me their king. I gave them this land, and I have given them every freedom and all the prosperity they can ever want. But what they will *not* do is get in the way of my mate. You are a gift worth all the kingdoms this ancient land has ever seen."

I swallow, though crippling guilt makes it difficult. I manage a feeble nod, his hand still not releasing my chin. His eyes sweep over me, and I wonder when I will be seared alive by the flames that hold me captive and rob me of breath.

"Tryta himself gave me a power that should be forbidden. He has never done so in any recorded knowledge to date. He gave me such power so I might smite the world and rid it of anyone who would use it for nefarious reasons and undo the work he carried out with Siralto to give people the right to *choose* their life. Along that same vein, I am *choosing* you. I am not a mindless puppet who serves his people. I am also not a raging despot like your father. Alaric is the opposite of how I choose to rule, but don't mistake me for what I'm not, Adelaide. I am not some pretty king with a handsome smile and perfect hair... I may have some of those qualities, but I am still a tyrant, just like anyone else. I just choose to be benevolent. I grant my people life and peace because it is something I believe to be a fundamental right. But at the end of the day, it is merely a privilege... one granted by my power and my power alone."

I wince at his words, wondering how his soldiers and court might react if they heard them. But still, I cannot deny the awesome might of his power and the way his shadows hold the line between destruction and peace.

I want to know, now more than ever, what he gave to Tryta to get their familiars back. I want to know what would have been so egregious that the gods would take that magic away.

Or was it some other power... some curse?

"Would you be able to get me a notebook?" I ask once he finally releases my chin. It occurs to me that I wasn't breathing that whole time; I suppose a vampire doesn't need to breathe after all.

I wonder if there is a limit to that.

"Did I not bring you on as my scribe? As our kingdom's own personal historian?"

I don't detect any mockery in his tone, but I still take a step back and look at him with a hardness that gives him pause. "You forget, Mars, that I had to ask for everything in Sunfall. I am not used to the privilege of free agency, as you call it. I was only ever a pawn. You say I am to be a queen. Well, who tells a queen how to stop being a pawn when that's all she's ever known?"

Mars smirks at me. "You were never a pawn, Adelaide. You were a knight, through and through. But queens still wield swords; they just do so with more confidence and power. You can never be *just* a knight now. You can only be what you are. It will take time to grow used to it, but the time is coming when you won't be able to wait anymore. You will be required to make choices that are far more difficult than any you've ever had to make. And only the queen will know how to make those choices."

There is a mystery to his words that makes me shiver. He mistakes it for a chill and offers to find me a cloak, which I deny.

"Let me meet these scholars you speak of, then," I say. "Let me go with you to acquire a notebook – perhaps two – and some quills. I prefer gray or white quills, if you don't mind. I don't know the fowl that occupy this area, but I know geese are prone to leave such things behind. I would prefer they come from *live* donors, as well."

Mars laughs. "Shall I dye our sheets purple next? What an oddly specific request."

I laugh with him. "Well, you did say to start acting like a queen. I've never met one outside my mother, but what I *do* remember is that she was a particular woman who liked specific things. I figured I'd take some inspiration."

We break out into hysterical fits of laughter. I don't remember the last time I've laughed like this. He pulls me into his arms, our chests shaking with a mirth I think we've both been in dire need of. He leans down, still chuckling, and presses his lips to my forehead.

"The light you carry is far more potent than the power in your veins," he whispers.

Without another word, he takes my hand and we make our way to the library.

PROPHECY

AT ONCE, I REALIZE Velyasa's library was never far from our bed-chambers at all. My feet did not lead me as far astray as I thought. Of course, I don't mention this to Mars. His ego doesn't need any further stroking, nor any other part of himself. My cheeks flush red even thinking about such an idea. I turn away from him, hoping he does not notice the way I have allowed my mind to wander to such unspeakable acts.

The sinister smirk on his face implies that he might be more aware of me than I would ever hope. Before he can pester me, I think of something I haven't had the chance to ask before.

"You said your kingdom needs a records keeper... but how does the kingdom have tomes about the Shadow Folk if no one has ever kept an account?"

"There have been sporadic efforts here and there," he sheepishly answers. "I recognize the importance of having a recorded history and have hired people over the past few centuries, but I always find that their efforts are...

shrouded... in bias. Most of the people who have written about us have been prisoners or outsiders. I thought that by hiring such individuals and giving prisoners the chance to earn their way out that perhaps we would avoid sounding overconfident in our history. I did not want to wash over the bad or the good that we've done over the years. But unfortunately, all I got were several inaccurate accounts and many more critical ones that miss the things my people take for granted. Those are the issues I'm worried will be lost to history when we fall someday."

"When?" I ask. My voice sounds small.

"Everything dies, Adelaide," Mars answers kindly. "One day, you and I will be reduced to ashes and be returned home to Tyrladan. But our souls will live on, and mine will never leave yours again. That is the beauty of our bond."

"Indeed, it is," says another voice.

I jump, startled to see that Velyasa's library is not as sparse of readers and scholars as Sunfall's was. Where our knowledge was sequestered and reserved for the privileged, Velyasa's library is open to all. I spot a few peasants plucking storybooks for their children from the shelves. My heart pangs with guilt as I think of all the children in my kingdom who don't even know what letters are.

But the voice that spoke belongs to a woman with stunning, dark blue skin. Her long black hair falls to her waist, and her eyes are prismatic. Dizzying swirls of blue, pink, and white stare back at me from within her irises, lending an ethereal aura.

Her white and gold-trimmed robes give her delicate frame added presence, and I know at once that she must be a scholar. I've not run into one before here in the library, even during the many times I slipped here to take notes and ponder what knowledge I could find on the Shadow Folk and their habits. This knowledge now rattles around in my brain as I try to discern the identity of the woman in front of me.

She must be fae – the dark blue skin and pointed ears are a telltale sign. And from what I've learned, fae usually have magic of the elemental sort. Where the flower girls' gifts are obvious in how they wield flora and give life to even the most miserable of gardens, I'm not sure what element might be associated with a blue so deep.

But then I consider once more the trim on her robes and note the stars woven there. *Cosmic.*

"A star fae?" I ask aloud, blurting the question before I can consider how rude I might sound.

The woman, however, smiles with a warmth that dispels any fears of having insulted her. I note the way she has *two* sets of fangs and shudder.

Since when is it possible to have more than one pair?

"Some fae are equipped with fangs at birth," the woman purrs. My eyes widen. Beside me, Mars barks a laugh and claps his hand on my shoulder. I glare at him, daring him to say anything without thinking first. He keeps his mouth shut.

"Who are you?" I ask.

"I am Professor Roselle, one of the leading scholars here at Velyasa. I joined this kingdom centuries ago to lend what support I can. I chart maps of the stars, predict weather events, and keep my eyes out for prophecies and curses that might harm this kingdom."

I wonder if she knows anything about why the Shadow Folk lost their familiars. Even if she does, I doubt I can convince her to tell me. If she's been here for centuries, her loyalty to Mars is almost guaranteed.

I hope that someday they might be inclined to trust their queen and offer me the same level of respect. But blood is stained so deeply into the skin of my hands that I doubt I'll ever be washed clean in their eyes. Secrets will be passed to me only by Mars's lips — those very same lips I always seem to want on mine. Kissing is so much less damaging than talking. Talking can cause pain that cleaves the soul. Kissing derives pleasure, even if it is painful.

I scold myself for letting my thoughts wander like this. Professor Roselle doesn't seem to notice my sudden lack of attention, though her colorful eyes analyze me with a scrutiny that makes me squirm.

I don't like being under the microscope, so to speak, and would prefer to return my face to the pleasurable crook of one of the tomes lining the many shelves in Velyasa's library. Within those pages, I can forget about Mars, the kingdom, Sunfall, and all my responsibilities. Even better if I can find a good piece of fiction to learn about Velyasan myths, or more information on their magic system. I am an adequate self-study under the right circumstances. Still, Professor Roselle continues to stare.

Mars doesn't seem as perturbed as I am by her open scrutiny. In fact, the awful bastard joins in on the staring contest. It almost seems that he's taking this as an opportunity to ogle me, and I would slap him if it weren't for the audience gathering in the library.

"You're the Shadow Slayer," another scholar murmurs. Before I can answer, the man bows. His pale skin is almost the color of aged paper. I don't believe the man has ever stepped outside the library.

"Ludwig, you needn't bow to her yet. She's not our queen," Professor Roselle chides. She clears her throat, ignoring the scowl on Mars's face as though it is not the most terrifying thing anyone could see. I imagine that countless others saw that particular expression on his face right before they died.

Professor Roselle must either believe she is immortal and immune, or she is truly stupid. I doubt she has the *uncle* card to pull like Sherry does, either. I take a careful step to the side to place myself between the Shadow

King and his scholars as more of them gather. I had no idea so many Shadow Folk were hiding in this library. Do they lurk in the shadowy corners every time I come to visit?

A small crackle travels up my spine. I hold the Siraltona at bay, whispering to her in my mind that all is well, all is fine. I do not need to tear down souls today.

"She's not our queen *yet*, but she will be," Ludwig finally answers. He stares at me with blank, white eyes like I am a fine piece of art and not a monster.

I grin at him, letting my fangs glint in the light from the torches in the library. Light from the outside casts an eerie glow on my skin that complements the way the Siraltona glows within my veins.

Surprisingly, none of them step away. They inch closer, and my wave of confidence shrivels up, replaced by a gaping hole of insecurity. Behind me, Mars clears his throat.

"She is my Lafura, and you will all treat her as such!" he demands.

A few of them murmur and stare just as the nobles did. I wonder if any of the scholars also serve in noble roles. None of their faces is familiar to me. I make a mental note to learn their names and start speaking to the individuals who work here.

How do I not recognize a single face when I have been here so many times since coming to Velyasa?

The library has been one of the small joys I have as a prisoner — an open font of knowledge. It was my only source of information when I was back in Sunfall. Then again, I don't think my father knew that I understood how to read, since he hid everything else.

Unless he had already purged that library of anything he feared I would learn...

I swallow, deciding to consider that reality later. I can't afford to become emotional right now, when I am on display for curious onlookers who can only window shop. An attempt to purchase a taste or feel of my flesh will land them a headless trip to Tyrladan, delivered directly by the feral Shadow King standing behind me. I hear a low growl rumble in his throat and a pleasant shiver travels down my body.

I barely contain myself. But I do. I take a deep breath. "Does anyone have anything they would like to say or ask of me?"

Ludwig speaks first. "Why did you stop fasting? Did the king force you to violate your sacred path?"

I step backwards, almost stumbling into my Lafura's chest. This is not a question I was prepared to be asked again. I knew I had caused a stir — at least, that's what Mars told me in those first few weeks of begging me to take my first drink. I knew there was political and religious turmoil because of my choice, but I still don't understand the depth of why they view the act as sacred.

"He did not force me to drink," I answer. "Tell me, Ludwig... why does it matter that I gave up blood? Forgive me if the question is bold, but I am unfamiliar with the customs of your people. What about my choice to abstain serves as an indication that I was pushed by divine inspiration?"

I hope my question doesn't offend the growing crowd; I am relieved when Ludwig, with his graying hair and watery, pale eyes, doesn't seem offended.

He offers a meek smile. "You do not offend, Your Highness. You see, blood is our life. We do not produce it on our own, but it is where our magic draws inspiration. We are reanimated from death by Tryta's shadows. That is what keeps us alive. But life alone is not living. *Magic* is our way of living. To give up blood is to give up your magic. And, as I understand it, you have some of the most powerful and rare magic there is. Just as we do, as it was gifted to us by the First Creator."

"Siralto was a First Creator," I counter.

"Indeed, she was," Ludwig says, unbothered by my effort to defend a goddess who is dead by Tryta's hands.

"So, you believe my choice to abstain was a choice to defy the gods?" I ask.

Ludwig gently shook his head. "Your choice to abstain was an effort to *commune* with them — to renegotiate by rejecting their gift. You gave up your gift and were willing to let it be taken back by the very goddess who chose to gift it to you from beyond the grave. It seems that magic broke your will, which means it was always meant to be yours. The goddess rejected your desire to return it. You must wield it. It is the only way." Ludwig's face becomes pensive and his eyebrows knit together.

I notice for the first time the notebook gripped with firm assurance in his hands. The small quill in his other hand is flying across the page, documenting everything about our exchange. I wonder if he will compare notes with me or answer some of the thousands of questions rolling around in my head.

Professor Roselle takes the silence as an opening to raise more questions. "Why would you give up your gift so soon after receiving it?" Her eyes are full of what could be concern or perhaps grief.

"I didn't know I was giving it up. The Siraltona was screaming to be released, and I couldn't... I couldn't let her. I was trapped. I guess on some level, I was trying to give up what I never felt belonged to me. I did not acquire my powers until just before your king arrived at Sunfall's doors, ready to burn it to the ground. It arrived just in time to save me and save my kingdom from the judgment of those it had oppressed for so long."

A few of the scholars bow their heads and mutter blessings to Tryta before meeting my gaze once more, unfazed by my confession.

"Let me ask you a question," I begin tentatively. "I know it is probably improper for a future queen to ask such a question, but do you all hate me for what I have done?"

I am stunned when they shake their heads, almost unanimously, that they do not hate me.

"Why?"

Professor Roselle speaks. "Your magic is ours now. Our king wields *you,* just as you wield *him.* I knew of your coming, Adelaide. I warned our king as such before he bartered with Tryta for things I cannot repeat."

Damn. There goes any chance of ever escaping this kingdom and life. We're truly fate-bound, I think to myself.

The blue-skinned fae continues, "You were utilized as a deadly toy for Alaric's depraved wishes, and your choice to continue and kill was both your own and the choice of your oppressor. We were not the only victims of his tyranny. I saw your path before you were born. Many here will hate you, it is true, but scholars of truth and prophecy often know more than the average person." Professor Roselle shakes her head. "The task to win favor among the people here in Velyasa is up to you, though I sense your future will be rife with such opportunity. But take heart that we do not overwhelmingly hate you. We know you will serve us and our kingdom tenfold as recompense for the things you have done against us."

I swear I see a lick of flames in Professor Roselle's eyes, and I instinctively reach out my hand to grab Mars, who remains firmly planted behind me, a guard dog on the verge of attack.

Doubt clouds my mind. I know it's a fool's errand to even begin to think I can win the trust of a people whose families I used to slaughter on behalf of Alaric and his twisted rule.

"How can I learn to use my magic for reasons other than killing? I've learned a few tricks here and there... but you all have such artistic ways of handling your magic. Does it resonate with you as it does with me? Do you converse with it, or do you just follow Rites or practices?"

It is probably highly improper to ask questions like this. Sherry and Mars were shocked when they found out how I speak with the Selyento, but if any of these scholars can help me, I'm willing to take whatever criticism Mars might have for me later.

No one responds.

After a long, uncomfortable minute that feels like an hour, Mars presses, "Why is no one answering Adelaide's questions?"

It's the first time he's spoken in quite a while, and I wonder if he was even paying attention. Where did his mind wander? Is he normally so passive in the presence of scholars? My father was active in every space — speaking, ordering, commanding. Mars is quiet and almost unassuming, if it weren't for his hulking muscles and flaming eyes. It's hard to miss someone with those qualities. It certainly takes great effort on my part to pry my eyes off him. Sensing my blatant staring, Mars looks down at me and winks.

I give him a low hiss before remembering that everyone can hear. Surprisingly, no one reacts or says anything to address our playful banter. Are they accustomed to public displays of affection? Then again... if they can hear better than humans, they probably happen across it more often.

My cheeks threaten to burn again as I consider how many guards have probably heard me and Mars through the walls of our bedchambers. I wonder if Mars will let me fire them. Granted, I've never seen them, but I know they're stationed outside the room each night. I can sense the traces of their magic outside the walls, but it must be in their rules that they are only seen when summoned.

Velyasa, I decide, is a strange place. Their morals may not be as back-wards as ours were in Sunfall, but their customs are incomprehensible to a freshly-turned immortal and my mind struggles to keep up. Again, I utter a curse beneath my breath at my lack of a notebook or journal to log my findings.

"I would be happy to teach the young queen," Professor Roselle speaks up, offering her king a dutiful nod. "None of us spoke up because we like to be... careful and purposeful in what we say. And taking on a student is no small undertaking, let alone a student who is a future queen." She turns her attention to me. "Tell me, Adelaide, do you submit yourself to instruction well? Or do you tend to let your headstrong ways dictate your progression?"

I consider her question. "I guess it depends. I'm open to learning, but I admit I am a headstrong woman. I won't pretend or lie and say there will never be moments where I'm not willful, but I did teach myself the ways of the Siraltona without even wielding it until last month. I learned my way around a blade and became my father's greatest military asset. I firmly believe I was kept from his table of political power because I would have swallowed his spotlight and made it mine. I am headstrong, yes. But I will do my best to leave this attitude at the door."

Professor Roselle smiles. "I do not ask that you compromise who you are; just that you give things a chance and don't be afraid to listen to your magic. The fact that it speaks to you is a rare gift. It is not unheard of, but it is a sign of a high level of attunement. You should proceed with caution, though, Adelaide. This kingdom's success hinges on your mastery of magic. Should you fail, everything will fall to ruin. I cannot let you go untaught. Consider this my effort to help you repay this kingdom by saving it. As its queen-to-be, it is your duty." The professor offers a deferential nod, though it lacks warmth.

Behind me, Mars shuffles his feet. "She is not to burn out in these efforts, Roselle." I hear the sneer in his voice, the venom in his words so toxic it nauseates me.

"Your Highness, all due respect, but *burning out* is the least of her worries. The Siraltona is eternal. What is *not* eternal is the limits of her own mind and the life of this kingdom, should it fall into the hands of your brother."

I know Mars is about to argue, so I squeeze his hand tighter and turn to him. "I will not die, Mars. Just as you have not died in your grand efforts to save this kingdom. Let me learn. Let me help this kingdom. Let me save this place you've forged and prove myself as your queen."

Behind me, I hear fervent whispers of agreement.

"Whether you survive is a matter of making the right choices, Adelaide. I'm glad you've made the first of the right ones — coming to me for help," Professor Roselle says, her voice simmering with pride. "Report to me as soon as you both have completed the mating Rites. There is no time to delay."

I nod. "Consider me your willing student."

"And Adelaide? Students must have a notebook — several, really. I believe you'll be needing these." Roselle snaps her fingers, and two leather journals appear in my hands.

My hands clamp shut like vices around them, the sweet feeling of victory ripe against my fingers as I run them along their spines and inhale their comforting scent, committing it to memory. Tears fill my eyes, and relief floods through me. I don't look back up. "Thank you."

Without another word, I flee the library, the ripe taste of memory and creation now fresh on my tongue as I think of all the words I'm going to pen in these two journals. Behind me, Mars is hot on my heels, dedicated to keeping me safe.

THE RITES

I DON'T KNOW HOW long I've been writing; my eyes feel like they are bleeding across the pages. I am determined to commit everything I've learned today about the Shadow Folk, magic, and Mars's dealings with the gods to secure his kingdom's success. I explain how my body fades and fatigues when I endeavor to create, taking care to note the way the Siraltona speaks in my ears about everything. I reveal how Mars and I are effectively immune to one another's most fatal magics.

Mutual-thrall, it seems, grows worse with time. The more we fight our desire for each other, the more we both seem to suffer. Across the room, he sits and watches me, his head hanging heavy in his broad hands. Despite the obvious wear and tear of exhaustion, his eyes are full of intrigue and passion as he observes me like a trapped animal.

I even write about this in the journal, not caring what he might think when he undoubtedly pages through this later. I don't mind if he knows my thoughts anymore. He is the only Shadow Folk who might care enough to read about them. Except Sherry, perhaps.

I owe Sherry several apologies, though I have no idea where to start. I don't know how to apologize to the families whose brethren I slaughtered under the false pretenses of Sunfall's morality.

Still, my heart pangs for my mother and Finch, both of whom lost their lives on errant missions that amount to nothing now. I still have not made good on avenging my mother. Now that I live as one of the creatures who slayed her, I realize I probably never will.

And to avenge Finch? I have no idea how to slaughter a beast like Jupiter. He possesses magic forbidden by the gods themselves. Am I an agent of justice for them? And if so, why not equip me better in my efforts to hold him accountable?

I cannot begin to pass judgment on account of the god of shadows when I was forged by the goddess of light — the very same goddess Tryta killed in an argument about free will and consequences. Will victory require me to barter with him? Or, worse yet, to try and commune with Siralto when she is gone from existence?

I do not pretend to know how to commune with the dead and the gone, but I know there is probably magic out there that would allow such a thing. The problem is that I have no clue how to begin to accomplish such a feat of magical prowess. All I know is how to cleave shadows in two and return their souls to Tyrladan.

I grumble a curse as my quill snaps beneath the weight of my madness. My fingers fumble to find another on the table in our chambers, but they come up short.

"That's all the quills we have in this room, my fire," Mars chuckles. "I believe I'll have to pluck another goose to satisfy your endless needs."

I arch my eyebrow. "If that was a euphemism, good job." I'm laughing before I realize it.

"It wasn't, but now that you mention it..." Mars casts me a wild grin, which I match with one of my own.

"What does it mean to perform the Rites?" I look at him, pleading. "If I'm to begin studying, then we need to undertake that venture sooner rather than later, no?"

Mars nods, his face now grave. "You understand that, once you've committed yourself to me, there is no going back?"

I stare at him. "You do realize that choosing anyone other than you was never an option, right?"

Mars shrugs. "You could choose yourself."

Outside, the peeking rays of the setting sun flare over the horizon, turning his copper hair gold. His flaming eyes sparkle, and I admire the way the shadows of early evening play along his sharp jawline. I want to bury myself in his beauty and spend eternity pondering how I ever managed to end up in love with the man I hate the most.

I'm struck by the unsettling realization that he could very well be the man who killed my mother. What's worse is that my heart and soul can't be bothered by such a potential truth. Only my mind holds out hope for the resounding logic of fear and respect for Mars as a predator. The other two pieces of me are traitorous bastards, swooning for someone who would have drunk my veins dry in a fit of spite against my father not too long ago.

But he didn't... although he tried.

I look down at my hands and consider how my power nearly pierced his heart and deposed a king older than Sunfall itself. I flinch. It is the first time I have felt regret at the idea of such a thing. I look up at him, my heart full of the truth.

"I would have regretted killing you, knowing what I do now. I want to be with you forever," I confess. "Choosing myself over you would be to betray my very soul."

Mars blinks. "So, not wanting to kill me is your metric?"

It's my turn to shrug. "What can I say? I just know it; I can't explain it. You're everything I should hate, but I don't. Even as my mind keeps me wary of you, my heart and soul were yours from the moment we met in Sunfall... even if you lied about who you were." I'm smiling even as tears fall from my eyes and stain my cheeks with more truths than I could ever say aloud.

He walks over to me, pulls me up, and laces his fingers in mine. "I would lie again if I had to, if it meant having you here with me. I don't regret a single moment since you came to join me." Mars leans down and brushes away the tears still staining my face with his thumbs, paying gentle attention to each one.

I struggle to swallow back the grief clinging to my throat and robbing me of air. "What does it mean to perform the Rites? How do we do them?" I ask the question a second time, cursing the way my voice shakes. Warmth spreads across his pale cheeks and I wonder if the Rites are something sensual. Is it the act of consummating the marriage, or is there more depth to it than that?

"We stand before the nobility and the high priests and priestesses of Tryta and profess our eternal loyalty to one another. Then, we drink each other's blood in front of the crowd. Once we have done so, as my queen, my nobility will come forth and bow and pledge themselves to us as a new, united front. Failure to do so will constitute treason." Mars growls this last sentence, and the flames in his eyes climb higher.

"No, Mars," I argue. "I expect there to be pushback. And it is not a sign they are treasonous; it is a sign they are wary, which is a wise characteristic.

My task will be to prove to your people that I am as committed to them as they ought to be to me."

His eyes sweep over me, his lips trembling as though he, too, might cry as I've been. Instead, he plunges toward me. This time, when his mouth catches mine in our sensual dance, it is more desperate and loving than any other time before. I do my best to return his sweeping passion as my body lights up with desire and a hunger deeper than any I've known before.

"Mars," I sigh.

He pulls away. "You are everything to me."

My cheeks burn. It's foolish that I should be embarrassed anymore. He's seen every part of me in excruciating detail, yet he never fails to arouse a feeling of nervousness within my soul. As much as I want to wring his neck in moments of rage, the desire to be swallowed by his fire wins out every time.

"Does their failure to accept me negate the rites?" I ask, insecurity creeping its way into my heart, holding her back from her destiny of finding eternal solace in my mate's arms.

"No. I make the decision, as well as you, to accept you as my queen regardless of my kingdom's ultimate ruling. You and I then consummate the marriage, indicating our decision to remain dedicated and faithful, with or without the kingdom's blessing."

"Will they depose you if you do that?" I raise an eyebrow, daring him to make such a foolish choice on my behalf. If he does, I'll kill him before I let someone take his place over something as childish as love. Even still, that love grows so much more devastating the longer I stoke it in the hearth of feelings buried deep in the magic of my soul.

"They cannot. The magic holding up this kingdom is mine. To remove me would weaken Velyasa and hand it over to Jupiter on a silver platter," Mars murmurs.

"What about after we kill him?"

"If our united efforts to end Jupiter's tyranny is not enough to convince my people of our dedication to them, then I might as well not rule them at all. We would leave this place and forge a new fate in a kingdom far away from here and forget the ungrateful bastards who would be far better served as a memory."

I pale. "Mars, you can't mean you would abandon the kingdom for me… That is reckless! You're frightening me."

"Only now?" he asks, offering a wry smile.

"Yes, only now," I lie. I try not to think of the way the Falahle erupted in the dining hall or how he can transform into the massive black dragon I first encountered at Sunfall.

I almost wish to see it again. *Almost.*

It dawns on me that I've not yet acquired a familiar form. Part of me hopes to find one soon, while the larger part is afraid of the beast I might find lurking deep within the parts of myself best left buried.

"How do we proceed, then? Do we… just tell the nobility we are coming? When do we summon them?"

When Mars claps a hand to the back of his neck, I realize the truth he's been hiding.

"You've already informed them, haven't you? That's why you asked if I was sure," I say, confirming my suspicions aloud.

"Yes," he confesses. "I was hoping today would be the day, after you met Roselle and spoke with the scholars. Our union will help solidify our magics, not to mention it will help me keep tabs on you and make sure you don't kill yourself in your efforts to help this kingdom."

We both take for granted that it was such a short time ago when I was plotting this kingdom's downfall without even knowing its name. I'm anything but right for the role as his queen, but the stubborn set of his jaw tells me he's certain of his choice and there's no persuading him otherwise.

I'm sure the nobles will adore this. I almost roll my eyes at the absurdity. Instead, I lower my gaze to the floor and ponder what the night will hold.

What will the rest of my life look like?

With the sun running out of light outside, I stand and resist the urge to pull him back onto the bed with me. Distraction is not the only way to confront the impending doom of my future, but it sure is tempting. The faster I get this awful creature to marry me, the faster I can bring him back here and stop yielding to tradition over passion. Perhaps I'll get my wits back after I've let him have me in all the sensual ways I keep imagining when our hands brush together or as our lips paint portraits of passionate desire against each other's flesh.

Time will tell, but time has run out. I must have him, so long as he'll still have me.

I have to marry him before he learns something about me he doesn't like.

It's tough convincing myself that there won't be something down the line that he decides is unforgivable about me, but it's a risk I'm willing to take. Having him, even if only for a few moments, would make all this suffering worth it.

My eyes lock onto his, and I nod, motioning for him to lead me to where the nobles are waiting.

~*~

Outside the castle, I hear the familiar call of crickets in the hidden crooks of evening and sigh as the promising kiss of spring's warmth settles on my shoulders, although a cool breeze threatens whipping winds and rain come morning. I find it fitting that we should marry in the spring. One never knows what the weather will be, nor what warmth the day will or won't bring. Still, life breathes anew, no matter how fleeting, and flowers find their way to the loving gaze of the sun they all adore and worship.

Spring often kills impatient blooms before they have a chance to truly blossom, but it also holds their soft petals like delicate hands and fingers, leading them into the guarantee of a life limited by the urgency of the seasons.

Mars and I are a love much like spring. It holds promise yet breeds uncertainty and harshness. Still, our love prospers, despite the angry gales of changing weather. We were helpless against the pull of falling for one another — we are bound by forces greater than ourselves. Still, I would choose him even without the gods' meddling. I would choose him without the bond.

I look up at my betrothed and smile, then lean against his shoulder as we traipse into his gardens. Violet, Peony, and Rose are all waiting for us beneath a trellis woven with the first roses of spring and, unsurprisingly, sprigs of lavender in honor of their fallen sister. If their excitement at seeing me the first time was anything special, the way they greet Mars is akin to how a mortal might greet a benevolent god. Their eyes shine up at him as he bows low enough for them to whisper in his ears before looking at me and giggling.

When he stands back up, the smile he gives me fills me with a soft, simmering desire that I know will grow worse. Even with those sharp fangs of his, his smile is disarming. I wonder if I will ever grow used to it. Will the effects of mutual-thrall ever wear off, or will it remain a permanent consequence of our soul bond?

"They're excited to have you as their queen," he chuckles.

I smile. "They're among the few who are." I'm not bothered by what I know to be true. But it's a sentiment I vow to change.

These people are worth fighting for. Misplaced fervor or not, I equate them to the people of Sunfall whom I failed to save from my father's tyranny. A chance at retribution by proxy is still a chance, in my mind. But a small part of me whispers that I must one day return to Sunfall and free those bound by the chains of my father's oppression. My work is not done there, even if it takes centuries to return to them and fend off the ghosts of those left bereft and suffering.

"What's on that mind of yours?" Mars is so close to my ear that his breath tickles me. I pull away, folding my neck in on itself to deflect him from trying to sway me further. Goosebumps break out along my flesh, and I'm a helpless victim to the smile on my face. I cannot break it, try as I might.

"Where is the nobility?" I peer around, hoping to spot some of my soon-to-be step-children so I might orient myself with the crowd. Knowing their mood in advance would help my nerves.

"They're further up," Mars answers. "The priests and priestesses have a designated spot in the garden to hold ceremonies such as these."

"Shouldn't the rest of the kingdom be informed? Maverick and Beatrice had quite a spectacle for their wedding."

"Do you prefer such pomp and circumstance? I can arrange for that. We can halt this ceremony now and do it in that manner, if you prefer," Mars offers.

I whirl to face him. "No! I do not. I simply asked so I could prepare myself for a crowd of that size. I much prefer this."

I hear laughter erupt from just over the next row of bushes and hedges and steel my nerves, bracing for whatever sort of reception I might face. Trying to bask in the bliss of my beloved's presence isn't working. My nerves are winning out in the fight for my attention, and I wish the circumstances would permit a better relationship with his kingdom.

I am still the Shadow Slayer.

My hands can never be washed of the blood they have spilled. I can only hope to be absolved with time. Knowing that Mars had to choose to defy his kingdom's wishes today in order to complete the Rites does nothing to settle the butterflies in my stomach.

For once, I hate myself more than I hate him for this. I hate that I allowed myself to become a mindless weapon for a man who loved ale more than his own humanity. Father or not, I never should have given my will and fire to Alaric to use as he wished.

And for what? A chance to wield power that was never mine?

The light in my veins rumbles its disagreement.

Right. Power that was always *mine.*

The Siraltona recedes, settling its rage to be used another day.

My feet almost float the rest of the way. If Mars did not have his hand gripped so tightly around mine, I might worry about drifting up and away, never to be seen again. My heart thrums in my ears, threatening to burst from my ribcage and make a break for the tree line. Perhaps my heart would be accepted back in Sunfall, changed or not. But I know that is a childish dream, and besides, I could never choose a different fate from this one.

When I finally spot the cluster of nobles, I flinch at the sight of so many angry faces. I knew the reactions would be hostile, but it doesn't lessen the blow of realizing I will be a queen with a target on her back from the moment she says, "I do."

Is that what vampires say?

I quiet these questions before they spiral out of control. I can't pull at my wrists as I often do when nerves plague me, so instead I focus on my breathing to ensure I don't pass out where I stand. I feel Mars's grip grow stronger on my left hand and know he senses how faint I've become.

Or he's as nervous as I am.

I look over at him and note his unbothered demeanor — he is every bit the royal I am not.

I glance down at my dress and frown, realizing I've opted for something plainer than I should be wearing. All the dresses he's supplied me with are finer than anything I wore in Sunfall, but still, I would have preferred some appliques or florals to set off the occasion. Instead, a simple ivory gown hugs my frame, the corset more forgiving than what Sunfall would ever allow. But it gives my legs room to move. I can spring into action at a moment's notice, and the skirt is not so bulky as to prevent a sword from hanging in the scabbard cinched at my side. Indeed, I did bring it.

I never go anywhere unarmed. A blade is where I find my peace, even as I know a far greater power has settled in my soul to be used until I die.

It may be the reason I perish, too.

For once, the Siraltona does not answer when it is mentioned. I take this as all the cautionary fuel I need. Slow and steady wins most races, but Velyasa is out of time. I will do my best not to burn out for Mars, but we need his people's acceptance to ensure we rule and prosper long after Jupiter has been slain. I refuse to consider an alternative ending where Jupiter survives and leaves us as the remnants of a history long forgotten. It doesn't do in the world of conquering to consider the potential of alternatives. Failure is not an option in these scenarios, as they certainly spell death.

I admire the blossoming rose bushes, peonies, and exotic flowers I've yet to learn the names of. We proceed through the throng of faces, both new and familiar, friendly and hostile, their names loosely grasped within my mind. I recognize Charlotte and Adalius at once in the crowd. They are the only two of his children I spot, though the size of this crowd could easily conceal the rest.

I spot Kaycee, the bosomy servant from the dining hall, weeping in the audience, and my chest swells with pride. I readily admit it's a stupid feud to have with a woman who bedded Mars decades before me. I wouldn't have stood a chance against her when I was off slaying his children and brethren.

I wonder if I have killed any of his children? It's a possibility I don't want to consider any more than the idea of him being responsible for my mother's death.

Taking a deep breath, I return my mind to the Rites. At the head of the crowd stands a group of people wearing black and navy robes, all etched in stars. They're reminiscent of Roselle's robes, but these are far less grand. All their faces are veiled.

"Trytala and Trytalo, I, Mars, present myself and my beloved, Adelaide, to perform the official mating Rites to honor the gods and their gifts to us. They have presented us to each other to have and hold for eternity, our souls having been bound by fates greater than our own." His voice, deep and booming, projects over the crowd and settles any remaining whispers with heavy authority.

The tension in the air grows thicker in the silence, and I almost beg them to return to their whispering. They can't focus on their hatred for me if they involve themselves in the idle gossip that nobles tend to revel in so much. This is a constant that applies in Velyasa as well as Sunfall. I hatched several plots, once upon a time, betting on this fact.

"Have you the evidence to support your gods-given bond?" the priest-esses and priests speak in unison.

The eerie clashing of their voices gives me pause. I'm compelled by a growing urge to flee — to run from this place and never return. We don't have priests and priestesses in Sunfall. Since Siralto is dead, we supplement our prayers with hard work and a dedication to observing the Rites of the dead. Souls return to Siralto, in our minds, and life is up to us in the meantime.

Here, belief is alive and well, but rests with the god who buried mine in the Neylka, never to be seen in one piece again.

"Yes, we do," Mars answers while I remain silent.

His hand, still holding mine, thrums with power, and his shadows erupt across the garden to douse the world in darkness. I needn't speak; my power erupts to greet his in a sensual dance of life and death, dark and light, a bond unbreakable for all the nobility to witness.

Gasps of disbelief and awe erupt through the crowd as they witness our powers melding, even stronger now than the last time we gave them a demonstration.

Am I losing myself to him? Will I only ever be a piece on a chessboard rather than the one playing the game?

But when Mars turns to look at me with a radiant smile and tears staining his cheeks, I know he doesn't see me like that at all. In the mirror, I see a failure who is bound by powers greater than her. When Mars looks at me, he looks at me as one might look upon a goddess, a hero, or a saint. There is awe and adoration in his features as he gazes at me with unmistakable desire, both lustful and reverent. Even in the absence of my body, his soul cries for mine.

It will always answer his call. Whether I like it or not is a separate consideration.

Our demonstration dies only after our magics have danced all through the crowd, leaving the nobles with no room to contest the strength and sincerity of our devotion.

"We accept your evidence," the crowd of priests and priestesses says, the chorus of their voices sending another chill down my spine. "You may proceed with the Rites as they are written."

I stare at Mars with unmasked fear painted on my face. I have no idea how to proceed with drinking his blood. Do we cut ourselves open? Do we bite each other's necks as he did mine not long ago at my execution? And who goes first?

Sensing my distress, Mars pulls me close and presses the tip of his nose to mine. "Follow my lead, my fire." He raises his voice to thunder over the crowd. "Velyasa, I present to you your queen. From a distant land she hails, her hands stained with the blood of so many of our own. My own hands, and many of yours, bear the blood of her people all the same. I know many of you see this as an act of defiance or desertion. You may even think I am acting with lustful interest at the expense of my people."

His words evoke assent among the nobility. Many nod their heads. I catch Charlotte rolling her eyes and shoot her a glare. Her flinty blue eyes would boil mine alive within their depths, but I won't let myself drown in them. I'm already burning in her father's eyes. That is suffering enough for any soul.

"I promise you, though, my people of Velyasa, that I have fought this bond with everything I have. You all watched as I condemned her to a life as one of us. It was a fitting punishment for someone responsible for so much slaughter of a people she did not understand. But since coming here, it has become apparent that this bond is undeniable. Over the past weeks, she has begun to learn about us, document our practices, and has a renewed vigor to learn more. She wishes to use her power to save us, rather than condemn us. Our souls are bound. I know these things to be true. Tell me, Velyasa, who are we to defy the gods?"

At this last question, many of them flinch. Some make gestures of supplication, repentance, and shame, but for every noble who seems swayed by this challenge, there are two more who remain skeptical of me, many of them looking at me with unapologetic hate.

I don't blame them. I would hate me, too, if I stood in their shoes. I know their position because I once occupied it from the other side. In many ways, I still do.

Taking this opportunity, I clear my throat to speak. By now, the sun is nearly gone. I hope it won't be a necessary participant in our ceremony, or else we are almost out of time.

"Velyasa, I come to offer myself as your willing and humble servant. I cannot pretend or sweep away my past, nor would I ask you to overlook it or let me act as though it never happened. To do so would be to spit upon the Velyasan legacies I culled in an effort to pursue a moral high ground that does not exist. A decade ago, my mother lost her head to one of your own, and I spent every moment doing my best to avenge her. Only after coming here did I see my folly. It is easy to say, as one of you now, that I understand more fully the beauty and complexity of your practices and culture. I know that war breeds difficult decisions — my mother's head was always doomed to roll from her shoulders in that awful moment. I cannot change the way I responded, nor how I let myself be manipulated by my father, King Alaric, to achieve ends that were never mine to determine. But now, I vow to spend every breath moving forward to secure this kingdom's future in spite of what I did in my past."

My voice, for once, does not shake. I have never held an audience such as this one, and I am emboldened by the look of pure, unabashed pride in Mars's gaze.

"And why should we accept such pretty words when you spent every moment up until the last week trying to behead my father? You can't sleep your way to the top!" Charlotte sneers. She steps free of the crowd, glaring at me and licking her fangs, eager to lunge at the woman who would steal her father away from her.

"I don't expect you to," I answer, my tone cool and composed. I somehow bury the rage with which I would normally respond. Today, I am calm. Today, I am a queen. I must answer those same questions Mars warned me about not long ago. A pawn would respond with limited focus. A queen can see beyond what's in front of her. Charlotte is only the first of many reactions I'll face on my journey to become their queen in more than just name. Hearts and minds must be won with action. How I respond will set the tone for my entire rule.

"The pressure is on me to prove my dedication. How I will do so remains to be seen. I have ideas, but I cannot make open promises until I have results to demonstrate. In the meantime, Velyasa, I not only pledge myself as Mars's eternal mate, but as your steadfast protector, just as I once protected Sunfall. My blade shall now rise and fall upon the necks of those who threaten Velyasa and its people, no matter the cost. And of this I am certain: I am a far greater threat than any one of your enemies might realize, including the people of Sunfall."

I don't wait for Charlotte or anyone to respond. Instead, I step back and let Mars have the stage once more.

"There you have it, Velyasa. Your queen. She may not be who you expected, but she is devoted all the same. I have no doubt that with time, she will alleviate any of your lingering concerns. You will accept her as my mate, whether you like it or not."

While in Sunfall, the nobles might have blanched at this bold statement and given my father a political headache. But in Velyasa, Mars's people bow their heads in respect, despite their personal misgivings.

Except Charlotte.

Her eyes blaze. "I don't care, Father. I will *never* accept her! You can continue with this foolishness, but I am leaving!"

A few gasp and murmur as she turns and stomps from the garden like an insolent child. I almost laugh, but the grief that twists Mars's face makes me pause. I reach out a hand to comfort him, and he accepts it. His eyes stay locked on mine as we share a silent resolve to finish what we've started, even if his daughter is absent from the proceedings.

"Adelaide," he starts, "do you accept me as your sworn Lafura?"

"Yes," I answer.

Silence carries between us, and I realize I must ask him the same.

"Mars, do you accept me as your sworn Lafura?"

"Yes," he whispers.

From his pocket, he pulls a dagger, silencing the questions in my mind about how we will consume each other's blood. He lets the sharp blade glance across his palm. Dark blood rushes to the surface.

I take the blade from him and slice my palm, noticing how my blood looks brighter, even as the sun finally dies beyond the horizon.

Instinctively, I bring my hand to his mouth, and he brings his to mine in response. We drink. His blood is sweet, thick like honey with a note of that same cinnamon I catch in his scent. I wonder what mine tastes like as he licks the last drops pooling in my hand. I polish off his and we clasp our hands.

"She will never be our true queen," Adalius sneers, breaking the silent love in our moment and shattering my hopes for a romantic evening.

At once, Mars is swarmed by nobles who bustle and jostle me aside to plaster him with their concerns. The Rites completed, I am an after-thought and a curse that the Velyasan nobility would rather stamp from the record. In the crowd, I even catch the courtesans who would steal my husband from my marriage bed swirling next to him.

I catch the questions as they hover in the air.

"How can she rule over us when our blood is on her hands?"

"Does she know what it means to be a queen?"

"Does she even know how to use her power?"

"Do you think she's pretty?"

The last question, coming from the barmaid Kaycee, rings in my ear and echoes with the chorus of angry wasps that buzz and flit in my head, threatening to wipe out the nobility where they stand. But I can't start the Velyasan nobility from scratch. I have no idea which ones are Mars's children, and which are his brothers in arms who helped him found this very kingdom.

With everyone's attention distracted and my wedding ruined, I turn on my heel and leave. I don't run. I don't give them the satisfaction of a runaway bride with a broken heart. I hold my chin high, ignoring the tears streaking down my cheeks.

The Siraltona screams to punish them for defying the will of her gift — the gift of my bond with Mars. But I won't let her seek vengeance. Not today. Not any day. Instead, I make hummingbirds of light with her. They guide me, distraught, back to the bedchamber I swore I would never find on my own.

Turns out I do know how to map my way home.

Distressed, I close our bedchamber door and sob.

QUEEN OF SHADOW

I LIE BENEATH SILKEN sheets, my bare skin smooth against the soft mattress. The scorching heat of the day and its scalding stressors still haven't left me; warmth lingers in my fingertips. My chest is sore from hours of sobbing. Mars has been absent for some time, and clothing seemed too much to bear. I know Mars will be busy for a few more hours before he deigns it necessary to deal with his fledgling mate — *if* he ever deigns it necessary. I know the nobles have been peppering him with question after question about why he chose me or even dared to give me the title of Queen. I'm hopeful he'll pass on seeing me altogether. I do not deserve him or this kingdom. My heart aches, and I am nauseous.

The words of the council members still ring in my head. I'm not fit to be a queen, let alone the Queen of Velyasa. Mars and I spent the better part of our lives hating each other.

Okay, the better part of mine.

The realization of how *old* Mars is sits heavily in my gut. He's been around for at least a millennium, taking wife after wife and creating hosts of children. He never should have taken an interest in me. Siraltona or not, I am a liability. I'm certainly not stunning, like so many of the courtesans I've seen fawning over my husband. Mate or not, I can't compete with the offerings on the market.

I don't know when I started crying again, but I curse myself. I'm not the person I was when I first got here. Fiery, angry, unapologetic. When Mars first saw me, he called me his *fire*. Now? I've fizzled out. I'm a shadow of myself. The change from mortal to damned creature of darkness killed the part of me I treasured the most. I never, *ever* let my looks or status hinder me in my view of myself. Granted, I never had the chance to entertain thoughts of romance. Love was a farce, and marriage nothing more than a business contract.

Mars changed all this. I want, yet again, to hurt him for it. I ponder all the weapons secured in our shared armoire and imagine how I might use them against him as a means of revenge. Before I can get up to open the doors, I hear the telltale footsteps of the Shadow King, and I frantically pull the blankets up higher around me.

"Adelaide?"

His voice is like soft thunder in a summer storm. The sound leaves me breathless. I'm relieved to know that mutual-thrall is a side effect of early mating, but it still bewilders me. The fact that he and I have such a hold on each other is a source of constant frustration.

"Yes?" I manage to squeak. "I'm... give me a moment."

I start to dart to the armoire where my pajamas are stored, but I fall back beneath the sheets when he swings the door open, his flaming eyes sweeping all around to take in the view.

I imagine he thinks I look small—stupid, even—buried beneath so many covers as the sweltering heat of this hot spring day threatens to suffocate us all.

"Are you falling ill? You can't tell me you have a chill." Mars walks to the bed, his brows knit with concern.

"No, I..."

Before I can continue, he strides over to me and places a cool hand on my forehead. "You're not warm to the touch — no more than the rest of us." He cocks his head to the side to look me over, and I'm stunned at how wonderful he is to behold. "Are you hurt?"

At the mention of such a thing, I notice that his eyes, despite being flames, have grown darker — they're more intense in the low light. "No," I whisper.

"Why have you been crying? Don't lie to me, Adelaide. Whoever hurt you will pay for their sins. Don't tell me those idiots at the Rites got to you."

"Mars, I—" I quickly shut my mouth when he pulls back the sheets, undoubtedly to check for wounds. Instead, he quickly realizes I am stark naked.

"... Adelaide?"

"I was hot!" I say. "I didn't feel like I could be much help at the Rites ceremony with your advisors and beautiful women everywhere, so I decided to come back here and cool off." I shrug off my feelings of inadequacy and yank the sheets back from him to cover my nakedness.

He snatches them back, unabashedly ogling me in my vulnerable state.

"Are you no better than any other man?" I demand. "Give your mate and failure of a wife her sheets back and go take up with someone more worthy tonight."

I choke over the last words, nauseous at the very thought of him entangling with someone else, giving them all the pleasure I've so desired from him. Each time we've come close to completing our bond, we've found every reason not to indulge—not all the way, at least. I'm not confident enough to ask him, and I know I'm not worthy of claiming him that way. I've only begun to care for him in the last month. It's odd not wanting to tear his throat out all the time. Those homicidal urges resurface only some of the time now. It's even stranger now that I am his *wife*. He took me as his partner in front of a kingdom that wanted anything but to acknowledge me as their queen.

I start to cry again and turn away to hide my tears. I make a feeble attempt to cover myself again. This time, he snarls.

"You will stop this madness right now!" he demands.

Without warning, I am pinned to the bed, his large frame looming over me and his eyes peering deep into my soul. At some point, he lost his shirt. Vampire or not, I'll never get used to how fast they move. *How fast I can move.*

"What is this nonsense about others? And not being enough?"

"You heard your advisors today. Your children. Your people," I say, my voice soft. It quakes a bit, betraying my fear. With my arms above my head, I've only my legs to try and keep him at bay. I start to snake them up, but he catches me, sidling right between them so that the only thing I'll do if I raise them is invite him closer.

So close.

I swallow.

"I care not for what my advisors say!" he seethes. "A mate is a precious thing that cannot be denied. You are my wife, royal or not. You are my wife, vampire or not. You are my wife, whether the kingdom likes it or not. You were delivered here to me by forces greater than us; we cannot deny the gods their gifts. We must take them."

Without warning, he descends on me, his lips finding mine and his tongue curling into my mouth with wicked heat. The feeling of his cool skin pressed flush against mine sends tremors of anticipatory pleasure all down my body. I moan into his kiss, and my legs slide farther apart. I yield to him without further protest.

When he finally pulls away, I gasp for air and beg him to return to the lovely games he was playing with my tongue. "You shouldn't take me," I manage to hiss. "You should take anyone else. I'm your enemy, remember? How long ago was it that I nearly pierced you with my light? How long ago was it that I lied to you about Jupiter and how he tried to forge an alliance with my father? How long ago was it that I cursed your very existence for changing me? I am your enemy more than I am anything else!"

With a dark, sultry chuckle, Mars slides his hands lower, one perching at the swell of my right breast and the other snaking much lower to the peak of my pubic mound. He rubs in small circles down there while his left hand plucks at my nipple. I shiver.

"But what fun would it be if I didn't bed you when we've come so far? And what's a little love between enemies, hmm?"

If Mars cares that, once upon a time, I wanted to kill him—maybe even a little bit now—he does not show it. Instead, his eyes are fixed upon my sex. He slides his fingers even lower.

"You really don't think you're worthy of me?" he asks, his voice coated with lustful want. "You really don't think I want this from you?"

I try to answer, but am cut off when one of his fingers finds purchase on my sensitive bud. He begins to rub and I am putty in his hands. I don't care who he once was to me. I only care what he is to me now. He can ravage me on this bed. I'll thank him and beg him for more.

Siralto, damn this mating bond!

My chest heaves as his other hand gently pulls on my nipple. I cry out.

"Look at my pretty wife, all out of sorts for me," Mars chuckles.

"I'm not your wife yet, right? We haven't completed the bond, like you said. We only exchanged blood. We have time to stave this part off before you're stuck with me forever," I grit out.

"Don't ever suggest such foolishness, Adelaide. I am not *stuck* with you. There is no going back from this. I love you. You love me. And that is enough."

He silences further protest by adding a second finger down there, rubbing them up, over, and around my clit in the most delicious rhythm. Wet heat begins to pool, far more scorching than the heat of the sun that's long since left in favor of the moon that hangs high overhead. The cool moonlit rays casting over us make it so much more serene and intimate.

"Mars," I whisper.

His eyes fall on my left breast. He grins. "We can't leave any part of you out of the fun, can we?" He lowers his mouth and begins to suckle my left breast, his tongue running gently over it, and I bite back a scream.

"Mars!" I beg, gripping his back and tugging his hair. His ministrations become more desperate, and I'm certain I'm going to tear his skin and hair asunder as I mewl his name, squirming and writhing beneath him. *For him.*

Just as I find myself getting lost in something like paradise, Mars pulls away.

"Mars—what?" I reach for him, but he grabs my hands and pins them above my head.

"Repeat after me," he commands.

Desperate for him to continue, I nod.

"I, Adelaide," he starts.

"I, Adelaide," I repeat. I snake my legs around him, but he doesn't crash between them to continue the sweet songs he was playing on my now wet, quivering center.

"Am worthy of Mars," he continues.

"Am—" I stop. "Is that what this is about?"

Mars starts to get up.

"Am worthy of Mars!" I shout, desperate to keep him here.

A spark of mischief kindles in his flaming eyes. "Good girl," he purrs. Let's see how much of this we can work out of you tonight."

"What?"

"Keep repeating," he whispers. He releases one of my hands and returns it to that sweet song he was playing earlier, and my attention is latched on the way his crooked grin becomes so much wider as he watches me fall apart for him.

"Yes, Mars," I answer, willing to do anything to have him continue in his quest to ravish me tonight. I'm tired of denying how badly I want this from him. How much I want *him*.

"I am the Shadow Queen," he whispers.

"I am the Shadow Queen," I repeat.

"That's such a good girl," he croons, his other hand releasing mine as he returns to touching and suckling my breasts. He lets one free from his mouth with a pop. "I love my mate, Mars; he loves me and me alone."

"I love my mate, Mars; he loves me and me alone."

His lips plant onto mine again and I groan into his mouth as his tongue snakes along mine. I start to climb, pleasure overwhelming me as he continues to play my core like a skilled musician. Slick, soft moans escape me with desperate want as we continue our mating frenzy.

"I love you," he whispers as he pulls away.

"I love you, too," I answer, my head stretching back on the pillow, my hair a halo of sin and sweet pleasure.

"Let me take you," he demands, and I tremble as I nod my head for him to continue.

He removes his hand from my core, but any sadness from its removal is soon swept away as he frees his cock from his pants. While I've seen it before, seeing it positioned and ready to plunge into me fills me with an eagerness that makes my whole body shudder.

"Take me," I plead. "Make me yours. Make me your mate."

"You always were," he answers, a soft smile now plastered on his face as he presses the head of it against my clit, taking his time to rub against it and elicit more horrid noises from me. "My precious fire. My Adelaide. *Mine.*"

He plunges his cock into me, filling my core with slow, deliberate force. I'm grateful for the slick I've built up down there, or else I'm not sure how I would've been able to take him all. I knew he was big, but this is something *else* to feel for the first time. Any fear of pain at being breached is swept away as he puts a thumb back over my clit and begins to strum at it while he thrusts into me.

In and out, he begins at a brutally slow pace, taking pleasure in watching my eyes almost roll back into my skull with pleasure.

"Mars," I whine, "deeper."

I'm ecstatic when he finishes pushing into me, fully embedded now. His thrusts become more forceful and intense.

I scream his name, not caring what guards or passersby might hear us.

"Mars—*fuck*—MARS!" I scream.

He leans down and gives me a searing kiss before leaning down to lap at my breasts again, using his free hand to grip them with more voracity than before. My legs are as high up as I can get them to let him in as far as he can go. I grip him tightly, clawing all along his back and neck. I want to keep him here like this forever.

"Mine," I croon back.

His fangs glitter in the moonlight as he smiles widely at my declaration. "Yours," he moans, his own pleasure getting the better of him. He pounds into me harder, our skin slapping together and making the vilest sounds.

My mind goes wild with the thought of him spilling his seed into me.

"Fill me. Make me yours," I whisper.

My demands are desperate whimpers, but the message is well-received as he proceeds to kiss and suckle along my neck. I hope he leaves his marks there for everyone to see—especially the courtesans and advisors who hate me for taking their king. *My* king.

I groan again as he picks up the pace even more. I fear he might fuck me to pieces on this mattress. *There are worse ways to go*, I decide to myself, determined to let this man finish me off. A delighted squeak leaves my lips as he nips along my neck and nibbles my earlobe, his pace never slowing. I try not to think about how many women he's bedded to allow him to bring these skills to our bed. Instead, I savor the ecstasy he doles onto my body.

I feel the peak of my pleasure coming. He notes the change in my moans and adds more fingers against my bud. A bolt of pleasure wracks my body as an orgasm tears through me, his efforts finally yielding reward.

"Look at my sweet mate—my beautiful queen," Mars says, his voice laced with pride. "You come apart for me and me alone. Understood?" A thumb slips up to my bottom lip, pulling it down so he can take it fully in his mouth. He bites down just enough to cause small pricks of blood to rise to the surface. I swipe my tongue over it.

"Understood," I hiss back. "So long as you only do this stuff for me."

"Good girl," Mars hums. "And always."

I'm overwhelmed by how good he makes me feel — both physically and emotionally. I don't know how he sensed my need tonight, but I'm indebted to him.

"Fill me," I beg. "Mate with me all the way."

"Anything for my queen," Mars chuckles. He thrusts into me a few more times, removing his other hand so he can grip my breasts while he fucks me. With a final grunt, I feel his seed seep into me.

We stay locked like this as it drips into me. I don't release the vise-like grip of my legs around his waist until I'm certain that he's filled me. When his cock slips from my core, he stops to give it a wistful look before settling beside me. He pulls me into his arms and presses soft kisses along my jawline while running his hands through my tangled hair.

"You are so good for me," Mars says, his voice a deep rumble.

I shudder against his chest and settle deep into his arms. He leans in to kiss me, his lips soft and kind. We fall into a slow sigh of kisses; I don't want to give him up. His love is like poison.

"You will be the death of me," I whisper.

"And you will be the death of me," Mars whispers back.

His forehead rests against mine, and I want to stay here like this. I know the morning sun will come before long, but I wish it would stay away. Wrapped in darkness, I know I'm his, and he's mine. Then insecurity brews within me again, flashing thoughts of another woman capturing his attention or some advisor convincing him to take a more worthy queen.

"You promise you're really mine?" I ask, fear tinging my voice.

"Shall I remind you again?" His voice is dark with lust again, and I shiver with excitement.

"Maybe you should."

He pounces, then spends the rest of the night reminding me over and over again just how stuck together we are. By morning, I'm deliciously sore and wonder how he can possibly stand and dress himself with such little effort. I watch, unashamed, at his sculpted frame as he slides on a fine robe. It's a deep black like the scales on his dragon form, and I'm struck by just how muscular Mars is. Were it a battle of physical effort only, he would snap me like a twig. I grin.

"Stay there, my fire," he commands. "I'll be back in a few hours. And don't bother with clothes. I intend to continue our most ravishing discussion when I come back. Be warned that whatever you're wearing will simply be torn off. I'll have breakfast sent up—only the finest moose and deer blood for you."

Without another word, my king is gone, leaving me wanting more.

Bonded

My eyes peel open, though they protest at having to focus on the rays of light streaming through the window. Outside, birds chirp and a few even land on the sill to trill happy songs at us. *Us.*

I roll over, my body sore and spent from the past few days of being wrapped up together, writhing in pleasure. We took few breaks, save to drink blood. Since I first tasted his, nothing else compares. Mars has explained to me that craving the taste of your Lafura's lifeblood is a sign of a strong bond. We have swapped a few drops here and there, but I refuse to take anything more than that. I don't want to risk becoming any more addicted to him than I already am.

I crawl to him, his chest still rising and falling from behind the veil of sleep and dreams. I rest my head on his broad chest and sigh at the feeling of his rippling muscles against my cheek, finding solace in the way he breathes.

His skin, cool to the touch, soothes me. I feel his arm twitch before it clamps down on me, crushing me against his side. He rests his chin on my head, and for a moment, we bask in silence together.

"How is my queen?" His voice is hoarse with sleep.

"She wants to go back to sleep," I moan. "I am exhausted."

He chuckles, shaking me against his chest. I scowl and pull away to look at him more closely. I know my hair is a tousled mess, judging by his disheveled copper locks. But the fire in his eyes sparkles like stars.

While the desire between us is still present, for the first time since meeting him, I can *breathe*. The mutual-thrall is, apparently, appeased. The Siraltona no longer screams at the sight of him, begging to be loosed to meet his shadows. Instead, she rests, content and purring like a cat that's caught a mouse.

Indeed, I've trapped him. I've fooled him into thinking I'm anything worthy of being called a "wife." I am everything a man should fear. I am headstrong and independent, and I tried to slay him on more than one occasion.

"How does it feel? Knowing I've duped you?" I dare to ask aloud.

He looks down at me, raising an eyebrow as he settles me into the crook of his arm. "Duped me?" He yawns without even a whisper of alarm.

"You've got *me* for a queen now. A loud-mouthed murderer who doesn't know her limits," I laugh. But it feels hollow and bitter as it leaves my throat.

"When will you learn that I admire your spark, my fire? Why do you think I call you my *fire*? You don't think I knew what I was getting into when I met you?" He presses his forehead to mine, our bare flesh warming up as we stay pressed against each other beneath the sheets. But there is no lust now — only comfort and respite.

"But the gods forced us together. You wouldn't have chosen me if you'd been able to reject the bond and defy the gods," I murmur.

At this, Mars brings a thumb to my lower lip and pulls down on it, strumming a silent tune. A tune of sorrow and regret, no doubt.

"You really think I would have chosen differently? That hurts, Adelaide. Never have you wounded me as you have now," he says. By the tone of his voice, I know he's speaking the truth.

I look up at him, my heart twisting. "I'm sorry, Mars. I... I love you. I do. I just don't know how you can overlook what I've done. I don't know how you can choose me when I cause so much strife. Look at how our wedding went! The Ayesa children and Sherry were too optimistic. Your people are not ready for me. They do not accept me at all, and you will spend countless hours sorting through them just to solidify your choice."

I look down at my hands again and imagine how much softer they might be had I not spent the better part of a decade wielding blades and hatred rather than gowns of silk and lace. I could have been such a good princess. Then, maybe, I'd be a real queen.

"Adelaide, many of my people have expressed *joy* at my choice. The nobility will always be rife with discontent because that is how they are. Their goal is to acquire more power, and, quite frankly, you've upset their chances of gaining something invaluable. Do you know how many pro-posal offers I received each year as a single king? They're upset that you've taken that empty slot at my side — that a stranger should rule. And my children are angry that their father is with his enemy and not an ally. Their role in ruining our Rites will be punished, but you were right. Resistance was inevitable. But since coming here, you have changed so many minds, just as your own has changed. Sherry was right — your choice to help the children and ask questions and learn magic from her helped them see *you* and not the Shadow Slayer. Are there those who decry your presence?

Absolutely. But the scholars and Sherry and the fae children all speak the truth when they tell you that you have more allies than you realize."

My eyes widen in disbelief. "I've barely left my bedchambers except to fight with you in the woods about hunting and to visit the garden once to see the children!"

"Your choice to spend time with those children and give them a light show spread like wildfire, Adelaide, and you have been walking around this castle without shackles. You haven't slaughtered anyone since you arrived. The nobility knows that you've shared information about Jupiter's attempts to ally with Sunfall, even though it fell short. Your intent was still pure. That time we spent in the library? People heard you say you were unsure of your magic and how you admired ours. You forget — vampires have superior hearing. I didn't have you quiet your voice because I *knew* they would hear the truth. Just as we are not the monsters your people painted us to be, you are not the monster from our legends and storybooks."

I pause. "I'm in legends and storybooks?"

"Adelaide, you've slaughtered thousands. You're something of a bogeyman here."

"Touché."

Mars laughs hard enough to make the bedframe shake. I cling to him, reveling with delight at the sound of it. It's rich and heavy, laden with a sweetness that makes my teeth sting.

"Don't doubt my choice in you, Adelaide. Do you doubt your choice in me?"

I look at him, gifting him a wry smile. "Only when you deserve it."

He rolls his eyes, but I'm glad to see mirth return to his handsome features. It's refreshing to see him smile rather than scowl. He has enough worry on his plate to last the next few lifetimes. I'd like to be responsible for lessening that, even if only by a little. Any amount of respite counts for someone like him.

"I love you, Mars," I say. "I only worry because I want you to be happy. As much as I hate you sometimes, my heart still wants you to know what it means to find joy."

He looks down at me, his expression somber. "I love you, too, Adelaide. Don't ever doubt that again."

I believe him, and that is enough.

~*~

"What are you doing?" Mars's voice echoes from the other room as I stand in the bathroom and stare at my features. I mourn the silver no longer in my eyes, eaten alive by the molten gold of the Siraltona.

My hair is as ratty and twisted as I feared. I stare at the hairbrush on the counter and pray several prayers to Siralto before picking it up, daring to try and comb through the matted strands.

Would it be acceptable to brush my hair between love-making sessions in the future? Or would that kill the mood?

I hate that I'm even considering these questions as the bristles reach the ends of my hair, eliciting a loud crunch. I wince, knowing that several minutes of pain are ahead.

Except this time, I pause and consider what Mars asked me just the other day.

Is my magic only capable of destruction?

I look down at my palms. "I think I'm going to try non-destructive magic today. You say it doesn't cause as much strain on the body?"

"That's the idea, yes," Mars answers.

His voice is closer now, and I know he's about to join me. That's fine, except I'd rather spend my time trying to look presentable for him and his court—whom I'll undoubtedly face today, along with Roselle, as promised—instead of swooning over my husband. But he steps into the bathroom before I can make my first, grand attempt at non-lethal magic since creating the light figures in the garden.

The figurines are easy to procure. I'm still channeling the energy *away* from my body; I'm just not infusing the light in weapons or using it to fend off shadows.

This time, I keep the energy contained within my body and let the light in my veins snake its way to my hair. I gasp aloud as the light travels from my roots down to the tips of my hair. Behind me, Mars stands and watches, his attention fixated on the way my magic moves through my body.

The crunching knots in my hair, those dreadful tangles I've grown to loathe, bow beneath the weight of my magic. I'm careful not to think of burning, fire, or destruction as I coax the light across my hair like waves in a placid sea.

Come on, Adelaide, I think.

Delight spreads across Mars's features as he watches me tame what I thought would be the most difficult bedhead I've ever seen. In mere moments, soft, silken bolts of auburn hair grace my shoulders. I release the light. My body, untaxed, feels refreshed.

My fingers shake as they rise to grasp a few strands with disbelief on my face. But that disbelief is wiped away when it greets a softness I used to envy in the other noblewomen in Sunfall. Everyone else seemed to have healthy, shining hair while mine was sacrificed on the battlefield in favor of saving the kingdom.

Now, I have the health and smoothness I've always coveted. I don't look Mars in the eyes. I can't let him know that something as stupid as my *hair* makes me emotional. But his hands slide around my waist. He tucks me into his embrace. Neither of us speaks, instead resting in the fact that we *know*.

Just as I know I'm about to ruin this moment.

"So, I can use magic for non-destructive purposes... and it doesn't tax the body," I say aloud.

His grip tenses, and I know it will take a silver tongue to wrench myself free of him now. The cobblestones on the bathroom floor grow cold, weary of the shadows threatening to pour from his veins and lock me away.

I wonder if it is a side effect of being bonded, but the growl rising in his throat is almost pleasant as it vibrates against me. Almost. Even so, the fire in my soul yearns to be loosed and I cannot spend my life in a cage, no matter how spoiled and long that life might be.

"Mars..." I start.

"Don't argue. I know what you're going to say, but I will not lose you in an insane effort to protect the entire kingdom with baubles and trinkets!" he scoffs.

Outside, I hear birds calling. They remind me of the freedom I stand to lose if I don't find a way to barter with this man I call husband. Oddly enough, his efforts to protect me and keep me tucked away still don't feel as oppressive as living beneath my father's tyrannical rule. I know Mars means well. I know that instincts are a bitch to beat. I can tell by the way the fire in his eyes flickers that he is fighting himself even more than I'm about to. But only with words now. My heart grows weak at the thought of laying hands on him or flicking a blade at his face. I almost flinch at the memory of how many times I nearly murdered the love of my life.

"Mars," I whisper, "if I am to be your queen, then I must start making those difficult choices you warned me about. Is it not fair that I should share the burden of ruling with you?"

He sighs, loud and deep, and buries his face in my hair. "I admire your bravery more than you'll ever know," he murmurs, his face still buried between strands of hair. "But please, let me help you find some alternative or compromise."

I want to hear him out — I do. But time is running out. I sense the magic in the air and its shift. One of the gifts I *did* have before the Siraltona was the ability to feel when magic was coming. And something heavy is hanging in the air— something evil, dark, and twisted. I know it is not coming from me, nor from the Shadow King who clutches me as a child might hold onto their favorite stuffed animal. I know he senses it, too, or else he would not be so frantic to keep me trapped here in a bathroom, rather than stepping outside to handle the kingdom.

"You're not one to hide from a fight," I say, my voice hushed in the sweet morning light that creeps across the bathroom floor, bathing us both in the dawn. The birds outside grow louder as Mars pulls back to look at me, his eyes boring into my soul.

"I do not hide from fights, but I will not risk my queen," he says.

"And I will not risk my king," I retort. "You and your people are everything to me. Mars, you built this kingdom. You turned it into what it is today; you gave your people a home. Isn't that what you told me when I first came here?"

He groans, finally releasing me enough so we can step out of the bathroom. I ignore his glower as I sort through our armoire, seeking a new dress to wear. It is odd standing here in bare skin. I flinch at the thought of some noble or guard or worse, Sherry, barging through the door to ask a question and finding us both wearing nothing but our love and shame.

Mars joins me in sorting through clothing; he chooses a soft, black tunic and trousers, and I decide to match him with a dark charcoal gown that's lithe and breathable. I can stuff a sword against or even beneath the skirt, depending on how I feel. He's dressed in an instant while I still fumble with buttons and zips, and strings.

"Let me help." He steps over to me, his eyes pleading to be allowed to assist me in something I find so trivial. I humor him and inch closer so he can help me with the last of the zippers I can't seem to manage.

It occurs to me that I could use magic, but robbing Mars of something he seems so intent on doing would feel... wrong. I smile and wait as he grabs hold of it and slowly snakes it up my back so as not to pinch my skin.

"No scars anymore, Adelaide," he murmurs.

"I still miss them," I admit.

"I know."

"But I would trade them every time, knowing how much better things are now that I am with you," I declare.

He pulls me to him. "You say this now, my fire, but here in a few hours after we have bickered some more about how you can use your powers and what limits I require, you won't be so keen on me then." He grins.

I roll my eyes. "I can't kill you anymore, so you should be far more careful about enraging me, Your Highness. Death is a mercy you can't be afforded. That means you're stuck with me."

I don't wait for him to think of a retort before I walk to the bedchamber door. "I believe I owe Roselle some lessons, do I not?"

"No, you do not. Not yet. *First,* you will accompany me to the grand hall and discuss strategies with me. Nobility is barred. Only Sherry and I will be in attendance."

I turn to him, raising an eyebrow. "Won't having Sherry raise suspicion about your loyalty?"

Mars shrugs. "I'd rather see my niece. The nobility will pay handsomely for ruining your splendid day."

"*Our* day," I say.

"Yes, but I got what I wanted in the end," Mars chuckles, his eyes sliding shamelessly down my body. The clothing clinging to me doesn't feel as modest anymore, and I shiver.

Duties first, Adelaide, you've taken enough time off for that as it is.

I can't, however, resist the chance to get under his skin just as he does mine. "You don't think I didn't get what I wanted?" I laugh, the sound low and sultry, and confidently stride from the room.

I'm certain my feet can find the grand hall just as they found the bed-chamber after that awful humiliation I suffered at our Rites. All I have to do is let my magic lead the way. Just thinking of her has the light rising to the surface of my veins and, true to her nature, the Siraltona makes clear exactly where I should go.

I smile.

~*~

He's right — I do want to kill him. Gone are the feelings of wedded bliss as I glare at my husband, seated on his throne. Beside me, Sherry reaches out to grab my hand. I can't tell if it's in solidarity with me or with Mars as she squeezes it, begging me to calm down.

"You can't tell me to simply *stop* using magic until we figure out how to 'tame' it!" I shout.

He's reached a point of extremes. He wants so badly to tuck me away and keep me sheltered from every possible danger. While Alaric wanted to toss me to the wolves, Mars wants to bury them all alive before I'm allowed outside again.

"Is this a side effect of being newly mated? Please tell me it wears off." My tone is pleading. I don't care if I sound desperate. If I do, it's because I *am*.

"I can't afford to have you harm yourself if you aren't willing to be reasonable," he argues. "If we have to cut you off until you are, then so be it. You promised me, Adelaide, that you would put your safety first. I cannot lose you now that you're here. I refuse to live another millennium without you. If you die again, you will *never come back*. I can't bring you back from death a third time."

His voice is shaken with grief, and I pause, considering what to say next. I hate how considerate I'm trying to be, especially since lashing out is so much easier. Now? Now I'm responsible for how *he* feels as much as I am myself. It's easy to be miserable alone. It feels terrible to add to someone else's pile of woes.

"Mars." My voice is soft.

Between us sits the pile of swords I got the wild idea to infuse. It was a moment of rage that I can't take back, and all it did was ignite his fears. The sweat staining my forehead is impossible to hide beneath the light streaming through the windows of the grand hall.

With the nobles absent, our voices echo. I can hear mice scratching behind the walls and birds fluttering in the rafters. I wonder how Velyasa could deal better with pests. Mice? I detest those. Birds I can live with, but I know they would be much happier out in the loving rays of the sun, rather than the shadows of the all-consuming ceiling of the castle.

I still cannot see the top. I wonder if it would be stupid or foolish to ask Mars to fly me up there. *Would his dragon even fit in this space?*

I think back to when I first saw the creature circling above the battlefield at Sunfall and wonder if he could pull off such a feat without shattering the walls. I wonder if his familiar was ever small enough to fit in this room, as Finch might have. Just thinking of my brother-in-law tugs at my heartstrings.

"Are you paying attention, Adelaide?" Mars demands, his chest heaving. "You just spent yourself to the point of exhaustion. You're not willing to see my side or even hear me out?"

I shake my head. "I... got distracted thinking about where the ceiling is. And thinking about whether your dragon fits in here — and if maybe you were small once, like Finch."

Beside me, Sherry gapes at my outburst.

Mars freezes. I expect him to hurl into another fit of rage. Instead, I am met with booming laughter.

"Of course! How could I be so stupid to overlook the possibility that you would be thinking of my familiar, or if I have always been old?"

I can't tell if anger or amusement makes his chest shake more, but I am mesmerized by the flashing smile painted on his lips, even if his awful fangs peek through. Those very same fangs are the reason thirst burns down my throat, crying out for more blood.

When will my greed meet its limits? There won't be enough life in the world to sustain me if I try to protect the kingdom this way.

"How are *you* able to use so much power?" I ask, returning my thoughts to our fight. My mind needed the rest to wonder about things like ceilings and birds, and I'm grateful I was able to find it, if only for a moment.

"Adelaide, I am *far* older than you, and I brokered a deal with Tryta, remember? Many things work in my favor to allow me to draw on my power more. Even then, when I fight you, I do wear thin faster than I would like. There *must* be limits. You are still mortal at some level, and you can still be felled by a blade. Perhaps you'll live if you spend yourself with your magic, once you've matured. But it takes *decades* for a vampire to become fully fledged. You can speed up the process, but that requires quite a lot of blood, determination, and a blessing from the gods themselves. You really think they'll bless you a second time when the power itself is a blessing for you?"

Regret etches into his face the moment the words leave his mouth, but I'm unfazed by his unintended cruelty. "If it's not a blessing, then I'll barter. It's what you did, is it not? Tryta first blessed you with his shadows and power. Then you went back and bartered to get your familiars back. That means they went somewhere — you must have angered them somehow. What did you pay, Mars? What did you have to give up to get that kind of magic back?"

Mars flinches like I've slapped him.

"That's not for you to ask!" Sherry scolds, interrupting our spat.

I whip my head to the side to stare at her. "Am I not his queen? Is his soul not my concern?"

My eyes flash with defiance, but she doesn't back away or flinch at the rage rising in my tone, the angry monsoon on the verge of breaching the surface. I feel my skin growing hot, but I've almost run out of energy. If I don't center myself soon, I fear I'll collapse. My mouth and throat are like sandpaper. I know Mars has wisdom to offer in telling me to slow down, but the image of Jupiter cleaving through Finch and spilling his guts in that clearing burns the back of my eyes. I wonder how long it will be before he does the same to Mars, Sherry, the flower girls, or anyone else I've grown fond of. In none of those scenarios do I worry about myself. I can live with the thought of dying. I can't live with the thought of losing *them*.

The irony of that fear isn't lost on me. Mars is afraid of the same thing. I know it isn't fair to ask him to let me die when I can't begin to fathom letting the same happen to him. But it's been hardwired into me for so long — I am expendable. I am the fighter, the protector, the flame that keeps the lights on in Sunfall.

Velyasa can stay alive if I can only protect it. I might be accepted as their queen if only I can figure out how to win their trust. What better way than to put my life on the line for them? Mars has already done as much by protecting them with every breath. But I'm not sure he will survive if I die. The way he looks at me now gives me pause, and I almost give in.

Almost.

I need a plan to bypass my weaknesses. I need a way to work with my magic that doesn't involve expending my breath and energy with every waking move.

I think back to how I felt when I untangled my hair earlier. That magic was effortless and, if anything, relaxing. I start to think of how I might be able to use my magic to replenish what it takes.

Is such a thing even possible? Can I ask to take back from the very thing that took from me in the first place?

"Adelaide, I am begging you." Mars strides toward me.

I look up at Sherry. She throws her hands up in exasperation. "He's right. You can't risk yourself the same way now, Adelaide. You're *bound* to him. Your souls are intertwined. Who's to say he would even survive if you die?"

I swallow, realizing my suspicions might be more correct than I'd hoped.

He places one hand on my shoulder and nudges my chin up so I have no choice but to look at him.

"If you two start getting gross, I'm leaving," Sherry threatens.

"How come she gets to know the truth, Mars?" I ask, my voice a whisper.

"I must atone for sins that I cannot speak aloud just yet. Please don't ask me to... I will tell you when I am ready, just as you told me when you were ready about your writings and your fears and so many other things that I won't speak aloud in front of Sherry. She only knows the truth because she witnessed my barter. And she holds that secret close for me, not to keep you out." His face is wan with exhaustion, the strain of arguing with me wearing him thin. "Please, Adelaide, stop with the madness and stop trying to use your magic at the expense of *both* of us."

I take a breath and slowly let the fire die from my veins. The dryness of my tongue halts me in my tracks. I've no choice but to stop. I want so badly to outsmart this bastard king in front of me, but the cool touch of his skin and the sorrow that haunts me from those flaming eyes is enough to get me to concede.

For now.

"I won't rest until I find a way to save Velyasa and avenge Finch." It's the first time I've admitted the second reason — the *realest* reason — for waving my banner of destruction.

"I know he meant a lot to you," Mars whispers.

Surprisingly, I don't detect jealousy in his tone. I hope he doesn't think I am waging war for a lost love. Finch truly was a brother to me.

"You mean more to me," I admit. "I hope it isn't sacrilege to say that out loud."

Mars grins. "Not at all. I should hope I do. I can't go unbury him and kill him again."

I scoff.

"Okay, but can we get back to the very real problem of figuring out how to get sunshine here not to burn herself out?" Sherry's interruption pulls us back to the here and now with a thud.

My soul feels bruised from the impact. I'd much rather keep things lighthearted, but I'm no fool. I know better than to stay wrapped in the arms of delusion, no matter how soft and inviting they may be.

"This morning... I... I used my magic to fix my hair, and afterward, I felt refreshed." I clear my throat, realizing just how dry it's gotten as I stand here, my thirst still unquenched.

Sherry rolls her eyes at me. "Great. You can do your hair. That magic is *soft*, Adelaide. It exists to refresh the soul for a reason. You can't go making weapons of war under the guise of self-care."

I glance down at the sword strapped to my hip and chuckle. "I mean, that depends on who you are, Sherry. Maybe it was self-care for me. Maybe it still is."

"Until you remember who you were waging war with," Sherry sneers.

I can't forget the lives of so many thousands of Shadow Folk I felled without regret, but my body aches with the remembrance of what it felt like to set loose the rage that builds within it. Now, when I cut my anger free of its chains, it halts me in my tracks and leaves me weak.

A small part of me almost wishes I'd never been given this power in the first place. Almost. Selfishly, I'd still rather have the strength of the strong king by my side than be left as a breeding mare in Sunfall.

My mind still ponders this possibility, even as Sherry snaps her fingers and hands each of us a goblet of blood. It's surreal that I've grown to accept this as a normal part of life now. Were my morals and beliefs so easily won?

Or maybe I never believed in those things in the first place.

Whatever the case, I tilt the metal cup back and let the blood race down my throat, draining it to the last drop.

Mars finishes his drink and makes a startling announcement. "I'll see if I can't wager with Tryta again." He says it as though he's planning to go on a hunt or perhaps waltz through the gardens.

Sherry and I stare at him, wondering if he's gone mad.

I carefully choose my words. "Mars, I appreciate your desire to protect me, but... your power isn't the reason you're immune to the Falahle... Tryta granted you that. What more can you ask of him? I have the natural power to protect. Yours is borrowed. You can't go asking to borrow more, surely? What will he ask for next? What will you be forced to give up?"

"If it keeps us alive, then I will make any sacrifice necessary," Mars grumbles. His tone says the decision is final. Sherry bows her head, though I sense the trepidation that rolls from her in waves.

I am not so submissive.

"No, Mars. If you won't allow me to wage my magic this way, then I won't allow you to barter with Tryta again!" I soften my voice and grip his arm. "Please, dearest. Let's re-evaluate and see if there aren't less taxing ways for me to use my magic. Let me train with Roselle first. I'm sure there's *some* way. Maybe I can work with the scholars and try to find a way to channel my magic?"

Mars blinks. "You mean to give them power that would kill them? The Siraltona would kill me where I stand were it not for the bond we share! It's out of the question."

I huff. "Maybe channeling it is, but what I'm trying to point out is that there are other options; we just haven't discovered all of them yet. How long do we think we have before Jupiter marches down here to take us on?"

Sherry shrugs. "He's got the element of surprise, Adelaide. Getting our familiars back stayed his hand, no doubt, but for how long? He may not get through you and Mars, but he'll easily take the rest of us if you two can't figure out how to keep his magic at bay. What we don't understand is *why* he hasn't marched on the castle yet. With each passing day, he takes more of our people from the outskirts. His efforts have grown even more aggressive since his horrid alliance fell through with Sunfall."

"Then why were you ever focused on Sunfall if you knew that the alliance wouldn't come to fruition?" I ask. I'm astonished that they would waste their time on people such as us.

"Because while we can restore *wills*, we can't restore lives taken. And without our familiars, we were running out of ways to hold down both fronts. We couldn't know for sure when we first arrived – we were waiting to see the signs that Jupiter had taken up with your ranks. Of course, they never came, but we couldn't know that for sure. We had to come and try to stamp you out. With him there, it would have been a two-for-one effort. Without him there, we could have at least given ourselves the chance to snuff out Sunfall and focus solely on the real threat at hand. The Siraltona at least grants us the mercy of death. The Falahle damns the soul. I was more concerned with having full attention to the latter."

Mars looks at me, his face hard with a pain I'm finally beginning to understand. We had them pinned. Sunfall *might* have won had he not loosed his dragon from its chains and made a terrible bargain with Tryta. But that brings me back to the question: How did they lose them in the first place?

"Has Sunfall moved on Velyasa since?"

He shakes his head. "No. Our scouts indicate that they are still looking for you. With the alliance gone and their powers dwindling, you would be the only thing left to solidify their rule. That's the other reason I haven't cared – you were the real threat. Maverick is wounded, and Alaric is dying, whether he knows it or not. And don't worry, I have bound our kingdom under a magical curse to prevent the people from revealing your location, or else I'm sure Maverick and Alaric would be here, demanding your return so they could punish you for desertion... well, at least Alaric. I'm hopeful that your brother would at least have the sense to believe you."

I pale. I hadn't begun to think of the ramifications of my actions. I always assumed being turned would be the worst possible outcome for me. Flexing my fingers, I feel the whistle of white-hot light and soft shadow swirling through my veins.

The love in my heart tells me I suffered far from the worst option as I look at Mars and then Sherry, two people for whom I would fight and die. One for whom I would even go so far as to bear children.

Not yet, though. Not by a long shot.

"Let me try *something*, then. I need to be strong enough to keep them at bay when that curse inevitably slips. Let me help you, Mars. Let me try."

Mars crosses his arms, staring at me as though I am a battle map. Gone is my husband, replaced by the strategist who has kept this kingdom from crumbling for longer than Sunfall has ever existed.

"I'll give you until the end of the week. After that, I am due to make my pilgrimage to the temple to thank Tryta for his most recent gift."

A week?

I look at Sherry, and she shrugs.

"He gave you another gift?" I warily ask.

Mars smiles. "You. And I must thank him for such a kingly gift."

My stomach churns. I wish more than anything that I could thank Siralto for her gift to me, but thanks to Tryta, my goddess is dead. All I have is the ghost of her power that, by some miracle, found me even beyond the grave.

I just hope that power is enough to save Velyasa.

Training

A

FTER DRAINING THREE MORE goblets brimming with blood, Mars finally relents and lets me leave with Sherry to find the scholar, Roselle. For once, I'm grateful he's responsible to the nobility. My heart aches to be outside his presence, but my power knows it is being summoned — challenged — to rise to the occasion and save Velyasa, and I'll be damned if I don't go down swinging. I can't let my husband barter with the gods a third time. They might take it as a sign of greed and strike him down, leaving me without a husband. Worse yet, they might accept his offer and leave him with one more debt to them.

I don't know why Tryta would be so forgiving and relenting, or why Mars has gotten away with as much as he has. To barter with the god of the dark twice and walk out unscathed is unheard of! Then again, bartering with a Creator at all hasn't been documented, to my knowledge. The world is full of tomes I haven't read, the number of which expands far beyond the years I have left, but I'm certain I would have heard of such a possibility if it had been accomplished.

"I'm glad he's letting you try," Sherry says, sidling closer to me as we walk to the library. Our steps are urgent, eager to see if I can stop our reckless king from harming himself to save the kingdom. I realize I put him in this spot by nearly doing the same to myself, but his position is more important. He is the spirit of his people, whereas I am the reason their spirit has been crushed for so long.

"I would rather die than him." I don't add anything else, but she reaches out to grab my hand and pulls me to a stop.

"That's not what I mean," Sherry says.

Her golden eyes search mine, and I notice a fine mist has settled over them. The daylight streaming through the castle windows sets her pale white hair aglow in the dim space, and I almost wonder if I'm staring at an angel. I want to pry and ask about her mother — about her life with Jupiter before coming here — but I hold my tongue.

"I don't want you to die," Sherry starts. "I don't want you to lose your soul in a vain effort to save him or this kingdom. But the way you speak — the way you wield... if anyone can save Velyasa, it's you. Not him. He's done enough to save us. There *must* be a reason the gods brought you to him. To protect him from the very thing that is supposed to be his weakness and to make his mate the wielder of said weapon? That is *profound*, Adelaide." She shakes her head, mystified. "I am not a fool. I know when the gods have chosen to bless us. The rest of the kingdom will see it soon, I'm sure. All they have to do is witness the same dedication and devotion that I have seen."

Discomfort churns in my bones, and I think of all the times I've been terrible to her. How I put her needs and wants beneath my own and left them in the dust. I'm not proud of it. She was right to call me out on this strange journey of mine. The crown on my head is new, but the magic we share as friends feels far older than anything in this kingdom. I trusted her long before I trusted Mars.

"I don't hate you," I blurt. "I've been a real ass about everything, but I want you to know I don't believe the nobles when they doubt you. I think they're selfish to ignore what you've overcome, and I was wrong to hate you all for what you are. Shadow Folk are vastly misunderstood where I am from, but I hope to rectify that image with time. Even if I can't, I want you to know my eyes are open, along with my ears. Thank you for letting me in on your story, even when I wasn't willing to acknowledge it."

Sherry swats at me. "Don't you *dare* make me cry, you fool."

But her arms find their way around me, and we hug for a few moments. I ponder the fact that I finally have a friend. I never had another woman to confide in back in Sunfall. Beatrice was always busy tending to Maverick and his ailment,s or expected to rest while failing to produce heirs.

I grimace when I think of my poor, suffering sister-in-law, Beatrice. I hope she finds peace in knowing that her lack of children is not her fault. Maverick is to blame, but even then, he is an unwitting victim in a scheme set forth by the gods. To use magic is to ruin one's life. It is a path to death and despair. Yet, for Sunfall, it is a necessity. Even as my father's thin veneer of control cracks and he drowns himself in ale, I know his soul has been claimed by something far more complex and powerful than he'll ever fully comprehend. I almost pity him. But the starving peasants of Sunfall and how he leaves them to die of hunger and cold don't absolve him of his crimes.

I've yet to pay him a visit for justice. I vow not to let that charge die, no matter how much I may understand his cruel motives. It's a bitter pill to swallow, knowing that I can commiserate with a creature so foul.

But he is my father, and I am still his daughter, changed or not.

"You can't die on me, Adelaide," Sherry says, snapping me from my thoughts.

She doesn't seem to mind when I get broody. I suppose it's a consequence of serving her uncle as long as she has.

"I hate to be a bother, and you don't have to tell me if you aren't comfortable, but how did Jupiter, of all people, learn to wield the Falahle? If the gods are so opposed to it, how did he master it?"

Sherry frowns. "I wish I knew, Adelaide. There are whispers... rumors... that the gods got bored when Tryta stepped back and Siralto died. They began to experiment with the very gift that the Creators gave them. I'm not sure who unlocked such a power or how... but my father got ahold of it. That is the greatest crime done by the gods that I know of. I know the power is not from Tryta or Siralto. It's... something far darker. If I ever could scorn and punish a god, it would be whoever left something out there that my father could use as he has."

We reach the library, most of our trip there a blur as I try to understand how Tryta and Siralto would leave such horrible magic lying around. But they believed in free will. The right to choose. So much so that Siralto wanted a world with no consequences. But Tryta's justice prevailed. Siralto paid with her life.

At least, that's how the story goes.

A twinge of doubt sparks as I consider all the ways the Shadow Folk have been misrepresented in text.

I notice the scholars gathering at the doorway. Roselle stands in the midst of them, her eyes bright with delight at the sight of me. Any hope of pressing Sherry for more answers dies in my throat.

"Are you ready to begin learning, dear scholar?" Roselle asks. "Our kingdom depends on you, and time is of the essence. Let's see if we can't tap into that divine light of yours."

I don't know how Roselle has guessed the urgency of my task, but I chalk it up to her being a scholar of prophecy. I wonder how she forged a deal with the goddess Aynda and what it cost her. Dealings with the gods cloud my mind, and I push past the temptation to dig into those questions as I struggle with the basic task of picking up a book from across the room using nothing but magic.

It sits on the table, unmoved. I finally curse aloud and fling my hands up, my throat tight with grief. "I'm going to fail this kingdom! I am a horrible patron of the Siraltona. Why the *hell* this goddess's dead magic would choose me is a mystery we will never solve! It'll be left beneath the rubble of this place when I fail to save it from Jupiter."

Sherry places a reassuring hand on my shoulder. "Adelaide, maybe you need a break. You've been at this for hours."

"She cannot take a break," Roselle answers, her voice firm.

I agree with her, nodding that I want to continue.

"You have spent the better part of your life living and breathing the ghost of magic used for destruction. For protection. For violence. You must change the way you shape it in your mind. You can do so with the little people and dragons you make with it, no?" Roselle's voice rises from across the room as she paces behind the table where the book sits. It mocks me, just as her tone does.

The temptation to take out my rage on Roselle grows with every failure, but deep down, I know these mishaps are my own fault. The glass dome above the library, something I'd missed before, allows the light from the setting sun to bathe the room in a soft, golden hue. This light from the sun is the tender kind that caresses and heals. I wish more than ever that I could wield that light as my own. The shadow present within me helps some. It can coax the Siraltona to choose peace, but it aggravates me that I feel more controlled by my powers than the other way around. Why else would I give them personalities and responsibilities, like they are truly running the ship?

Maybe they are.

I close my eyes again and pull on the power that rests in my veins, begging her not to come to the surface with fangs and blades, ready to cut through the universe.

I hear the whines and cries of it as it echoes in my ears, begging to be loosed for justice on Finch's behalf. I see him die again and again. Every now and then, for good measure, my mother's head slips to the floor with the same sickening thud that has ricocheted in my ears for sixteen — almost seventeen — years now.

By the time I manage to put those grievances to rest, I will have let this kingdom fall into the clutches of a madman who defies the gods and their magic.

I grit my teeth and valiantly resist the urge to send some violent prayers up into the atmosphere. My goddess is not alive; she cannot protect me from their wrath, and I'm not sure I'm on good enough terms with Tryta to rely on him to step in, either, should I affront one of his children.

"I can't do it." My breath comes in gasps. I can't push air into my lungs fast enough to keep up with the exhaustion in my body. My problem is not in the power, but the will to control it.

By the way Roselle grimaces at me, I can tell she knows how weak I am. I won't be any use to this kingdom if I can't manage my emotions enough to simply lift a book off the table.

"Yes, you *can*."

Roselle's tone is far from encouraging. It is scolding. Harsh. She has high expectations, and I'm far from reaching them.

Angrily, I fling my hands in the air. "What would you have me do differently? I cannot change how I was shaped! I cannot unforge myself from the fires of weaponry and destruction! My gift is in *death*, not life. I can make pretty things that dance and have no bearing, and I can fuse weapons with the wrath of the dead goddess herself. However, I cannot lift books and be calm and kind and patient with my magic!" I fume.

"Yet you got your hair straightened out this morning," Roselle counters.

Beside me, Sherry stiffens. She senses the shift in my magic before Roselle does. But I refuse to release it. I refuse to give them the satisfaction of showing my might rather than my patience.

Instead, I let the light curl off me in angry waves of smoke. Several of the scholars gawking nearby step back, hiding behind the winding columns that hold up the library's ceiling. If I don't get myself under control, no amount of marble or granite will keep the ceiling from being blasted to pieces by my power.

Closing my eyes, I do my best to whisper to the Siraltona. I beg my power to listen. I beg her to do as I bid, rather than have her bid me to do as she wishes. It's selfish, but necessary. Too often, I have been trapped by the world I cannot control and the men and monsters who would have me bend the knee and give up at the first sign of trouble.

My body yearns to give out. I have been given flagons of blood that I don't care to know the source of. They all tasted different — different victims have given me life so I might save the lives of many more. I lick my lips, pondering the souls that might yet die if I don't learn to wield my own power.

I am a shameful excuse for a wielder.

I drop my hands to my sides, my power spent and my eyes blurred by tears I can't control. I know that, by the end of the week, my husband's soul will be further in hock to the dark god who killed my goddess. Her power is a testament to so much love and light that was lost and will never be recovered. And yet here I am, using it to kill and nothing more. Brushing my hair is little to be proud of.

I look at the book, forlorn when it doesn't move from the table. With a last heave of effort, I let the pang of regret for my husband's plight pull on the magic one last time.

The book flies into my hand. I scream with relief and collapse to the floor.

~*~

Sherry and I lie on the floor of the library. Mars still hasn't come to retrieve me from training, though I know it won't be long before he comes to rescue me. I can't count the number of flagons of blood I've consumed. He'll suspect the worst, no doubt. Ever since the book moved, things have only gotten more difficult.

Roselle now expects me to be able to move *anything* in the library, and I've grown more than frustrated with her. Even Sherry seems tired of listening to Roselle devise differing creative reasons to do anything but learn how to wield my magic with any purpose.

Move this. Move that.

The longer we go, the more numb my rage becomes. I half wonder if this isn't Roselle's strategy. Perhaps she's taken a page out of my father's book and chosen to wear me down first and then shape me from nothing into a pupil worthy of her image.

I pity her if this is her plan. It turned out so well for my father, after all.

"Sherry," I begin, "do you still believe I'm capable of saving the kingdom now?"

Beside me, she starts to laugh. "You know what, Adelaide? I do. If anyone is going to figure this out, it's you. I would've stomped out of here hours ago if I had been asked to move my magic like this. This stuff takes time, and these people commit *years* to studying."

"But I don't have *years*. I have one *week*." The words leave my lips, soft and deadly, a reminder of how much work I have yet to do and how little I understand how to use my magic in a way that doesn't exhaust me.

I won't be able to cage my fury when I'm out facing Jupiter. I cannot walk onto the battlefield, calm and unbothered, and expect to save Velyasa like this. The stakes are higher than ever. I can't simply equip each person with protective wards. I must find a way to endure in battle without falling apart. Mars, I know, has gone easy on me. Jupiter will not.

I can't rely on the explosive display that saved my life back in the clearing where Finch died. It came much too late, and I doubt I can recreate the occurrence. I'm not keen on trying, either. I'm rather fond of this library with its grand, towering shelves and the open atmosphere. Watching everyone partake and read as they wish is a warmth I've never known.

"Get up, Adelaide," Roselle commands.

I roll my eyes. "What am I moving now?" I sit up from the cold marble floor and throw a wan stare at my instructor, whose name I could spit like a curse word about now.

But her eyes are full of mischief, sparkling in the light of the stars now peeking through the glass dome above us.

"What are we doing?" I ask. "Something different, finally? Or are you giving me false hope?"

She laughs. "We aren't going to move something. We're going to read." In her hands sits a dusty book that looks like it might fall apart at a moment's notice. "I asked my fellow scholars to look for this while we trained. It's been buried in the lower levels of the library for centuries, but I thought it might be of use to you."

I stand and approach Roselle with a growing sense of apprehension in my gut. I don't think she's going to hurt me, but I wonder what sort of knowledge was so sacred that it had to be hidden in the bowels of the library. I wonder if I'm even allowed to see those lower levels.

Against my better judgment, I hold out my hands. When she passes it to me, I try not to let my mouth gape open when I realize I'm holding a copy of the book of the gods. There are only so many copies in circulation. They are rare, coveted, and almost never complete. Translated from the lost language of the gods, they contain important information about the pantheon of Tyrladan.

I slide my hand over the front cover, and my eyes meet Roselle's as understanding slides into place. "I need to pick a god, don't I?"

Roselle shrugs. "I'm not saying anything."

For the first time, Roselle leaves me to sit with a book and think alone. I realize now that Roselle understood the truth this whole time. I cannot master my magic alone. Just as Tryta blessed Mars, I must now barter with a god to save my kingdom.

Sherry walks up beside me and we stare at the tome for a long time before she moves her hand with mine to flip open the front cover. "Are you sure you want to do this?" Her voice sounds small — she is as shaken as I am.

"I'm the only one who can do this, Sherry. If we don't stop Jupiter, who will?"

Her eyes fill with tears. "Don't give them anything you can't afford, do you understand? Your soul is *yours*. Your life is *yours*. Don't give them anything that leaves this kingdom without her queen."

I take a deep breath. "I promise." The lie tastes sour in my mouth, but I let it worry there in my teeth all the same.

I turn over the first page and begin to read.

HUNGER

S HERRY AND I HAVE exhausted the book, and I write down a few likely candidates in my notebook. More than once, my eyes glide back to the page where Siralto sits. Her golden glow evokes a pang of longing in my soul that I can't ever squash out.

I owe her so much, and she'll never know. Her eyes were long closed before I was born; yet her magic fills my veins to the brim with hope, love, and knowledge I never could have had without her. Part of me wants to believe it was she who sent me the fruit that cured me. I want to believe she is the one who returned my power to me or filled me with it in the first place.

That's not possible.

Sherry and I spend the better part of the night trying to figure out who would have given me the Lasira fruit. Which god would want to bring back something so dangerous and rare? And why did they give it to the Sunfall royals in the first place?

I haven't really considered this fact as much as I should. A sneaking suspicion in my heart tells me it was acquired through less-than-favorable means, but I don't know anything about how to rob a dead god or use her power for nefarious purposes. My father, on the other hand? Anything is possible. I know nothing of the kings and queens who came before him, only that his light was the loudest. It was the light that secured Sunfall's freedom from the clutches of the Shadow Folk.

But as I gaze at Sherry and Roselle and all the gathered scholars, I wonder if that is the truth. And why would the people of Sunfall play along if it weren't so?

I've been gnawing at my lip with worry, and thin drops of blood stain my chin. I raise a hand to wipe it before Sherry notices, but when she turns to me, she shakes her head.

"You'd think you'd break that habit after one too many mishaps, but here you are." She reaches into the pocket of her dress and hands me a handkerchief. I thank her profusely and clean myself up before anyone else notices.

The sound of heavy feet behind me makes my heart flutter. I turn to find that Mars has finally returned from his meeting with the nobles. I smile at him, my eyes weary with fatigue. As much as I would love to let him ravish me tonight as he has so many times, I don't think my body will withstand it.

From the way his own head hangs heavy with exhaustion, it doesn't look like he's up to the task, either. He extends a hand to me, which I gratefully take, and pulls me from the old wooden chair I've been occupying, ushering me into his arms.

His voice is heavy with sleep. "Come to bed, my fire. We can return you to your studies in the morning. I trust the fifty flagons of blood were enough to keep you standing?"

I look up at him as shame floods my cheeks. "I did my best, my king. I did. But I confess... my anger got the better of me at times. I made sure to rest when possible."

Behind me, Sherry speaks up. "She was a hell of a sight to see today, Uncle. She was... otherworldly."

I scoff. "I moved a few things here and there. That's hardly extraordinary."

"Many take years to master such a simple act, and that's when they start as children!" she argues. "You've only had your power for a few months now, Adelaide. It's damn impressive."

I brush off Sherry's praise. "Yes, but it won't save our kingdom."

"No one can blame you for trying, my fire," Mars says, his voice soft.

I detect a hint of pride there, but I am ashamed that I still leave him empty-handed of the power he needs to save his kingdom. I cringe as I think of how Adalius and Charlotte will celebrate when their father's newest wife fails to fulfill the one duty she swore she could uphold.

I vow never to brag so boldly of my power again. This lesson of humility is too much to bear. I can't fathom the consequences of failing now. Tears threaten to spill from my eyes, and I take a shuddering breath, burying my head in Mars's chest.

"No one will judge you for trying," Sherry echoes. "You're not failing."

But her words do nothing to ease the blow to my chest — the reminder that when the end of the week comes, my husband will barter with a god who murdered the one goddess I needed to make this entire blasted plan work.

"I think it's time you come to bed," Mars whispers.

I don't protest as his hands trail down my back, but I shriek when he flings me up into his arms and tucks a hand beneath my legs to steady me.

"Make sure you bring her back in the morning. She and I are going to figure this out!" Sherry calls as Mars sweeps me from the room.

I relish in the warmth of his skin, usually so cool. But then I pause, realizing what I'm feeling.

"Why are you warm?"

"I may have tried my hand at wielding some Siraltona today," Mars confesses. "I thought maybe I could help you."

I look up at him, my chest swelling with love and pride. "I wish I could have seen it."

"I wish I could have witnessed you pick up books today." Mars looks at me with heavy longing in his eyes, a longing that goes deeper than anything I've ever known. The yawning chasm of loneliness he feels swallows me up. I only hope I'm enough to fill the space and keep it from eating us both alive.

But as he sets me on the bed and helps me undress, his fingers gentle with the buttons and zips of my dress, I know more than ever that I am right where I belong, and I am exactly what he needs.

How could it ever be any other way?

I know tomorrow will bring inevitable bickering, especially if he catches wind of my plan to make a deal of my own with a god or goddess of my choosing, but for now, I settle into the comfort of his embrace as we slide beneath the covers, worn and spent by the trials of the day.

I only hope we'll both wake in the morning. If we don't, I pray to Siralto, wherever she is, that he and I will wake together — wherever there is in the After.

~*~

Mars is furious. Sherry and I stand in front of the book, guarding it with our bodies to prevent him from destroying it with the shadows snaking from his hands. If ever there was a day I expected to meet the dragon lurking beneath his flesh, today is it. And I know for sure that the library can't hold a creature that big.

At some point today, in my training, Mars decided to join us. And, at some point, he figured out from the scholars exactly *which* book I'd been reading from. Discretion, as it turns out, is not something I've earned with the scholars. *Or they were dumb enough to think he wouldn't be angry at the prospect of me bartering with the gods.* My husband is in the throes of a heated debate now; his one goal is now to destroy the book of the gods before I can manage to strike a bargain.

I flinch as I realize how real the possibility is that thousands of years of knowledge might be caught up in the rage of a flaming serpent any moment now if we don't convince him to calm down. I've never been one to get down on my knees and beg, but today might be that day. I step closer to him, my heart pounding in my ears.

"Mars, please. I am trying to think of a middle ground," I plead.

"NO!" he roars so violently, I swear I see fire rise in his throat. "You will *not* sell your soul to some common god to fix this mess!"

"Your Highness, a patron deity might be just what the doctor ordered!"

I'm astonished to hear Roselle's voice rise above the throng of concerned chatter that's broken out in the library. His outburst has caused a scene, and citizens are pouring in faster than I can count to witness their king argue with his new queen. They stare at me with eyes full of sadness as my plan is leaked for all to hear.

"She would sell her soul for us?"

I hear the question murmured from different corners of the room and curse my enhanced hearing. I wish I could not smell their fear and taste the way they still doubt me as more and more of them file into the library.

When Adalius and Charlotte sidle in towards the front, I refuse to look at them — refuse to let them see my failures.

Frustrated, I fling my hands out to my sides. "What is an acceptable way to save your kingdom, Mars? What is an acceptable way for me to use my power to save us all?"

Mars stomps his foot, not unlike a child throwing a tantrum. A gust of fire snakes from his mouth. The world tilts on its axis; my power screams for me — screams to be drawn on and to halt Mars's power in its tracks. The edges of a whisper, ancient and soft, urge me. *"Put out the flame."* I can't tell if the whisper is real or if it is the weight of my own exhaustion, but it beckons me.

Without thinking, I let light pour from my hand to stop the flame. It extinguishes on impact, saving the old wooden table standing beside us.

All around us, everyone freezes. I look down at my hand, astonished by the act, and even Mars's rage is temporarily sated by curiosity.

"Do that again," I mutter.

"What?"

"Breathe fire again," I demand.

Mars looks at me, puzzled, but he obliges and once again, I shoot the Siraltona from my hands and stop the fire from scorching the marble floors, the shelves, or the rows of tables and chairs upon which scholars have made their livelihoods here in Velyasa.

Relief floods through me. I don't feel the familiar ache or pull of a magic that's too much to bear. Looking up at the shelves, I spot some titles I might want to read and reach for them.

The gathered crowd gasps as I use my magic to grab them, one by one, and pull them to me. They line up in my hands. I let the light flow through me like music. It whispers and sings old songs and tales that I've yet to understand.

Something shifts in the atmosphere. Some god has answered my call; I've yet to find out who. I haven't even brokered a deal yet, either. I've not called anyone by name or practiced any of the rituals required to meet with them. It's not lost on me that Tryta's page is missing from the book of the gods, either. I know who has that page.

But as my eyes meet my husband's, he reaches a different conclusion. While I ponder which deity met my cry for help with benevolence instead of demands, he lets out a jubilant shout.

"You!" he cries. "You found a way to wield without expending yourself!"

I look down at my hands and smile. I think back to the necklace that I fused with light and let more light pool into my hands, focusing on creation and not destruction. There in my palms, I let the light and dark meet once again in a symphony of creation. In the wake of their union, a glinting metal chain winks at me in the sunlight streaming down through the glass dome above. I look up, and the sun bathes my face.

I don't see anyone lurking in the skies, but my skin creeps with disbelief. *Someone is watching me.*

But I can't turn my head to look because a crowd of people rushes to meet me. Mars can barely keep them at bay, as many throw themselves at me and cry out their thanks and admiration.

Above the throng of chatter, Sherry cries out, "She would have sold her soul for us. The gods heard her pleas. She can save us!"

The shouting around us grows, and I try not to cry; not from relief, but from how overwhelmed I feel at the faces all moving in on me, seeking me out as though I am a new goddess here to save them from the clutches of damnation.

"Enough!" Mars barks.

Everyone steps back.

"Your queen is doing her best to save us. We must honor her efforts by giving her some space and letting her breathe. She is still young—a fledgling. She must be given the space to grow safely if she is to save us as we believe she is capable. But know that she is the Shadow Slayer no longer. She is the Avenger of Shadows and the savior of Velyasa. Just as I have given you peace, she will defend it with her life. As will I."

His voice doesn't shake as mine would have, and I envy the brevity of his voice even as we silently acknowledge the truth: we still might die at the hands of the same bastard who slew Finch. And even if we win, there's still the matter of Sunfall.

But worse still, I possess the horrid truth that *I did not wield this magic alone*.

Something—*someone*—helped me today.

I only hope their generosity does not run out. A thick blanket of nausea coats my throat. Sweat breaks out along my forehead, but no one around me notices, save for Sherry. Not even Mars catches the way I stumble when stars dot my vision. A deep, gnawing hunger threatens to claw through my stomach, and I look to Sherry for help. I don't know how to ask; I only hope the pleading in my eyes is enough for her to understand why I've grown pale and sway beneath the raw sun pouring in from above. I wish, for once, to be bathed in Mars's darkness to save me from the clutches of the bright light that hurts my eyes.

"I think Her Highness would do well with a hunt. She's been studying in the library for quite some time," Sherry smoothly says. "Please let her through."

I detect a layer of honey in her voice — magical, no doubt — and all around us, people move. I turn to her, puzzled by how she managed to do such a thing, but she doesn't stop to abate my confusion as she ushers me from the room, Mars hot on our heels.

"What went wrong?" His voice carries after us as she rushes me to the entrance of the castle.

My vision grows darker. I feel myself start to slip and crumple to my knees the moment we exit the building. The soft grass of the garden outside caresses my feet, and I almost weep.

"I think I got... overwhelmed," I mutter. "I've never had that many people come at me at once outside of battle. No one ever crowds me like that — ever."

My heart races. My hands feel clammy and shake around the hilt of a sword I never pull. I can't find my way back from the battlefield I never left. I can't claw my way back from the clearing where Finch was disemboweled.

Mars and Sherry both kneel beside me as I struggle to figure out how to return to the present.

"No one here is going to harm you, Adelaide," Mars whispers. "I didn't even think about how a crowd like that might... trigger some unwanted thoughts."

I swallow as bile rises in my throat. I worry I'll expel my guts right here in the garden. The acid will harm the plants, I'm sure, so I do my best to hold it in.

But I fail.

Mars runs his hand up and down my back to soothe me as I empty the contents of my stomach. My body shakes.

Both he and Sherry sit with me in silence after I finish, neither speaking nor asking me why I had such a sudden onslaught of terror. I've never really been among crowds like that. Dances, yes. Hearings, yes. But I've always been left to the side. Never have I been the center of attention unless people were trying to kill me.

Even my wedding was easy to slip away from. Mars was the centerpiece on whom everyone focused, whereas I was the villain. The irony of my light and power is that it has always left me in the shadows. Always, even before I possessed it.

"It is a shame, the weight you have been asked to carry for so long," Mars finally says. "I'm sorry that we are about to ask you to do it again. When this battle is over, I promise you will never have to wield a sword again, and we can rule in peace."

I look at him and laugh. "Don't make promises you can't keep."

"I keep telling you that, Uncle. When will you listen?" Sherry chimes in.

"When I firmly believe there won't come a day where I don't burn down everything that harms my fire to the point where she becomes ill when she meets her subjects. No one should be forced to live a life where reliving it is a nightmare, such as that."

I sigh. "Mars, I love you. But let me help you keep your enemies at bay. You can't fend them off alone."

"For you? Of course I can, my fire." He smiles at me, and by the gleaming of his fangs, I know he speaks the truth.

But so do I.

"And for you, I'll do just the same." I feel my fangs scrape my upper lip as I smile.

The three of us stand near the tree line. We agreed to go on a hunt, not just for the blood, but for the relief it provides. My legs cry with relief as I stretch them, releasing the tension that has built up within them. My throat still burns from retching earlier. I lick my lips, eager to fix the sour taste in my mouth by drenching my tongue and teeth in the blood of some poor creature.

Without waiting for Mars or Sherry to follow me, I bolt, snaking through the trees and letting the beams of sunlight and shadow caress me into the empty space and thought of the hunt. It's a natural instinct, just as Mars told me the first time he brought me out here. I was just too ignorant to hear it. I will never be forcibly deaf to my needs again. Not when my soul cries for the replenishment it needs after bearing the weight of so much angry magic.

I tilt my nose to the sky, ushering in the scent of a vast array of options. I focus on the subtle thrum of heartbeats and footsteps, careful to consider every potential meal. Would some of them live to see another day if I chose them over something else? I needn't take *all* their blood. Perhaps I could drink from more than one — make a true game out of it.

When I meet my first victim, a doe, she writhes and thrashes as I take from her. She's not willing to let me feed without a fight. I'm thankful to her for the rush of adrenaline a good scrap can bring. I don't kill her, instead taking just enough to sate my thirst before letting her go. Her hoof swings out and barely misses me, one last, angry kick of defiance being all the doe has left to offer as I bask in the warmth lodged in my throat.

Then I'm off again, seeking the next challenge. I tangle with a bear next. Its swiping claws are relentless, but they're not enough to deter me as I immobilize it, my power holding the creature hostage as I drink. My throat is greedy, but not enough to let it die. I allow it to live, and I'm gone before it can take another swipe or bite, its teeth meeting air instead of flesh.

This is the fastest I've ever raced before. Animal after animal becomes an unwitting part of my healing. Satisfied for the moment, I rest against the side of an ancient, gnarly tree that reminds me of the one that bore the Lasira fruit. This tree is lifeless, barren of any leaves or fruit or flowers, but it serves as a good resting point as I pull the pendant from my pocket —

the one I forged from the Siraltona and Tryta's darkness. Both are nestled neatly within my soul.

I don't think I'll ever understand the shadow as much as the light, but it's bizarre how it serves as the perfect canvas for the light's creations. I hold it up, studying the way the amber pendant winks in the stray beams of sunlight carving through the shaded canopy of trees. The chain is gold, rich with promise and hope for the kingdom. It could save so many souls. I just need to make more of them.

Before I know it, I'm weaving them; one by one, I create, finding new versions of the pendant dangling in my hands. I wonder how quickly I could dispatch them to the soldiers who keep Jupiter and his henchman at bay. How long will they hold up against someone who has wielded the Falahle as long as he has?

Each time the same amber gem attaches to the ball, I wonder if that is the resulting color of dark and light manifesting into something new. But then I ponder the sun, the trees, the ocean, and the creatures that inhabit my world and recognize just how limited my ability is compared to that of Tryta and Siralto.

I wonder how much control it takes to create.

I lose count of how many pendants I weave before deciding I have a good bunch of them. I know it's not enough, and I try my best to ignore the way my heart flutters, strained by the amount of magic I've just used. As relaxing and refreshing as creation magic feels, I discover in this moment that there is *still* a task in using it. It is impossible to be fully calm and centered when creating, and, immortal or not, I am not infallible. I am not a god.

As I consider which being helped me back in the library, I catch a new sound on the wind. It's the thrumming of a heartbeat — a heartbeat I know and love well.

I half believe I'm dreaming. I'm on my feet and running — hurtling toward the sound of the thump, thump, thump that I've missed more than breathing itself. My heart shatters as I consider that this may be a trick. It could be the worst possible thing to happen to me, a deceitful dream denied to me once realized. But I must take the chance that this might be *real*.

I crash through branches that snap and twist, smacking me in the face and cutting my flesh. My skin heals as quickly as it opens without spilling a single drop on the forest floor. Once upon a time, I would have been left striped and stained by such reckless behavior. But not now. Not in this body.

The sound grows louder — the creature doesn't move as I crash into the clearing where I find him.

Challenger.

His great, chestnut body is not worn by starvation. He has eaten well in this wood and wears no tack to hold him captive or signs of branding by another owner. Instead, at the sight of me, his ears flick forward. A smile, by a horse's standard.

"Where have you been, friend?"

His voice, smooth like velvet, caresses my mind. I sink to my knees as tears blind my vision. "Here," I whisper. "I've been here all this time. I thought you were a goner. I thought Jupiter had stolen you from me forever!" But as my eyes trail up his neck, I note the faint scars from where he *should* have died. Yet here he stands, breathing in defiance of Death itself.

"You're sharp. I was brought back to you. A gift," he whispers.

I blink. "Am... am I hearing you?"

My horse, my beloved steed, saunters over to me. Somehow, his flesh and fur look new, just as my own do. I don't doubt that with time, his scars will fade as mine have. I know I should be wary — I should run before I let this ghost of a creature touch me, but my heart pangs with grief at the thought of turning away from him. I can't leave him behind again. He carried me to Hell and back and never once led me astray. If I die by some wicked apparition meant to make me think it's him, then so be it.

Kingdom be damned, Challenger is worth the whole of it.

It's an irrational thought driven by grief. As the warm breath from his nostrils caresses my face, I bask in the way his presence radiates calmness into my own.

"I am no trick. I came back from the land you know as Tyrladan. The goddess who sent me meant to offer me as an olive branch — to let you know she means to bring you peace."

"Which goddess, Challenger? Is she the one from the library?"

Even as the question slips from my tongue, I know it to be the truth. Some patron goddess has chosen me. That narrows the options, of course.

"That is for you to discover. She will meet you when you've been readied. There are still some things you must learn, but she will guide you in the meantime. It is good to see you, old friend."

A low, grief-filled neigh rings through the clearing. I throw caution to the wind. I fling my arms around his neck and weep into his coat. I'm still back in that clearing. I'm still watching him get away and be taken into the arms of Death. I'm still watching Finch be claimed all the same, along with the phoenix Sira, whose fire died protecting me on that awful day.

But here, now, my horse has returned to me, a gift from the very goddess who vowed to help me.

"What does she expect in return?"

"Nothing, dear friend," my horse answers, his voice choked. *"Your mission is the same. Will should not be taken — choices are meant to be in the hands of mortals. It is the only magic that was never denied to them. It is*

the most important aspect of the spirit you all possess. It means that your fate is yours to wield and decide, the consequences determined by others. But the choice should always belong to you all."

I wonder when a horse becomes wise, or if their souls are born with it. Anyone else might find it absurd that a horse could understand such things, but I know better. He's been in the presence of those long dead now for months. I'm surprised he's not speaking other languages and telling me tales of souls lost to time.

"There is always a price, Challenger."

"Is not the blood and life you've already lost enough? Rest in this, Adelaide. I relay to you the truth."

My breath hitches. I start to argue when I hear the telltale sound of Mars and Sherry's footsteps behind me. I turn to find them both cautiously standing at the edge of the clearing.

"Whose horse is this?" His voice is rolling thunder.

I know the next lightning strike is not far behind. I must answer before he kills my horse. "Challenger. He's *mine*," I declare. "He was given back to me by the gods."

As a show of trust, Challenger lowers to the ground, allowing me to take my seat on his back. Without a saddle, my legs hang looser than they would if I had some stirrups, but it's always a treat to feel him move without the burden of tack between us. It allows me to truly *know* how his muscles move and appreciate where his gravity lies.

Challenger moves towards Mars, unswayed by the way he stands — a predator waiting to pounce. It is not the way of a horse to move towards danger, but Challenger seems to recognize that Mars only wants to protect me.

When he reaches Mars, Sherry lets out an unmasked noise of delight and slides a hand down Challenger's slender nose. The horse does not bolt, bite, or buck at the gesture, further proving that he is not a mirage or a trick.

"Getting up there was stupid, Adelaide. Reckless. Foolish," Mars scolds.

I can't hide my tears, and the flames in his eyes soften when he realizes I'm crying.

"I am glad he was returned to you. Do the gods say why?"

"A goddess has ordained to help me. For free. I must confess, Mars. I felt someone watching me in the library today. Someone was there and loaned me their aid. Someone gave me the push I needed for my magic. I made no deal and struck no bargain," I hasten to add. "They brought me Challenger as an act of good faith to reassure me that their help is 'free', paid for by the sacrifices I've already made."

Mars's skin pales. "No god acts for free."

"I know," I answer. "The cost thus far has been my blood and energy, which I've been told is enough. I don't expect that to last forever, and when they reveal to me the true cost, I will let you know at once before making a choice."

It's the closest thing to submission that I can offer my husband. I know I am not a good queen where that is concerned. But this is the chance we've all needed.

I reach into my dress pocket and procure the bunch of necklaces I made while pondering in the forest mid-hunt. I toss them to Mars; he catches them so swiftly I almost don't notice his hand move. Were it not for my supernatural eyesight, I wouldn't have seen it at all.

Sherry eyes them with a deep want. I know, more than anyone, how much she wants one of those necklaces. I pull on my power and fashion one, this time thinking about the color of the gem that I want. Purple, for the rich color of her skin. For everyone else, I could not care less about the color I grant them. But for Sherry, the gesture will mean more.

When it settles in my hand, freshly forged, I examine it to ensure it is sufficient before tossing it to her. When it lands in her hand, she stares at it for a good while before slowly sliding it over her neck.

When it rests there, she lets out a deep sigh. "Thank you."

I don't need her to say anything else. By the way she stares down at it, thumbing it with awe, I know it means far more than her soft thanks. I have given her protection against the very thing that nearly destroyed her the first time. I can't imagine how a reunion with her father might go, or what he might do to her if he ever breached our walls. I hope the chain holds up against his awesome, terrible power.

"Don't ever let him take that off. No matter what happens," I declare.

While I don't want to consider the reality that we might die, dying is something one never plans on. The least I can do is make sure that the people I leave behind are armed to the teeth against their foes.

"I won't." The steel in Sherry's voice forges a promise between us. Mars doesn't speak, instead focusing his efforts on peering at Challenger as though he might grow a third head or start spitting fire.

I do not know how to gain this man's approval, but I shall seek it all the same. Challenger doesn't sound bothered by my husband's hesitation. If anything, he almost seems as if he expected it.

"Do you hear him speak to you, Adelaide? The same way your power calls your name?"

Mars's eyes meet mine, and not for the first time, I wonder if he hears my innermost thoughts. I don't know what the extent of our bond is, or if it will continue to push against limits I never stopped to consider, but my blood runs cold. There are thoughts in my head that would shame the worst of sinners, and I can't begin to let Mars traipse about in there.

But when I do not hear the siren call of his deep, booming voice, I hide a quiet sigh of relief. While everyone has things to hide, I'm not sure I'm ready to be laid bare to him like that. Being naked in the flesh is far less terrifying than being naked in the mind.

"I do," I finally say, careful of my tone. I don't need him to see any weak point by which to attack me and my horse.

Mars nods. "We shall see how he acts. Will he consent to being stabled with the others? I will have to keep him separated for a while to ensure he does not spread illness to them."

"I do not mind. I would like some hay and grain. Hunger has returned to me. It will not leave until I die again."

My heart lurches. What a wonderful place he must have been in if there was no need to eat until returning to this mortal plane! I pity him for being forced to come back. In Tyrladan, he was free.

"Why did you come back when you didn't have ailments like hunger, Challenger?"

"You needed me. I will not leave you until it is the right time. I have been with you through the hardest of battles. I'll not miss the hardest one yet."

Mars turns his head, puzzled by the flash of grief and gratitude that slides across my face. I slip from Challenger's back and slide my hand along his broad side. I am frightened he will disappear like a fine mist if I release my hand from him, yielding the sense of touch to some horrible dream before I wake.

"He will go. But he needs food," I say.

Mars smiles. "We won't deny the boy his meal. He will be surveilled to ensure he is safe, as you say, but I will trust your judgment in this."

If ever there was a time I wished to repay Mars his favor, now is the time. But I won't do that in front of Sherry and Challenger. Maybe later. I can't tell if a fight is brewing between my husband and me first. He sounds like he agrees with my choice, but there is hesitation in his flaming eyes all the same. I sense I am not done defending the nameless goddess who has chosen to aid me, even though he was willing to barter again when he had nothing left to give but his life.

I reach out and grab his hand, gripping it tightly. I will all the love in my bones to creep through his skin and into his soul. I hope it takes root there and never leaves, even after I am long gone, should it come to that.

FAMILIAR COMFORTS

W E LEAVE CHALLENGER WITH a full supply of hay and fresh water. It takes several minutes before I feel comfortable enough to leave him behind. No part of my mind, magic, or soul has come to terms with the fact that he's *back*. Back from death, no less.

Sherry leaves us once we reach the castle. My husband and I walk in silence. Tension swirls in the air between us, despite how much my heart craves him. I know I've angered him, somehow, and he's too kind to take it out on me.

The silence drives me mad. I need him to speak to me. Yell at me. Curse me as he did when I first arrived here. I have no idea where I stand or why he's upset this time. I have several good guesses, but the uncertainty crawls along my flesh like angry, pinching needles.

"Mars, please. I did not summon a goddess," I blurt. "Not on purpose. I did not defy you. I did not risk my life against your wishes."

He looks down at me and raises a dark eyebrow. "Do you think I'm angry with *you* about all of this?"

I look down at my hands and swallow the lump lodged in my throat. I hate the way sweat beads along my skin, betraying my nervousness. "I know you didn't want me consorting with the gods."

"And yet I asked you to let me do the same." He shrugged. "I know you did not forge a deal. I know that whatever deity this is... they have chosen you whether you like it or not. *That* is what enrages me."

He puts out his hand for me to take again and I, ever greedy, take it for the lifeline it is.

"Besides, since when do you care about sparing my feelings?" Mars asks.

I blink and peer into his enigmatic eyes. "I've... been considering the possibility that we might die. It haunts me. As much as some ghost of myself still hates you for the bastard you are, I don't want either of us to leave this plane without you knowing that, in the end, my soul cries for you. Through it all, it is yours, along with my heart and mind. I may not have chosen this path, but it is the truth."

Mars stops in the hall, halted by my words.

"I am so scared that we are going to lose," I continue. "I cannot get the image of Finch's brutal death out of my mind. My horse had to be pulled back from the clutches of Death itself! I have power, but it comes at great cost when I let myself be eaten alive by the rage in my body because I am not *old* enough to wield it. I am not seasoned in the immortality that has blessed my veins and freed me from mortal woes, yet those woes still haunt me and hold me back when my kingdom, new to me, needs me most."

I curse myself for the tears that course down my cheeks. I have never been much of a crier. I don't see shame in it, but the overwhelming reality of all that's happened to me in less than a year is catching up and the weight is becoming too much to bear. Even so, I cannot give out or falter, because

I've never had this much to lose. I look up into flaming eyes that brim with tears and curse him for giving me the one thing I never had.

Someone to have and to hold. He's mine.

I take a shuddering breath and look down at my feet. I trace the wear of my boots and wonder if they'll stand empty on a battlefield before long. Will the blessings of this unnamed goddess be enough to carry me through the challenges ahead, or will my head hit the floor as my mother's did?

"Adelaide," Mars whispers, "I am only sorry I did not find you *after* I had already slain my bastard brother. It is a shame that you must share that burden with me."

Outside, I hear the aching cry of a mourning dove. The sound anchors me in the here and now as I look back up at my husband. It's so strange — he is everything to me and yet, he is the monster I've feared longer than any. I am amazed that he stills my heart as he leans in close, blocking the sunset behind us from view. Muted light streams in through the window and basks us in the heather of dusk.

"It's not your fault," I whisper. "If my kingdom hadn't... If *I hadn't...*" I can't finish my sentence. I fall silent, letting my tears do the speaking.

"And it is not yours," he earnestly says. "Listen, Adelaide... there is more to that story than you've been told. Of course we are not the monsters you fear, but we are not blameless in the conflict. I am as fallible as any man. Someday, you may hate me when you learn what I bartered to get where I am. You may hate me when you learn how I lost our familiars in the first place, as I alone am responsible."

I swear my heart stops beating. I peer up at him, startled to see his exhausted, wan pallor. "Mars, I killed thousands of your subjects. I can forgive whatever you've done, even if I hate you in the moment when you finally tell me what got us to this point."

He shakes his head. "I fear the day you decide you don't love me. All your hate has been superficial, to this point. Our bond has always won out. I fear the day it doesn't. I fear the day that you hate me for pulling you into this nightmare and you learn how I've done so. The gods blessed my wretched choices and gave me a lesson in humility and love by bringing you to me."

I let out a shaky laugh. I don't like where the conversation is going, but I don't think he'll let it go further. His fear of losing me trumps any chance of learning whatever horrible truth he's hiding. But for once, I don't care. I shove aside trepidation in favor of reckless forgiveness.

"I swore an oath to love you even beyond what most married couples do," I say. "Whatever happened *must* be forgiven. Siralto's light — the only thing left of her — has forgiven Tryta. She cries for the darkness, even after he slew her. What greater evidence of our bond is there than that?"

Mars presses his forehead to mine and we stand together in the dying light of the day. I know that someday he will tell me what he's done, and my proclamation will be put to the test. But just as he put his kingdom in my hands after all I've done to destroy it, I know I owe him that same forgiveness in return. I only hope that my fire will be doused the day he stokes it with the truth.

We share a knowing look as he descends on me, his lips claiming mine with passionate need.

"I need you," he gasps, crushing his tongue into my mouth with forceful want.

I let him in, greeting his tongue with mine. They dance together, fast then slow, as our gasps echo along the castle walls. "We should get to our chambers," I manage to breathe. "I don't think the kingdom needs to witness this."

Mars nods, scooping me into his arms and rushing me towards our bedchamber.

"What do I do? To... to prevent conception?" I ask, uncaring if passersby hear as we make our way to a night of passion. I meant to ask Sherry, but she is gone now and there's no sense in being ashamed of asking the would-be father of my children. "I don't think it's wise to have an heir right now. We have bigger things to handle. I want to give them to you, but I want to slay Jupiter first."

Mars nods before leaning in for a deep kiss. We near the bedchamber and desire bursts at the seams of my veins as I watch the way his eyes drink me in. I will be consumed in those flaming eyes of his someday.

"I have a medicine you can take. All women in Velyasa have access to it. When you take it, the effects last a month. I will have Sherry bring more tomorrow."

When he sets me on the bed before making a mad dash to the armoire, I begin to remove my dress. I don't need him to start on the festivities — I can handle those myself. He returns with a small glass vial in his hands. I take it without complaint. Once the contents are emptied, I don't feel any fear in proceeding with our night's plans.

"Let me finish undressing you," he begs.

I oblige, allowing him to slip my dress from my frame. Once my clothes are lying on the floor in a rumpled heap, I move to unbutton his trousers. He stops me.

"No," he demands. He stops to look me over, admiring the slopes and curves that have returned since I started eating as I should. My breasts are fuller and my legs and belly are no longer gaunt from starvation. "You are so beautiful when you are healthy. You are beautiful always, but you positively glow now." He grins, a deep purr rumbling in his chest.

"Take me," I beg.

He smirks. "I will. But I will take my time."

I could kill him.

He still doesn't unbutton his trousers as he moves over me and begins to suckle my breasts. They seem to be his favorite feature, though I'm not so sure when his hands slide to my ass and thighs, gripping and grasping with unfettered desire as he gently nips the mound of my left breast. I squeal and he smiles without ceasing his attention on my breasts.

"Mars!" I gasp. I try to slide my hand to where I need it most, but once again, he stops me.

"Patience, Fire," he commands.

I want to scream, need burning in my core in ways I can't begin to fathom. My hands, still shaking, reach for his trousers. This time, he lets me help him take them off. His length springs free and I stare at it. It's a decent size, but not so intimidating that I worry about being impaled. A bead has formed at the tip, and I lick my lips.

"I believe I owe you a favor."

I don't wait for him to protest, though I don't hear anything of the sort leave his lips. I slide from the bed and plunge to my knees, one hand grabbing his length and fondling him at the base with the other. I hesitantly move my mouth closer and place my tongue, gently, on the tip. He lets out a soft groan.

"Adelaide," he murmurs.

Taking this as my cue, I slowly begin to take him into my mouth, cherishing the taste of him on my tongue. I don't move fast, careful to look up and gauge his reaction. When I note the way the vein along his shaft begins to protrude more aggressively, I take one of my fingers and run it along that vein and he bucks into my mouth.

"Sorry," he gasps.

But I don't stop. I bob my head, taking as much of him as I can before sliding it back out. In. Out. In. Out. Every time I let it out again, I let it pop against my lips and drop tender kisses along the tip. He gasps each time, and I feel his hips try not to send his length slamming into my throat.

I relish how much control I have at this moment. Even more, I adore the sight of those flaming eyes rolling back with pleasure with each new thing I try with him.

Just when I think I'm about to get him to climax, he pulls free and throws me back onto the bed.

"I'm taking you," he says.

Not an ask, but a demand, and one I'm more than eager to oblige as he puts his knee between my legs and props them open.

When he takes me to the hilt, I cry out. The ecstasy and pleasure are almost too much as I writhe around him. He is desperate today. I know he needs this even more than I do, but I am far from complaining about the way my body responds to him.

Every time he drives himself in or strums a new tune with his fingers, I start to black out and see stars. When I finally let loose, my body shakes around him, helpless to do more than gasp. But I don't mind. I feel safe as I reach my peak and I know he will care for me, even as I fall apart.

He follows suit and we stay locked together in silence for many moments, refusing to move or separate.

"I will love you despite it all," I breathe. "Even when I hate you."

Instead of answering me, he gives me another tender kiss, the taste of our love lingering on his lips.

I smile.

~*~

Freshly bathed, we both tumble into bed, still bare save the sheets we throw over our skin. It's still not warm enough to ditch the fur comforter, but the promising warmth from earlier today gives me hope for summertime. Summer is the season I was born, which is fitting, as it is the most fiery month.

I wonder when Mars was born. I look up at him and smile, realizing he is still watching me. Though his eyes are heavy with the wear of the day, his spirit is unwilling to fall asleep first. I've noticed this about him. He always goes to sleep last, as if he feels compelled to ensure I am comfortable and safe before he can rest.

I lean up to him and rub the tips of our noses together, ignoring how my body aches from the desperate love we shared moments ago. I know by morning I will feel fresh and renewed, as though I remain untouched. Such is the reality of being in this body — the body of a predator meant to live in the shadows for centuries, if not longer. I consider how long Mars has been alive and wonder how he has managed to keep himself busy all this time without growing bored.

I don't blame him for taking lovers before me. Living alone is hard enough, let alone for hundreds of lifetimes. I reach up and run my hand through his hair and wonder how many women have done the same to him before meeting an early grave or leaving him in favor of someone else, his heart still empty.

I count my lucky stars that I did not have to live so long before meeting him. Even with the strangeness of how we met, I would still rather have things angry and lethal as they were in the beginning because they led to this end.

I only hope it is not truly the end. I hope that we might live on despite Jupiter and Sunfall and all the things that seek to end our enjoyment just as it is getting started.

"When will I get my familiar?" I ask, my voice a soft murmur in the night. Even as sleep tugs at my eyelids, my mind wanders into the world of magic.

I wish so badly for something like Mars's dragon to awaken within me. Perhaps then we could breathe Jupiter to ash and bathe the world in our fire.

"You are close," he whispers. "Speaking to animals and gaining control of your power can be a sign. Normally, it takes years, but since some deity has ordained to bless you... it could be any day now."

"Oh." The word is a soft punctuation, declaring that my mind has reached its limit and needs to shut off. As I rest my head on his broad chest, the sound of his breathing lulls me to sleep. My dreams are full of dragons, fire, and victory. I go to sleep smiling.

When I wake, Mars is still sleeping. I don't dare wake him. Instead, I revel in the way his skin almost glows when at rest and the sight of his disheveled hair against the pillows. As his chest rises and falls, his breath a gift I cherish with each passing day, I consider once more what it would be like to have a familiar form to aid us in battle.

Even if I were a dragon like him, it would take centuries to grow to his size and be of use. I curse the laws of magic and prowess for robbing me of another great plan to save the kingdom. Frustrated, I use this time in the quiet to forge more necklaces. I let the chains vary in length, color, and even choose different clasps for each so that the soldiers have options.

It feels like a feeble attempt against the inevitable. Jewelry should have little bearing on how well we fare against an evil as terrible as Jupiter. It occurs to me that I know very little about my brother-in-law outside of the fact that he is Sherry's father and he killed Finch and Sira. And Challenger. I shudder.

"Are you cold, my fire?"

Mars's deep voice rumbles against the morning light and a warmth settles in my chest.

I look up at him, mid-spell, and smile. "No. I just realized I don't know very much about Jupiter. I know who he is, but... outside of being a murderer and an evil bastard willing to rob people of their choice, how did he come to be? Like, has he always been one to seek power as he does? How long has he threatened your kingdom, and what drove him to those ends?"

Mars sighs. "I was wondering when you would ask. You've been so eager to help the kingdom..."

I catch a faint chuckle on that last word and glare at him. "What are you implying?"

"Nothing, nothing at all."

I lightly smack his chest and he laughs harder, his mirth rocking the bedframe.

"I just admire your willingness to jump right into action."

I roll my eyes at him, but he's right. I do tend to act first and think later, despite my role as a strategist back home. In my efforts to assimilate myself here and survive, I've thrown caution to the wind and become impulsive. Now Mars plays the role of forward thinker and I act as the mindless sword who would protect the kingdom at any cost.

Is that the type of queen I want to be? A blind weapon used to protect the masses?

I don't have time to fret over my shifting role. Right now, I need answers about who Jupiter is.

"Jupiter is my younger brother. Different fathers, but same mother. When my father died in a battle, my mother remarried and had Jupiter. He is far younger than I, as my mother didn't remarry for centuries after my father's passing. It almost killed her to lose him. I'd long left home to search for a kingdom to call my own when I received news of her union with a new man. The first time I met my brother, he was already five years old. I had been out on a campaign. I was newly turned and vampire slayers were far more common then than they are now, and I had intel on a network of them that I was keen to take out."

When I realize that Mars is speaking about a life that is centuries before my time, my chest tightens. It's hard to fathom the battles he has won and lost. Tyrladan has reclaimed countless lives, and he has witnessed much of it.

"Was your stepfather cruel to him?" I can't help but ask the question.

Mars shrugs. "If anything happened to him while I wasn't there, I don't know of it. My stepfather was not long-lived. Nor was my mother after he passed. I don't think she was ever happy again after my father died. I wonder if this is what led Jupiter to be different. My mother was not a queen by birthright. Nor was my father. My kingdom was one I forged with my power alone... but my brother saw the legacy I had established and began to crave that for himself. That's where things went wrong, I believe."

"Did he learn of your kingdom and come to stay with you, or did he watch you from afar and grow jealous? Once he was grown, I mean." I'm doing my best to paint a picture in my head. I am eager to understand as much of my adversary as I can, even if only through second-hand accounts. Mars's absence for most of Jupiter's childhood puts a damper on my ability to understand motive, but I'll take what I can get.

"He came to me when our mother died. He was distraught by her passing, so he threw himself into a role as one of our lead generals. Jupiter proved to be a mighty foe in battle, which was helpful because I was still working to secure land and titles. I had heirs, but none were old enough to replace me, should I be felled by a blade."

He has children almost as old as the kingdom?

The more I learn about my husband, the more I realize just how out of my league he is. Were it not for the gods, I wouldn't have even registered as a potential mate to him. Maybe a night or two of fun and a way to secure yet another unneeded heir... but never a wife. My heart winces.

"He served me for a few centuries, though it was only in the last hundred years that I noticed things had begun to change. It was subtle at first. As you saw, I tucked away the book of the gods deep in the library. I do not make a habit of hiding knowledge, but I realized some things must be kept away for the sake of everyone's safety. An important lesson, but one I learned too late. My only saving grace was that I hid Tryta's page long before—for my own selfish reasons—and that Siralto is dead, and her page is useless."

I wince again at the mention of my goddess's death. To think of her as a useless memory on a page... it stings.

"Did he barter with someone else?" My heart is thudding so loudly in my ears that they ring.

"We don't know who he bartered with. None of the gods in that book would even begin to think of giving him the Falahle. He acquired it just before he left, which I discovered when I caught him using it to command soldiers. Right around then, Tryta gave me the rest of my powers —just enough to resist Jupiter's. When I went to barter for the return of our familiars, Tryta gave me that same power to use against Jupiter. Tryta does not like to be involved this closely with mortals, but he felt it necessary that someone should possess the power to shut Jupiter down."

I chew on this. Something in his story doesn't add up. I know he's hiding things from me — details about his bargains with Tryta —but I'm sharper than he gives me credit for.

"When did you exile Jupiter? Or did he leave of his own accord?"

"Of his own accord. He and I... we saw things differently. We both envisioned different worlds for our kind. I believe we should live freely and without oppression, whereas Jupiter relishes the influence of shadows. I would much rather my people be free to choose to go about their lives at whatever time of day they see fit. Why can't we live as the mortals do? The sun does not scorch our skin — it makes us a target to those who fear us. I damned us further when we lost our familiars."

I pause. Something clicks in my mind, though I'm not yet sure of all the pieces of the puzzle Mars has given me. Is he leading me astray by giving me only the parts of his story that he wants me to hear? Or has he given away more than he intended? Or maybe he wants me to figure out the mystery of the familiars on my own. He loves a challenge... is this a game between us?

"Jupiter and I parted ways the day we lost our familiars. He got his back within no time at all through dark means. I... was not so lucky. Tryta had seen my foolishness and demanded justice. Where Jupiter's patron does not mind cutting corners and allowing mortals to die in both spirit and body, Tryta cares that his creation remains authentic."

What did you do, Mars?

I don't speak the question aloud. I don't have to. The look he gives me speaks volumes as understanding stains itself on his handsome features.

"You're thinking into this too much, Adelaide."

"On the contrary, I think I'm just starting to think at all."

The first question I've failed to ask is *when* they lost their familiars. I always knew they didn't have them until recently. Only when Finch returned did I realize the Shadow Folk had gotten them back.

If I can trace their history to figure out *when* they lost them, I might be able to figure out *how*.

"You'll be the ruin of me," Mars breathes.

"Consider it payback, love." I wink, refusing to be dragged beneath the waves of sorrow that radiate from him. He truly fears he'll lose me when I learn the truth. Whatever he's done, he did it while Jupiter was still with him.

This alone makes my blood run cold. For the first time since our Rites, I am wary of my husband.

I need to uncover the truth, and *fast*. I only hope whatever he's done is not enough to make me regret taking him as my mate. I don't know if I could survive the blow of something so treacherous.

Mars doesn't elaborate further on his younger brother. Instead, we sit in the uncomfortable silence of morning for what feels like eons. I don't look up at him again. Instead, I let my mind do what she does best — I unspool her to piece together the mystery of my beloved's greatest sin.

~*~

We haven't spoken to each other since this morning. Mars, I fear, has grown wary of the sharpness of my mind. As much as my heart longs for him to say something — *anything* — I know I will have to solve this mystery on my own. I wonder how long it will be before he turns into another Alaric. How long will it be before he begins to fear me for my mind far more than he fears me for the blades and power I wield?

When he leaves me to meet with the nobles, my lungs tighten and I decide to stroll through the gardens. I would rather dive into the library's vast collection of books, but now I know he's hiding more knowledge than he lets on. Who's to say he hasn't hidden more of the volumes that might hold the answers I seek?

He's desperate to keep this secret from me, but he knows that my light tears through more than just shadow. It has laid bare every mystery before me thus far and will continue to do so.

Two can play at this game. An unknown goddess has harkened to my pleas. She is waiting to help me, even if she cannot give me her name.

The problem is that I don't have a clue what sacrifices she demands or how I might consort with her. In the distance, I spot the temple that Mars plans to visit soon and wonder if it might not be worth trying to speak to Tryta myself. I may not have the page to understand his needs, but I do hold the power that once belonged to his dead wife.

Will that be enough to gain his attention? Will it be enough to get the attention of the goddess already vying for a spot to help me?

It feels treacherous to think of myself as being worth some divine competition, but desperation is a powerful drug.

With no one watching me now, for the first time, I make a decision that isn't about Mars or Sherry or even Velyasa. I turn my feet toward the temple to try and summon the gods who will help me, because now I have more than a kingdom to save. I have a secret to unearth.

The weather is blessedly warm and I take deep breaths, letting the sweet scent of flowers coat my throat and warm my veins. My skin begins to glow as I busy my hands and mind by making more necklaces to give to the soldiers. I wish I had brought along a satchel to carry them. By the time I weave through a row of tall hedges and the most beautiful, vibrant flora I've ever seen, I am burdened with the weight of what must be a hundred of them. Not a single bead of sweat trails along my skin. I am not spent. I am renewed.

Before me stands the temple of Tryta. The statue of a man shrouded in dark shadow stands just outside of it, along with a marker to tell everyone who they worship in the land of Velyasa.

The dark marble columns along the entrance leave gaping shadows between them, bright white veins coursing through the marble and giving way to light through the unyielding dark.

My breath comes up short and my lips tremble. I've never spoken with the gods. Siralto can't speak to me, so praying to her was always a safe bet. *Dead gods can't listen.*

This god, however, is alive. Just as the goddess who wants to help me is also alive. A sob rises in my chest as fear begins to take over in favor of the push to try and save myself and the kingdom.

I wring my wrists, still angry with myself for trusting Mars so easily. I know it is due to the strength of our mate bond, but the way he hides things from me gives me even more reason not to extend mercy or understanding.

He's just like any other king. Power is all that matters.

But that statement doesn't feel right in the depths of my soul. Mars has been an open book up until this point. The purpose of hiding his knowledge was so he could keep it from Jupiter. He didn't even mind that I found the book he hid from his brother.

Why is he acting so strange now?

I don't know when I decided to step inside the temple. Perhaps my curiosity came to life, but now I stand in the midst of it. The temple is mostly barren with no artwork, stained glass, or religious literature to be found. At the center of the temple stands an altar.

None of the prophets and priests from my Rites ceremony are here. I wonder if they only come out at night since Tryta is god of the dark. But I am not afraid to make my pilgrimage in the day. His wife was woven of light itself — given that context, I have nothing to be ashamed of.

At least, I try to tell myself this even as my skin grows colder and my heart more terrified that it may yet be broken by the very man I knew better than to trust.

"He may not be who he seems, but he loves you."

The voice speaking now, to my terror, is a man's. If I thought Mars's voice was deep, this voice scrapes along the edges of the darkest parts of the universe itself. It's so deep it feels more like a whisper in the night, a creeping nightmare straight from Kohlu that's come to claim my soul.

But the fear in my soul stills and at once I know I have no reason to be afraid of Tryta.

"Yes, my little light. My wife's magic chose a beautiful vessel. It suits you well. Your mate was well-chosen. He will not steer you wrong. Your heart will be broken, no doubt, though he does not mean to deceive you. But the choice will always be yours."

"What did he do to lose the familiars?" I ask, tears coursing down my cheeks. I can't stop the aching sorrow in my chest or the feelings of betrayal that snake their way up my spine, sending shivers all down my back and arms. I sink to my knees and grip the cool floor, hoping it will give me peace.

"Your husband alone must answer for that. But you will discover the truth one way or another. I took the familiars to make him pay for an almost unforgivable sin. But who am I to deny my chosen son a second chance?"

Son?

"I thought... I thought he said his father died."

"His mortal father passed. Mars himself passed. I breathed new life into him, for I am where all Shadow Folk lay claim to their lineage. He found life in my darkness, just as you have through him. In a way, you are like my daughter, too. But you, dear petal, have more than what Mars could hope for. You possess the light that has long been gone from the universe. It has claimed your veins. Now you must ask yourself: What will you do with it?"

I want to keep pushing Tryta for answers, but I know better than to argue with a god. Instead, I consider how to answer his question, because there are so many things I want to do with the power.

I want to save Velyasa. I want to understand the horrible things my husband has done. I want to stop Jupiter and avenge Finch. Once, I was consumed by the need to avenge my mother, but that need feels hollow now. No amount of fighting can bring her back. I don't even know which of the Shadow Folk killed her. Chances are I might have already slaughtered the person responsible.

"I want to forge a path that's mine. I want to save this kingdom and be a real queen. I want to help my husband, even as he keeps secrets from me."

"That is admirable, Adelaide, but not the full truth. You are a free soul. You want to be powerful. You want to be honored. You want to be a force to be reckoned with and be treated as Mars's equal, do you not?"

I flinch. There is no malice in his tone, but the authority in Tryta's voice makes the accusation sting.

"I don't mean to conceal truths, but I don't think I'm truly aware of my motivations. In a way I *do* want to be a force... but how can I ever be seen as his equal? How can I ever earn my place on the throne as anything more than his wife? I am working double time to give him what I can — to help him where I can."

I lay the necklaces I've made at the foot of the altar. "See? I've been making these to protect the people from the Falahle. But will it be enough? Who cares for a girl who creates stupid, pretty trinkets? What if they don't hold up? What if they are not enough?"

From the corners of the temple, I hear a deep rumbling. Tryta is *laughing*.

"My, do you remind me of Siralto! Her power certainly chose a kindred spirit. Adelaide, these are powerful artifacts. You have mastered her light, but also my dark. You have begun to understand the secrets of Creation and have only had your powers for a few months. Is that not worth the recognition you seek? Your glory will be tenfold what it was as the Shadow Slayer. Why else would I have led you to the Lasira?"

I freeze. "That... was you?"

"The power you have now was begging to find you. Who was I to deny even an echo of my wife's wishes?"

I grimace. I don't know if it's safe to ask this next question, but at this point, with my heart shattered and my mind on fire with unending questions, I yield to it anyway.

"Then why did you kill her?"

Silence.

I lay my forehead on the floor as a show of submission. I squint my eyes shut, waiting to meet my end.

"I did not kill my beloved wife. The reason for her death was so much more than what the poets and scribes wrote. Surely, you've seen how the world rewrites most of its history to make monsters out of the things it doesn't understand? Do not be afraid to ask me questions, Adelaide. Your husband may fear judgment, but I have heard it all. It is the nature of my wife's magic to be curious. I will not harm you for embracing your gifts. To create is to be curious."

I cry in earnest. "Then who is helping me? Is it you? Challenger said a goddess brought him back."

"That, I cannot say, but your patron goddess will tell you when she is ready. For now, know this: You and your husband have much to confront each other over. You will have to decide for yourself if the sin he committed is worth forgiving. I cannot make that choice for you. But I can tell you that his intentions are pure. However, purity does not spare us of the consequences for our actions."

I swallow, nodding. I hope Tryta sees me agreeing, even if I don't speak. I don't know if my tongue can form words anymore. My throat is dry. I crave both blood and water and know it will take several flagons before I am sated this time.

"Trouble is coming to Velyasa, dear Adelaide, and only you can stop it. Not even Mars can stand against the evil coming — not alone. You *are the key. Your choices alone will decide the fate of this kingdom. As its queen, you must decide where your priorities lie. But know this: Do not believe for a moment the lies of the bastard Jupiter. His future is in Kohlu. Do not forge yourself in the flames of damnation, no matter the temptation."*

I swallow. *Why would I forge my allegiance with Jupiter? He killed Finch and then tried to ally himself with my father.*

But if Tryta says there is something to fear, I figure I'd best heed it.

"I leave you now, Avenger of Shadows. But come visit me again sometime. It is always a blessing to see my wife's light once more, even if it is borne by others. Mars does not wield it as well as you do. Be well, lovely one. Someday, when you come to Tyrladan in the end, you can come tell me firsthand of your adventures here. If you decide to stay with him, Mars can come along as well. I do love my children, even when they defy me from time to time."

If I decide to stay with him? As much as I want to trust Tryta that Mars means well, I hang on to this sentence and it lingers in my ears. *He really does mean that it is my choice. Can you undo a bond woven by the gods?* But I can't bring myself to ask it aloud. Instead, I bury that question to be answered another day.

"I will," I whisper. "But no offense, I hope I don't see you in person for a long time — long after the kingdom has passed to safe hands."

His laughter echoes in the temple, but then he is gone, and I stand alone. As I turn to leave, I notice that the necklaces have been packed in a satchel for me, just as I wished. I reach out, ready to pick it up, when fire erupts in my flesh and I scream.

My body is not my own as I writhe on the temple floor. The Trytalan priests have returned and all stand around me, though no one speaks. When one starts to move to help me, the others hold him back.

"Let her transform!" their leader demands.

They all take a measured step back and watch silently as I fight against the way my bones snap, click, and tear.

My familiar, my mind groans.

I hope that whatever form I take, I can survive the change. It never occurred to me that the first change would be so *painful*.

With Tryta gone, there is no god present to assist in the welcoming of my familiar form and I am left alone to fight. The Siraltona whines and screams in my veins, begging me to let her loose, and I warn the priests to move.

"Get back!" I manage to scream.

They barely step out of the way before the temple is bathed in light. It streaks from my skin and sweeps along the floors, erasing any echo of the darkness in the temple. The priests, thank Siralto, appear to have taken cover. The light does not burn them to ash. I pray this stays the case.

"One last gift for you, petal. You'll need this."

Tryta's voice is back. I don't know if he ever left or I just stopped listening, but I let his darkness bathe me in serenity as my fingers are traded for claws and scales. Relief springs up like a well in my eyes and I weep as my skin is shed for scales. Dark, ruby scales. Red, like Finch.

Fire. Light.

But then the red fades and becomes more like burnished gold. Another god is present. The goddess who blessed me. I feel her. I feel her working with Tryta and let the process overcome my senses.

I don't know how much time passes in this fugue state.

My heartbeat roars in my ears and when I open my eyes, I'm aware that my body is much *larger* than it was before. I feel heavy, sluggish, and the great wings on my back weigh me down.

I look down and behold the body of a great, amber dragon. Where Finch was small, I am not. My head stretches almost to the ceiling of the temple; I know if I were to spread my wings wide, I would knock the temple columns to the ground.

In my throat, I taste the fire that Mars would have burned Sunfall to the ground with, once upon a time. A great purr erupts from deep in my throat.

"Adelaide?" Mars's voice, soft but deep, carries across the temple floor. *"The choice is yours."*

Tryta's voice echoes one last time in my mind and the energy of the nameless goddess fades, leaving my heart pounding heavily in my chest and ears. Tryta claimed Mars means well, but Mars is Tryta's born-again son. Mars is also still responsible for the consequences of his actions. It's hard, though, to judge his choices when he still won't tell me the truth.

"Mars," I hiss. My voice is deeper, but soft, unlike his. A serpent's tongue is more my speed than the booming thunder of Mars's shadows. "Have you come to confess your sins to me? Tryta tells me you must. He and the nameless goddess who chose to help gave me my familiar."

It feels strange to address my husband like this. Gone is the feeling of forgiveness I harbored so close to my chest just the night before when we made love. In its stead is cautious wariness. He and Jupiter cost the Shadow Folk their familiars. It was a sin deemed almost unforgivable to Tryta, but Mars chose to atone.

It's even stranger to side with Tryta's judgments, but I sensed truth in his tale. He couldn't have killed Siralto. At least, not on purpose. I'm not sure if it makes a difference, but I owe him a debt of both gratitude and power. My thunderous wings ache to taste the skies as I have seen Mars do. I wonder why Finch did not grow as large as I have, but I suspect starvation and limited resources were to blame. I realize now that the blood we were giving him was not enough, and I curse myself further for being so ignorant of the ways of the Shadow Folk.

But the Shadow King staring at me now feels more monstrous and alien to behold. Our bond tugs at my heart, begging me to be still and silent, but the fears in my mind win out.

"I must go test my wings," I say, sauntering past him, careful not to clip the columns or ceiling. I don't want to disrespect the very deity that just gave me this newfound freedom. I say my first silent thanks to Tryta and the nameless goddess before stepping out into the light.

Mars follows along beside me, his eyes sweeping over me with cautious delight. If he senses any tension between us, he masks it well as we greet the people gathered outside the temple. Sherry stands among them and her eyes are wet with tears as she steps out to greet me.

"Have you seen yourself?" she whispers.

"No," I breathe back. "All I know is that my scales are red and gold."

Sherry beckons to the crowd; they bring me a mirror and I behold my new form for the first time. Eyes of blazing gold sit within the face of a dragon forged by the colors of flame and autumn. I have a slender, almost deceitfully kind face and twisting, gold horns that reach toward the sky for a sweet embrace with the clouds. The webbing of my wings is a symphony of reds, blacks, and golds that pale in the sun's dazzling light.

In the broad light of day, a living, breathing goddess of fire has taken a resting place outside Tryta's temple. But I am no goddess. I am an angry, deceived queen with mixed emotions as I consider whether to blame the people for the secrets Mars keeps from me.

I turn back and look at him, allowing my sorrows to carry over our bond. When he flinches, I know the message is received. "I must go test my wings."

Without waiting for anyone to agree or argue or tell me to wait, I step away from the crowds, careful not to trample anyone, and spread my wings, giving them the taste of the air they crave. My bones scream with relief as I give them a good flap. At once, I am separated from the ground. Airborne, I do exactly what I need. I take off, high and far above Velyasa.

I don't know if I will come back. But then I hear him. His great wings crack like thunder in the air and I look up to find that my husband is in hot pursuit.

There goes that plan.

"And you thought you could get away."

There, nestled in my mind, is the one voice I hoped I'd never hear within it. The familiar, it seems, was the key to finishing our bond.

You can hear me now?

"I can hear everything. What's this about trying to undo our bond?"

I roll my eyes and take off, leaving him in a wake of light and fire. I don't wait to see if he catches up.

Troubling News

WHEN WE LAND, IT'S in some far-off forest a good way from Velyasa. I need to rest my wings and find the comfort of flesh and bones again. When I touch down, it is smoother than I expect, and I return to my human body without incident. I suspect that the first transformation is unique in difficulty since it has never been done before. Now, I feel the great, scaly beast lurking beneath my skin.

I hear him change behind me and whirl on him.

"You almost didn't have Tryta's forgiveness!" I hiss.

"What happened to being willing to forgive me no matter what? A mate bond is unbreakable, Adelaide," he hisses. "Would you truly leave me?"

The grief in his cry is so startling that I almost fall to the ground and weep. I've not heard such a noise since my father discovered my mother's head, cleaved from her shoulders and left to rot by the Shadow Folk who ended her life.

"I don't know what I'm forgiving! And Tryta says the bond is a choice. I want to choose you, Mars. I want to choose you in every lifetime, but you won't tell me the truth! What are you hiding from me? Why am I not permitted to know what you've done? I am your queen. I have been so accommodating during all these changes. I was forced to become the very thing I swore to destroy once upon a time, and I have done so to the point that I now have *your* god's blessings! But he still leaves the choice to tell me the truth in *your* hands. So what is it, Mars?"

He paces, mad like a dog, and I wonder when he'll snap – when it will all come crashing down on him. I know I'm close to the truth. Whether he and I are still standing in the wreckage of whatever terrible confession he's about to make is another thing to consider.

He looks at me, a deep pain in his eyes, and I brace myself for whatever might leave his mouth next.

"Jupiter and I killed your mother," he blurts.

The world around me goes numb. My breath catches in my chest. I'm almost certain the world is coming to an end. I can't breathe. I can't hear. I can't see.

All I have is the sensation that I've just been glanced by a blade I didn't even see him carrying. But the blade was comprised of hateful words—his confession. The worst thing I could ever hear has left his tongue. I can't unhear it.

"Why?" I whisper.

Mars is on his knees. Tears pour down his face, and his features are twisted with so much grief that I can't bear the sight of it. Something about the way he cries in pain draws me to him. I don't know why I am comforting *him*.

I know it's a consequence of the mutual-thrall, something neither of us has control over. My soul coils with rage, grief, and betrayal. I consider once more if I shouldn't have beheaded the bastard standing before me, begging me for forgiveness for slaughtering one of the few people I cared about.

"What offense did my mother commit that would warrant her *life*, Mars?"

His trembling hands grab mine, and he looks at me as the ghosts of his choices haunt him. He looks haggard, worn. His voice shakes and cracks with so much rage and grief that I find myself crying with him. But I can't get past his startling confession.

He killed my mother. He and his brother killed my mother.

"Your father killed my eldest son. His name was Darius. He was next in line for the throne and went out on a mission to try and establish peace with your nation. Your father had him beheaded in front of the entire kingdom and paraded his body around like a puppet. All I wanted was revenge."

I hold up a hand to stop him from speaking further. I was too young to remember anything from that day, let alone a public execution, but it doesn't shock me because it was something my father would do. Still, my heart thuds. The very culprit behind my mother's death now begs for mercy in my arms.

Once upon a time, I would have jumped at the chance to behead Mars where he stood. Now? I'm not so sure. Agony and rage course through our shared bond, our souls still laid bare to one another. There is a truth in the shadows of his choices that has yet to reveal itself. My heart refuses to believe that he could have been the one to make such a choice. Gone is my belief that Mars is some cruel monster, but hearing him confess still leaves me breathless.

I try to think back to that day. I try to remember the vampires responsible, but my ten-year-old mind was not strong enough to hold onto anything more than the sound and sight of her head hitting the floor. I beg my memories to recall anyone else standing over my mother's decapitated body – begging them to find some other monsters drinking her blood.

But Mars carries on in his quest to explain. I must give those delusions a rest, instead letting the truth continue to shatter my world.

"I didn't even see you with her. I wanted to hurt Alaric. I wanted to make him burn for his sins. Jupiter knew this and promised that he could help me. That he and I could do the unthinkable and kill his wife. I went along with the plan." He shook his head, and his voice cracked. "I had fathered Darius right as I started the kingdom. My boy was with me for every battle, every victory… everything. He would have made a great king."

Mars is winded. I reach out to steady him, and he reluctantly accepts the feeling of my hands on his chest. We sit in a cool forest with the trees high above us, shrouding us from the burning light of day.

"Why my mother?" I ask, my voice choked. "Why not Alaric's son? Why not me?"

"Jupiter wanted to kill you. I realized it too late. My sin was that I used the Falahle on your mother to spare you. I never wanted to kill a child, just his wife. Jupiter was mad with the desire to kill everyone he could within Sunfall, and he had you in his clutches. We couldn't find your mother. She *left* you there, Adelaide. She left you as a sacrifice. I summoned your mother against her will and took her head from her shoulders. I used the Falahle on my brother to drop you and took the memories from your mind. Adelaide, I took your *power* by doing so. The darkness I summoned is what poisoned you. *I* am the reason you could not wield the Siraltona, though I swear I did not know that would be the outcome. I did not know another way—"

My mind swirled with the implications.

Mars took my power… and my mother left me behind?

I look at Mars – *really* look at him – and wonder how the gods chose him as the person I'm supposed to be with forever. Even still, I remember Tryta's revelation that this entire thing is still my *choice*. Still, I feel a deeper sting of a darker form of grief. My mother left me to die. The echo of that memory, while not mine, rings true across our tether. I fear how that nightmare will haunt me later. My mind cannot process grieving my mother a second time, this time for the person she wasn't. Instead, I focus on addressing my husband.

"Your brother preyed on your grief," I say aloud. I can't tell if I am reasoning with myself or unwilling to consider the alternative.

"No, Adelaide, I was a fool and let my grief prey on me. I would never have engaged in such a reckless act of revenge on my own. Our kingdoms had just started to settle into something like peace. I let the temptation overtake me. I sent my son into that place, even though I knew how foolish your father was. But Jupiter was so sure that we were on the brink of making peace with them, so I took the risk. Darius was more than willing to prove his worth to the kingdom, and now my boy's blood is long lost to the soils in Sunfall... along with your mother's. Then you were left there with that monster."

My breath hitches. I feel the dark embrace of Tryta's magic wash over my veins, the few shadows still lurking in my veins pulsing with a constant truth.

"My son was deceived, Adelaide, but it is your choice. Your choice is to forgive him or leave him. The choice is yours."

Tryta's voice booms in my head. I flinch. Mars reels back from me, his face still etched with grief.

Tryta's presence fades as quickly as it came.

So much for a choice, Tryta. I can't leave him after knowing he was deceived.

Deep down, I understand the choice, but looking at Mars now and seeing how overwhelmed he is with grief makes it almost impossible to choose anything other than to stay with him. Fueled by my love for him and the agony of being betrayed by my mother, I set down the blade of light that's been building in my soul since he first started confessing to this age-old truth.

My mind is made, despite everything I once stood for. Perhaps it is the shadow and light that now flits about beneath my flesh, standing at the ready to fight and die with me. Perhaps it is the strength of my bond with Mars that has grown deeper after completing the Rites. But I will not leave my soulmate. I suspected, even when I first arrived in Velyasa, that he might be behind my mother's death. Yet I still chose to be with him.

I grab his face, anger at Jupiter coursing in my veins. "Your brother duped you, and my mother is to blame for leaving me there in the first place." My skin is incandescent with rage, but to my surprise, my fury is not directed at my husband. "Why would Tryta punish you for saving a child? Why would he...?"

"For taking up arms with Jupiter in the first place," he answered miserably. "I *knew* he was consorting with dark magics, and I still chose to go with him. I allowed my rage and anguish to drive me to slaughter an innocent woman and almost cost a child her life. I had no idea that child would be *you*. I had no idea that one day, you would grow up and find the gift I stole from you. I had no idea that by stealing your power, it would come to reside in me and set us up for a bond. But the worst part, Adelaide? I would do it again. I would do it all again if it meant that you could be here with me right now."

I'm stunned by his admission, but my heart doesn't know where to land the rage and fury that storms through my soul. I hear thunder on the horizon and wonder if it's an echo of the power swarming inside my chest, threatening to crack me open and devour the world. It could swallow it up if I let it. All I have to do is yield to it.

But the agony in my husband's voice breaks me.

"You thought I would leave you for this? Mars, my father killed your son. You sought retribution. You forgave me, did you not?"

"Did you not hear what I just said, Adelaide?" he cries out.

"Don't you realize that power made no difference? Mars, they would have married me off *sooner* had I kept that power. You heard yourself, right? My mother left me. I'm not sure you robbed me of power at all — I don't ever remember wielding it. I was always a pawn to be sacrificed in service to that kingdom. If I *did* have the Siraltona, they suppressed it." I shook my head. "And here is where I disagree with Tryta. He of all people should understand what grief does to a soul. You are not a god. You are a man. A reborn son of Tryta, but still a man. How should you possibly bear the brunt of the wrath of the gods when Jupiter was even more responsible than you?"

I don't know where I find this font of understanding and forgiveness. Maybe it is due to how our souls are intertwined. Maybe it is because I understand better than most what it means to be swept up in a thirst for vengeance. But my heart cannot find the path of rage that he expects me to seek against him. Instead, my mind fights to try to recover the memory of that day. A small voice wonders if he's telling me the truth, but I've never seen anyone filled with this much anguish in telling their story. By the way the fire in his eyes dims, I know this secret has been killing him. I feel the ache through our connection and sweep my arms around him.

"Mars, I must confess that right before I took the Rites with you, I considered the possibility that you were the one who killed her, and I chose to marry you anyway. The reason I was worried about the strength of our bond was not because of that. It was because you were keeping a secret from me that was this important to you. Our magic is *bound* together by the gods. Tryta gave me my magic back through the Lasira, and he did that so we could unite. Why would you ever think I would leave you when I learned the truth?"

He looks at me, incredulous. "I *stole* your magic and *left* you in that hateful place. I let my bastard brother destroy your life in my heated pursuit of vengeance!"

I want to argue with him on those points, but I know it won't do any good. In his eyes, he is guilty. It is up to me whether he ever finds the relief of forgiveness. And I, of all people, know what it's like to wear guilt like a second skin.

"Yes, and I slaughtered *thousands* of your people and nearly killed you on the battlefield. I think we're even. I also chose you after you deceived me, kidnapped me, and turned me into a vampire. Don't you think we're past this sort of nonsense?" My chest heaves as anger finds its roost. I am angry at him for believing I could be this shallow.

He stares at me, his face stained with tears. He is bewildered by my answers, but I don't know how to answer differently. If anything, my blood boils and my power screams to be loosed on Jupiter for being the *real* reason for my suffering. I want to know how he escaped punishment, whereas Mars did not.

Is there still something Mars is not telling me?

I feel a shuddering shadow snake across the tether and realize that Mars is connected to my thoughts again. The emptiness and rage I've felt have, up until now, shielded my mind from his, leaving only echoes of our emotions to be felt. Our bond, while secure, was interrupted in our spat. But that interruption is patched now as I feel him settle back into my thoughts. I wonder how I might control that power someday, or if I want to.

"I can still hear you," Mars says in my mind. *"And no, it is the truth. I can share the memory with you, if you wish, but I don't want to. I don't want you to see that awful day again. Go ask Tryta again if you must, but please know that I am not keeping anything from you this time. That is all I have. Tryta took our familiars as penance for using the Falahle to harm innocents. Even though I was trying to protect you, I used that power in a manner most forbidden."*

"How did you get it back?" I whisper. "How did you get the magic back?"

After struggling to find the right words, he gives up and speaks once more over our connection. Exhaustion tugs at his eyes. I know this confession has robbed him of breath and power. I pity him. I pity my husband and the guilt he's worn, just as my hands have been stained with the blood and grief of the thousands of Shadow Folk I've slain.

"I prayed for forgiveness over and over, but I had to give Tryta something in exchange for my sins. I begged him to return your power. To make me weak. Instead, he kept me strong and gave you power and brought you right to me. My punishment was that my love would be filled with the power to slay me. That she would be someone who hated me – that she would have to choose against all odds to love me, lest my own mate be my downfall. Whether I lived would be her choice. That is the only way I could get my power back and the power of my people. My life had to be tied to the one I harmed. Whether I lived would be her choice. *I would have to surrender the very immortality that Tryta granted me to the hands of the one I wronged.* And that is the bargain I made. That is how I got them back. It is why we had to retreat after that fateful day when your mother died. *My life has always been in your hands, Adelaide. I meant it – you will be the death of me, my fire. I do not deserve the bountiful gifts I have been given."*

My heart heaves. Without thinking, I reach up and press my lips to his. He freezes before giving in to me. We grip each other, filled with a heady mix of passion and sorrow, desperate to find release in each other's arms.

I don't know where we are, but I hope only birds and deer are getting an eyeful right now. Then, something makes us stop. Just as he's about to lift my skirts, we hear thundering hoofbeats.

Mars immediately pulls me to him and shields me with his body.

"Where in Velyasa are we?" I whisper.

He puts a finger to his lips to shush me. I fear the worst and weave two pendants, not caring if the flash of light betrays our position. I'll cut anyone in half who comes after me and my husband. I slip a pendant around his neck. While we are both immune to Jupiter's foul will-stealing magic, I'm not about to take the risk that he's found a way around that resistance. With both of us wearing amulets, we wait in the quiet.

"I don't think they saw us," Mars says through our bond, though I detect annoyance in his voice.

"I'm not leaving us unprotected, Mars." I glare at him, grateful that we can speak like this. Just as I can't hide from him, he can't hide from *me,* either.

As the throng of horses rides past, leaving us concealed in shadow, I almost miss it. The sound of a voice I haven't heard in quite some time. My heart begins to race, pounding in my ears and throat as I get up and dash toward the party of soldiers passing through.

Mars gets up to chase me, but he isn't fast enough. There, in the clearing ahead, is Maverick.

My brother has come to Velyasa!

He looks at me. I brace myself, awaiting an incoming fight against my own brother. He must know the truth by the way he stares at me, horror etching his familiar features. Those silvery gray eyes of his — the ones we used to share — haunt me with the tales of so many missed months.

I miss the feeling of a blade at my side. Instead, I let the light in my veins hum to life and take a sharp shape of her own — a blade forged by divine fury. I prepare for the worst as Mars braces my side, his shadows alive and at the ready.

Maverick launches off his horse and rushes to me, his leg dragging behind him, still damaged from that long-forgotten battle. I wonder if it was Darius who struck a blow to his leg all those years ago. How many lives were destroyed in a war neither side ever had to fight?

I don't get to think about this further before my brother reaches me and crushes me into his arms, sobbing, "You're alive!"

The light in my veins dims. Mars keeps his shadows at the ready, but he stands more at ease. I hold my brother as he weeps and cast wary eyes over the people who rode so far, no doubt to find me. Among them sit Ronald, Jack, and Devon. My heart cries out at the sight of them. Where I expect to find hate and fear, I find warmth.

"We're so glad to have found you!" Maverick says as he pulls away from me.

"You're not angry?"

Maverick shakes his head. "Father was, but he's dead now, Adelaide. I killed him. *I* am the King of Sunfall now. As soon as I caught wind that he was trying to betray our kingdom to Jupiter, I took my vengeance."

Joy bursts in my heart, and I swear the rain that now falls is tears of joy from the gods themselves. "Thank Siralto," I whisper.

~*~

We follow alongside them back to the castle. None of us speaks, leaving an awkward, yet companionable silence woven between us. I have many questions for my brother and even more questions for Mars when we return home.

"Have my answers not been enough?"

I turn to look at Mars and shoot him a knowing grin. *"They have, but I need more from my husband. I still can't believe you thought I would leave you when I already suspected you might be responsible. War does not make for easy choices, my love. You had good intentions. You just… didn't choose the best responses. But what other options were there? I cannot blame you. If anything, your brother will pay for taking advantage of your grief in that way. You did not take away my power. Jupiter did, as far as I am concerned. And my bastard father would have used me even worse if I had the power."*

I give a slight nod to my brother's injured leg, which dangles at an awkward angle from his saddle. By the way he was dragging it when we reunited in the clearing, I can tell the injury has gotten worse. I wonder if Sherry could help heal him.

"I do not want to lose my wife because of past mistakes."

"You chose me even after I killed your people, love. I'm the daughter of the bastard who killed your son. I think we are past that, at this point. Or should I be worried about you leaving me?"

Mars squeezes my hand. *"Never."*

"That settles it. But don't ever hide anything like that from me again. I can't stand to see you buckle from the weight of such secrets."

"I can't hide from you anymore, Adelaide. I knew when Tryta gave you your familiar that he was forcing me to speak for myself."

I raise my eyebrows at the realization. Tryta knew that giving me my familiar meant I would be able to hear Mars's thoughts. Tryta really did put the ball in his court, forcing him to speak aloud.

"And you should know, he lied," Mars added. *"You could deny me, but our bond is truly unbreakable. Not even death can sever it. Why do you think Siralto's light is still so drawn to Tryta's darkness, even though she does not breathe anymore?"*

I nod. *"We would be distant, but still aware of one another?"*

"Yes. A soul bond is eternal. You can run from it all you want, but I have seen kings and even emperors driven to madness when they try to deny it."

I swallow. *"I'm not fond of madness. It didn't suit my father well, and I'm not one to play up the sins of my father."*

"I didn't pin you for the type."

Ahead of us, the castle draws closer. We must not have flown as far as I thought. Maybe my rage and sorrows were what made the trip feel longer. Knowing that Mars was hiding something filled me with an agony I never wish to feel again. By the way he looks at me, I know he won't ever do that again. I grip his hand tighter, hoping I don't crack any of his bones.

"They'll heal if you do."

I squint at him and stifle a laugh. Turning to the soldiers gathered outside our castle, I say, "Welcome to Velyasa."

The people of Velyasa have begun to crowd around us. Startled whispers travel through the gathered spectators.

Maverick. Ronald. Devon. Jack.

They've heard these names and learned to fear them, but ironically, none of those names strikes the same terror in them that mine used to. Which is bizarre, since between my brother and me, I was the powerless one.

Now, I address them as their queen. I can tell that Tryta's choice to bless me today won a good majority of them over. Now they look at me the same way they look at Mars, with few exceptions. I even see several of the pendants I wove sitting on the throats of the Velyasan soldiers that keep the crowds from getting too close. Ever vigilant, their weapons are drawn and at the ready should Maverick or his party try to strike.

I raise my voice to be heard above the agitated whispers. "My brother, the new King of Sunfall, has come to visit. He has slain Alaric. It is my hope that with my brother's visit, we can establish a new peace between our neighboring kingdoms. Today, we shall welcome them as guests. Today, we shall let them feast with us and share in our customs and ways. Please help me, as your new queen, to show them things not even I know."

Mars beams at me with pride before turning to his people. "Your queen and I hope to usher in a new era for Velyasa — one where we can live in the light of the day and the shadows of the night as we please. We hope that with your visit, Your Majesty, you will be amenable to such an arrangement."

There, in the tone of my husband's voice, is the edge of a blade I know too well. This time, I don't take offense at it.

Maverick detects the message and slightly bows from where he sits in his saddle. "Excuse me, as I cannot dismount as well as I used to, but unfortunately, I am here to say that Sunfall, while rightfully my kingdom, has fallen to worse hands than mine."

The crowd goes silent. I feel faint. I already know what my brother will say next, but it doesn't diminish the horror when the words leave his mouth.

"Jupiter has taken Sunfall."

Beside me, Mars roars.

~*~

We adjourn to the grand hall. Mars and I don't bother with separate chairs; I sit firmly tucked in his lap. He refuses to let me move away from him, his eyes darting along the walls of the hall as though he expects Jupiter to emerge from the shadows any moment.

"How did he take you down?" I finally ask.

"The same way Mars and Ivan managed to trick us the last time. You know, Father was always one to take drinks he shouldn't. I was so angry with his foolishness, I slew him when I found him, but the damage was done. It was too late." Maverick shook his head, perplexed. "Jupiter... his shadows are different. They possess the person, body, and soul, until they become mindless monsters who do his bidding. Our gathered party is the only one unaffected by his magic. The Siraltona led me here, Adelaide. It *whispered* promises to me. It promised me that you were alive and you had joined forces with the Shadow King. I see now that you married him." A ghost of a smile graces his lips. "Are we to believe that you can stand against someone like Jupiter?"

Mars clears his throat. "My brother is a force to be reckoned with in his own right, but I would never condone his actions. Velyasans believe in the free will and choice of the people, just as the gods intended."

Maverick looks at me and mouths *brother* with a look of terror on his face, but I shake my head. In my head, Mars chuckles, but the sound is devoid of any real joy or mirth. His head is already spinning, calculating our next move and considering how this blow to Sunfall might become Velyasa's problem next.

"How did you and your party escape unaffected?" Without waiting for them to consent, I let the Siraltona sweep over them like the tides along the floor of the grand hall. It sweeps along their skin, searching for the Falahle. It finds nothing, returning to me empty of the promise of battle.

Outside, the sun is setting and my eyes beg to close for the night. My body is sore, spent, and aching. But I am committed to keeping my attention on my brother and my men, whom I fought alongside time and time again to keep Sunfall safe.

To know that it fell within months of my leaving is a bittersweet feeling. I feel bad for my brother and my people, but the nobility and my father, the king, got what they deserved. Still, to be robbed of one's will is not a fate I would wish on anyone.

"Where is Beatrice?" I ask, realizing she's not here.

Maverick gazes at me with sorrow-filled eyes. "She was killed."

Grief consumes me, and I don't try to hide my tears. *My sister-in-law, sweet Beatrice, was murdered?*

"She's with Finch, then. Dead by the hands of the same awful creature," I hiss.

Through my tears, my rage still rings true, begging for me to fly down to Sunfall and unleash the fires of Kohlu on the bastard Jupiter, who has taken up residence in what was *my* castle. *Our* castle.

"I'm so sorry, Maverick," I finally add. He doesn't speak, and tears fall freely down his cheeks. He looks more haggard and worn than ever. I have so many questions for him, but by the looks of him, he needs sleep far more than I do. He is still mortal. Where I feel exhaustion, he probably feels like he stands with one foot in the grave.

"I believe your brother and his soldiers need to rest," Mars says aloud, his booming voice rousing a jump from all of them.

They still eye him like the beast they've grown to fear. If it weren't for my presence and endorsement, I don't doubt that they might pull weapons or even try to flee from him. But the sight of me gives them pause. I don't ask Ronald about his and Brenda's children because I don't want to know the truth. I know they, too, have probably been laid to rest or had their minds and spirits consumed by Jupiter's darkness.

I wonder if Tryta might reconsider his punishment for using the power he granted to Mars. Then again, that was why he gave it to Mars in the first place – to control Jupiter. Mars shares a look with me, and I know we'll be speaking about this later.

Still, the biggest fight I have ahead of me is not with my husband and the secrets he keeps. Instead, my fight will land me right back where I started. My future, after all this time, still rests behind the walls of Sunfall.

"Do we have rooms set aside for these fine people?" I ask. "We'll station guards for them and, if Sherry has the time, I'd like for her to look them all over and dress their wounds, new and old."

Mars nods. "We have accommodations at the ready." He scans the face of each man from Sunfall. "You will be watched closely. Any sign of treason or fight will be met with lethal force. Cooperate with us, and you will be handsomely rewarded for helping me cull my brother for his sins."

No one speaks, but the gathered party nods their heads in agreement. Maverick looks defeated, but I give him a reassuring smile. My brother has always been more prone to logic than my father. I pray this remains true.

"Adelaide, I have so many questions for you," Maverick finally says.

I hate how his voice breaks beneath the weight of so much loss. "I will be happy to answer them *after* you rest. It is not up for discussion. You all have traveled far to get here. I cannot leave you unrested and unfed."

I move to get up, and Mars stands with me, his hand reaching for mine, fearing that I might dance away like an apparition on the wind. But I don't dissolve into the dying light of the day. Instead, I squeeze his hand in return.

"Kitchen staff will be up shortly. Mars and I need to discuss strategies. We will debrief you in the morning."

The commander in me returns with little effort. I was always good at delegating in battle. I led with a firm understanding of what it takes to win against enemies who are stronger and more powerful than I am. This time, though, I have power, and a lot of it.

"Adelaide?" Ronald calls out to me. I turn to face my friend. "It's good to see you alive. I can already tell you make a great queen, little princess."

I smile, holding back tears. "It's good to see you alive, too. I hope to keep things that way. Take care of yourselves here and follow directions. They're kinder than we've ever been led to believe. Be patient and listen." Turning on my heel, I stalk from the room before any of them can see me cry. By the time Mars and I reach our bedchambers, I fall to the floor, sobbing. Mars sinks beside me and cradles me in his arms.

My mind is on fire with all I've learned in the last day alone. Mars killed my mother with Jupiter. He killed her to save me from his brother and took my power as a result, and somehow, I'm not even mad about it. I curse the change in my heart and how it has softened for the monster beside me, but my soul knows the cost of battle and war more than most.

Nothing is ever off the table. *Ever.*

My brother has found me, alive and well, and confessed that Sunfall was taken by the same bastard who killed Finch and helped kill my mother.

My breathing is heavy, and I fear I might falter. I wonder if the dragon lurking beneath my flesh could breathe enough fire to let the searing heat within my bones die down, but the rage in my soul never let me sleep, even before Tryta gave me my dragon form.

"Tryta. I met Tryta! And an unknown goddess helped give me my familiar. I can't take any more revelations today. I need sleep."

"I know, my fire," Mars whispers, his voice like soft rain inside my mind. *"One day, I will repay you for your struggles with peace and quiet. I will treat you to a life as a queen, well-pampered and without strife."*

"Don't make promises you can't keep," I joke.

But the resolve on his face tells me he believes in his promise. Despite it all, Mars holds on to hope that peace might be attainable. In all my years, I never expected the Shadow King to be an optimist. Even so, I willingly live in this delusion with him, pressing my lips to his and wrapping my arms around his neck.

Tonight, I decide to believe the lie that everything will be alright. By morning, the lie will dissolve, and the reality of the threat in Sunfall will become real.

But tonight, I let myself live in the fantasy of peace that doesn't exist. Sunfall and Jupiter can wait.

I close my eyes and sleep.

MANSALO CODEX

A

Ahklena: To redo; to relive. (Magical) The process of reliving your life after you have died (or during).

Ahleh: Return

Ahlura: Magic

Aleh Awlo: South West

Alti: Mountain

Altiya: Heaven/Elysium

Adan: Live/life (command, action, being, etc.)

Arke: happy

B

Barulatye: book

BarulatyeSelben: Book of the Gods

Ben: Soul

Bendala: Binding of souls

Bur: East

C

Chella: open/to open

D

Dya: Dream

** [Define this better] DyaChella: To open a dream – attach the name with a vision of their soul in your mind

Dehsa: equality, fairness

F

Fleckerleke: Meaning TBA -- compare to "fuck" / slang

Fal - Fate

Falahle – Will-stealing magic. Used to rob people of their souls and force them to do the bidding of the wielder

Falme - Fate string

K

Kohlu: Tartarus

Kreyuhl: The Passing Point/Place (The garden of the Selyento)

L

Lafura: Soul Mate (of the chosen variety)

Lafuran: Soul mates (plural)

Li: Water

Lia: rain

Lo: Language/ to be of something

La: Love

M

Mansa: war

Ma: You

Mar: your

Me: string

Marlo: Day

N

Na: Death (the concept, not the creature) - specifically of the violent sort, in most contexts

Narlasha: Special instrument in Tyrladan. Strings made of light that change with the time of day. Not playable at night. Brightness and tone of the strings rise and fall with the setting sun or sun(s), depending on where it is played in Tyrladan.

Neylka: Nothing (the nothingness between the worlds in the Afterlife)

P

Penda: North

R

Ralun: minor Mansalo god of darkness (accomplice to Terrence)

Rashia: squirrel

Rohk: Follow

S

Sel: music

Selben: Gods

Selbena: God

Selbeno: Goddess

Selyento: Tree of music

Sira: Fire

Siralto: Goddess of Light

T

Thma: Gift

Toines: (comparable to dollars--currency)

Tye: Paper

Tyrladan: Afterlife

Tryta: Darkness (the God)

U

Uht: place
Uhn: No

V

Velyasa: Window/Portal

Y

Ya: to
Yehta: Limbo/Purgatory

Grammar Rules

No conjugation for verbs -- context alone determines how a verb is used.

' attached to a phrase indicates an understood you. (Either in command or regular conversation).

Qualities of possession (their, your, etc.) should be conjoined with the objects they possess

Acknowledgements

I want to thank my family for their continued support. My mother has tolerated every cliffhanger. My brother has rolled his eyes as he watches me post over and over again about my books. And my father has always been there with a supportive grin when I tell him about what I'm up to and where I'm going to talk about my books next.

I'd like to thank my beta reader, Elisabeth Wiles, for her ability view my stories like a second set of eyes and revel in the enjoyment of this series with me.

I'd like to thank my ARC readers, my PR teams, and my community for so much of their continued support in getting this book out there.

This book was a labor of love and the longest and most complex I've ever written to date.

I would also like to thank my girls, Rachel and Journey. You all are the stars in my night sky.

ALSO BY

Tales of the Selyento

Remember the Stars

Beyond the Stars

Unliving Goddess of Stars

Tales of the Shadow Folk

Magic Bites

Sunlight's Shadow

Stay in the loop about new releases! Join my mailing list by going to linkt.ree/ErisMarriottAuthor